Leaving Cold Sassy

The Unfinished Sequel to Cold Sassy Tree

Also published in Large Print
from G.K. Hall by Olive Ann Burns:

Cold Sassy Tree

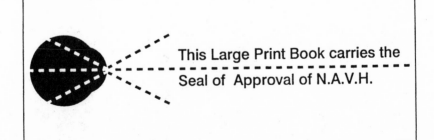

This Large Print Book carries the
Seal of Approval of N.A.V.H.

Leaving Cold Sassy

The Unfinished Sequel to *Cold Sassy Tree*

with a Reminiscence by
Katrina Kenison

Olive Ann Burns

G.K. Hall & Co.
Thorndike, Maine

Published in Large Print by arrangement with
Ticknor & Fields/Houghton Mifflin Company.

All photographs are courtesy of Mr. and Mrs. Nathan
LeGrand, Becky Sparks, and John Sparks, unless otherwise
credited.

G.K. Hall Large Print Book Series.

Printed on acid free paper in the United States of America.

Set in 16 pt. Plantin.

Library of Congress Cataloging-in-Publication Data

Burns, Olive Ann.
    Leaving Cold Sassy : the unfinished sequel to
Cold Sassy tree / Olive Ann Burns : with a reminiscence
by Katrina Kenison.
        p.   cm.—(G.K. Hall large print book series)
    ISBN 0-8161-5702-2 (acid-free paper).—
ISBN 0-8161-5703-0 (pbk. : acid-free paper)
    1. Large type books.   I.   Kenison, Katrina.
II. Burns, Olive Ann. Cold Sassy tree.   III.   Title.
[PS3552.U73248L4   1993]
813'.54—dc20   92-40634

Contents

A Note from the Publisher

AT THE TIME of her death in 1990, Olive Ann Burns had been working for five years on a sequel to her bestselling novel, *Cold Sassy Tree*. Since its publication in 1984, *Cold Sassy Tree* has become a phenomenon, taking its place alongside such American classics as *The Adventures of Tom Sawyer* and *To Kill a Mockingbird*. It is the story of life in a small Georgia town at the turn of the century, as seen through the eyes of fourteen-year-old Will Tweedy. In the course of three momentous weeks, Will mourns his grandmother's death and then watches as his grandfather scandalizes all of Cold Sassy by up and marrying a fresh-faced young milliner thirty years his junior.

In *Time, Dirt, and Money,* (the working title for her novel), Olive Ann picks up Will's story in 1917, just as he is falling in love with his own wife-to-be and grappling with the changes time has wrought in his beloved hometown. Fifteen chapters of the novel are complete, and Olive Ann had mapped out the rest of the story in her mind. Despite a long battle with cancer and congestive heart failure, she continued to write with tremendous energy and pleasure.

To the end of her life Olive Ann Burns was passionately interested in Will Tweedy's future—as were her thousands of fans, who have waited eagerly for a second book. In large part, we are publishing her unfinished novel for those readers. Anyone who came under the spell of *Cold Sassy Tree* will welcome this glimpse of Will Tweedy, now on the brink of adulthood; of the feisty young schoolteacher who captures his heart; and of Cold Sassy itself, a town that has claimed a permanent place in our imaginations.

We would not undertake such a publication were we not certain that Olive Ann herself wished it. For years, Olive Ann promised her readers a sequel; she dictated the first draft when she became too ill to write. She endured nearly three years of complete bedrest without complaint, for she spent long afternoons in Cold Sassy, Georgia, chronicling the adventures of our old friends. But during her last hospitalization, she realized that she might not live to complete the novel. Late on the night of June 22, 1990, while lying awake in the Georgia Baptist Hospital, she dictated a letter to her next-door neighbor, Norma Duncan. It said, in part, "I've figured out a way that if I don't get to finish the novel it might still be marketed as a small book." With this publication, we fulfill Olive Ann's wish to let people know what happened to Will Tweedy, and we trust that her many fans will welcome her final pages.

Time, Dirt, and Money

One

I THOUGHT I was roaring into Sanna Klein's life, but if I'd been on tiptoe instead of a motorcycle, it wouldn't have made any difference. She didn't even hear me coming. Everybody in Cold Sassy was at the watermelon cutting that Sunday afternoon except the bedsick, and to her, meeting them was more of an ordeal than a party.

The school board always put on a watermelon social the day before school started in September to introduce the new teachers to the townspeople. I'd never missed a one, but this year I wasn't going. I didn't much feel like facing that many homefolks. It was 1917, the United States had got itself into a world war, and I was twenty-five years old and not even in uniform. While some of the fellows I grew up with were already dying in France, I was working for the University of Georgia over in Athens, twenty-three miles from Cold Sassy. I told myself I'd outgrown a small-town watermelon cutting. But the truth is, I didn't have the nerve to go. Then on Thursday I ran into my old friend Smiley Snodgrass at the Athens Hardware Store. "Well, if it ain't Will Tweedy!" he yelled, slapping me on the

1

back. "Hey, Will, you go'n get over to P.C. for the watermelon cuttin' Sunday?"

I need to explain "P.C." Back in 1907 our town council decided Cold Sassy sounded too countrified for an up-and-coming business community, and they changed the name to Progressive City. My Grandpa Blakeslee wouldn't have allowed it, but he was dead. In the nearly ten years since, the town had progressed, but the new name still hadn't caught on. Progressive City sounded silly and took too long to say. Those of us who didn't keep calling it Cold Sassy just called it P.C. Old Doc Slaughter still had COLD SASSY, GEORGIA, on his office letterhead. "Anybody you hear callin' our town Progressive City," he said, "you know he's just passin' th'ew."

Anyhow, here was Smiley, come to Athens to buy some plumbing pipes. Smiley was bursting with news. "I done got you a teacher picked out, Will. Her name's Miss Klein and she's from over in Mitchellville. We ain't got but three new teachers this year," he added.

"Yeah, Papa told me." Papa was head of the school board.

"I reckon I'll see you there."

"Cain't make it this year, Smiley. I'll meet her later."

"Well, I'll gar'ntee you, Will Tweedy, if your later ain't soon, somebody's go'n beat you to her. She's a pure-T beauty, Will. Real foreign-lookin'. I-talian maybe. Or Spanish. Might could even be a Gypsy. Anyhow, she's got heavy black hair, and

2

black eyes, and her eyelids—law, they's so smoky-dark it's like she reached in the f'arplace and got herself some sut and smeared it on."

When I didn't say anything, he added, "I reckon you know that her and them other two teachers are rentin' the upstairs rooms at Miss Love's house."

"Yeah, I know."

"I built a bathroom up there so Miss Love could rent to'm."

"I've seen it. How'd you think up puttin' it on the roof?"

"Miss Love thunk it up, to save space indoors."

The bathroom was set into an L-shaped corner of the roof. From the street it looked like a play-house. Had a roof, a porch, a corner column, ban-isters, a door, and two little windows. Smiley had cut a door to the bathroom porch from the up-stairs hall. This bathroom was an improvement over the backyard privy Miss Love had to use when she married Grandpa Blakeslee, but nobody would look forward to going out there on a freez-ing-cold, rainy night.

The clerk came over to Smiley. "I've got up your order, sir, and toted the sum. You want to come see is it right?"

Smiley started to follow, then turned back to me.

"Well, anyhow, but . . . well, you know . . ." Smiley kept the conjunctions coming whenever he was trying to think what he wanted to say. "Well, ain't it about time you quit bein' hurt about Trulu Philpot or whatever her name was?"

3

"You tend to your business and I'll tend to mine."

He shrugged. "Well, so anyhow, yesterd'y I took Miss Klein's trunk and thangs upstairs to her room, and I'm sayin' you better latch onto her."

I picked up a tenpenny nail, tossed it, caught it, and put it back in the barrel. "I know I'm God's gift to women, Smiley, but you met her first. How come you're so willin' to give her to me?"

"Shoot dog, Will, Miss Klein is—well, refined as heck. She wouldn't give somebody like me a second look. Now I don't go so far as to say you're refined, but, uh . . . at least you're educated."

Smiley wasn't the only one who already had me matched up with Sanna Klein. The next day I got a note from Miss Love, my grandpa's widow. The word *widow* sounds like "old woman," but Miss Love was still high-style and beautiful, and looked young despite the fact her hair turned solid white in the month after Grandpa died. Every widower and bachelor in town would be courting her if she'd give them half a chance.

As usual, she began the letter "Dear Will Tweedy." Grandpa Blakeslee used to call me both names, and Miss Love had kept it up—in his memory, so to speak. Maybe it was in his memory that we both still called our town Cold Sassy instead of Progressive City or P.C.

Dear Will Tweedy,
You must come meet "my girls"—all twenty-two years old. The first to arrive was Miss

4

Isa Belle Hazelhurst, from Ty Ty. She has dimples and a sweet face, but is a little empty and silly, I'm afraid. You'll be interested in her south Georgia accent. She pronounces the "i" in "nice" and "ice" like the sound of "i" in "bicycle." Those sixth-graders will be mocking her from the first day, poor thing. "Isa Belle" is pronounced like "Isabelle" but she says just call her Issie.

She is sharing the large upstairs bedroom with Miss Lucy Mercer Clack from Clarkesville, a nice plain sensible young lady.

Miss Sanna Klein has the small bedroom by herself. I think you may be really interested in her, Will. She's a beautiful little brunette.

Judging by the quality of her clothes and her manners, she obviously has what your mother would call "background." She's from Mitchellville and is to teach fourth grade. Just a lovely girl.

See you at the watermelon cutting if not before.

> Hastily,
> Love Simpson Blakeslee

P.S. I guess you've heard that your Aunt Loma came in on the train Tuesday.

Two years before, Aunt Loma had gone off to New York City to seek fame and fortune on the stage, leaving her son, Campbell Junior, for my

5

parents to raise. She claimed to feel guilty about it and had just gone back to New York after being home for a month "to be with my boy." But from what I heard, she didn't spend any time with Campbell Junior except to tuck him in bed at night like he was still little bitty instead of twelve years old.

I wondered briefly why Aunt Loma was back again so soon. But I was more interested in Miss Sanna Klein. Sanna . . . Sanna . . . What an odd name. Vaguely familiar, though I was sure I'd never known a Sanna before.

Sanna Klein was exotic and beautiful. She was refined. Miss Love approved of her. Suddenly nothing this side of dropping dead could have kept me away from the watermelon cutting.

Usually when I went home, I took the train from Athens and used Papa's car after I got to Cold Sassy. But that Sunday I rode my motorcycle, with the sidecar attached so I could take two pillowcases full of dirty clothes for Mama's washerwoman to do up. There's nothing like a Harley-Davidson for getting around mud holes, rocks, and wagon ruts on dirt roads—or for making an impression on girls. I stopped by home, left the clothes on the back porch, and went directly to Sheffield Park.

Saddle horses and buggy horses were tied under trees on the far side of the baseball field. Cars sat in a straggly row near the wagon road into the park, so as not to scare the horses or make dust.

6

I stopped the Harley-Davidson between Miss Love's old black Pierce automobile and Wildcat Lindsey's new Model-T Ford, and lit up a cigar. Most of the university students smoked cigarettes, but I favored Tampa Nuggets.

Then I headed over towards the town band, already playing in the big eight-sided pavilion for the crowd gathered in the shade of some huge oak trees. The dusty, dried-up grass was thick with low-hovering yellow jackets, but I barely noticed them. My mind was on Sanna Klein.

Two

IT COULD HAVE been a scene in a moving picture show—except I was walking into the picture. And instead of everything being black and white or gray, I was seeing blue sky, green trees, and ladies in bright-striped or flowerdy dresses, dazzling in the sunlight.

It was a hot day. The very old sat on benches in the shade, some holding babies, all tapping their feet to the band music, and all smiling except for poor old Dr. Hedge Rufesel, the dentist, who used to travel from town to town, filling teeth and making dental plates right in people's homes. A year after finally settling in Cold Sassy, he'd had a stroke. Today Dr. Rufesel's wheelchair was parked beside the bench where Miss Effie Belle Tate had sat at the watermelon cutting in 1914, not long before she died. A Negro man was pushing bits of watermelon into his mouth.

Long planks had been laid across sawhorses to make tables, and people stood around in clusters, talking. Every few minutes they parted like the waters to let one of the Negro men get through with a huge watermelon that had been cooling in the creek. With much laughter and howdy-doing, the colored men would tote melons to the tables and slash them open with a flourish of their big sharp knives. The slices fell like red dinner plates on each table, as neat as place settings.

Loomis Toy saw me before I saw him. "Hey, Mist' Will! How you doin', son?" I loved Loomis, a very tall, very black man who had worked for my family for as long as I could remember. He taught me how to garden long before the university's School of Agriculture taught me to farm.

"I heard your little girl took sick last week," I'd never noticed the sprinkle of gray in his hair before.

"Yassuh, Mist' Will, but she doin' mo better now, yassub. And she sho 'preciate that doll Miss Mary Toy sont her. Lawdy, I 'member Miss Mary Toy playin' wid dat doll her ownself. Don't seem lak that long ago, does it?"

Mrs. Avery came up from the creek with some wet towels. "For when folks are ready to wipe their hands," she said, smiling at me. "Will, go put'm on that sycamore stump over yonder."

Near the stump I saw the Widow Abernathy and her eight children lined up at a table in front of eight watermelon slices, like dairy cows at their feeding troughs. The mother opened her purse, took eight spoons out of a napkin, and handed one to each child.

I wondered where Sampson was. Several young boys were dodging out from behind trees to spit watermelon seeds at each other, but he wasn't with them. Nor was he among the clusters of parents and children who stood with favorite teachers from years past. My own favorite, Miss Neppie, had died of appendicitis in the spring.

I headed for the biggest oak tree, where the rest of Cold Sassy would already be waiting in line to meet the new teachers. Snatches of conversation drifted in the air:

A young woman jiggling a fretful baby was talking to Mrs. Means. "I don't know if he's teethin' or just tired."

"Most babies are teethin' or tired, one. Unless they're hungry or wet. What I call a good baby is one that's asleep. I never have . . ."

"In the paper it says we 'sposed to join the Women's Army Against Waste. What in the world's the Women's Army?"

"It's just a way a-talkin', honey. What the gov'ment really wants, they want us women to serve less meat. They say raise more hogs and chickens, quit fryin' the pullets, let'm grow up to hens. Can more vegetables. They say quit cookin' light bread and biscuits. Save the wheat for our soldier boys, and . . ."

". . . seen that new teacher?"

"Miss Klein? The dark-complected one? She's a pretty little thang, ain't she?"

Mrs. Snodgrass, Smiley's mama, was talking to two women I didn't know. One had a voice like a crab. "You wouldn't think mill hands would come to a town social," she rasped.

"They got chi'ren in the school same as us," said the third lady.

"But they ain't comf'table here," said Mrs. Snodgrass. "Look at 'em, standin' off to theirselves, starin' at all us. Not to change the subject, but have y'all seen that great big diamond Loma Blakeslee Williams is flashin'? I hear her fee-ance is a rich Yankee banker!"

"It's all right to marry rich, Wi-nona, but anybody marries a Yankee is a lost cause. Loma's daddy fought in the War, for heaven's sake!"

"Sometimes I wonder bout Loma," said Mrs. Snodgrass. "It's like her corn bread didn't git done in the middle."

This was my Aunt Loma they were talking about. I paused to relight my cigar, took some slow puffs, tried to act like I was looking for somebody.

". . . Well, Loma left here two year ago to make her fortune in New York City," the crab-voiced lady commented, "and if'n that diamond is any measure, Winona, I reckon she has did it."

"She's also took up smokin'," said old Mrs. Calvert, joining the group.

"No!" exclaimed Miss Winona. "Who told you that?"

"Miss Hazel's cook smelt it on her."

Mrs. Tabor, walking by, heard that and said, "But y'all, she whistled for the Presbyterians at preachin' this mornin'. It was real pretty."

11

Miss Winona was incensed. "Now, Miz Tabor. What could a vaudeville whistler possibly whistle in church?"

"Why, Wi-nona, you should a-been there! She done 'Whisperin' Hope.' She whistled it in two-part harmony—like doin' a duet with herself!"

"What I heard was she looked mighty peculiar doin' it," said Mrs. Crab-Voice. "Kept pokin' on her mouth and cheeks with her hands and fingers the whole time."

"Well, she did look funny. But it was bout the prettiest sound I nearly ever heard. Sent chills up the back of my neck. Why, there's Will Tweedy! Where you been keepin' yourself, sugar?"

Greetings and handshakes came thick as I made my way through gaps in the crowd. "Hey, Will Tweedy, you old son of a gun! Come 'ere, boy!" "Goodness, Will, ain't seen you in too long!"

A group of excited boys and young men were carrying on about the war. Old Mr. Henry Botts put his arm around one in uniform and said, "We go'n have the Kaiser on the run in no time, ain't we, son?"

The Army boy was Harkness Predmore. Last time I saw Harkness he looked barely old enough to shave. "Hey, Will!" he called to me. "I en-listed!"

"Congratulations, Harkness. Take care of your-self," I called back, and walked on—faster . . .

Nobody had asked why I wasn't in the Army. They may have wondered, but nobody asked.

Fat little Mr. Homer Boozer was already eating watermelon at a table shaded by the big oak tree. Fat little Miss Alice Ann saw me, poked Mr. Homer, pointed in my direction, and called out, "Will Tweedy, come say howdy!" I went over and said howdy, then excused myself to join those waiting under the tree to meet the new teachers.

I couldn't see Papa for the people, but I knew he was there. When I did catch sight of him, I felt the usual twinge of shame, but I also marveled how he could keep on in his role as community and church leader despite what he'd done—as if it hadn't even happened. There he was, prosperous and dignified, standing with four other school board members. By craning my neck I could see two of the young ladies. But not the dark-complected one.

Instead, I saw Lightfoot and Hosie Roach with their four children, all holding hands as they headed for a plank table already set with watermelon slices. I wanted to go speak, but let the moment pass.

In high school when I was so crazy about her, Lightfoot was skinny, tow-headed, fresh from the mountains, eager to learn. But she had to leave school and work in the mill, and at fifteen she married Hosie Roach, a twenty-two-year-old mill hand who had gone to work for Grandpa Blakeslee at the store. Lightfoot was kind of fat now and her hair had darkened, but from where I stood she looked proud and happy.

I used to hate Hosie. He always was smart, no

denying, and a few years ago, he and Lightfoot had started a store of their own in a little shack at the edge of Mill Town. Townspeople called them uppity, which meant they were making a go of it. Their oldest child was about nine now, a pretty little white-haired girl named Precious.

Precious Roach. Good Lord!

Watching the family stroll away, I wondered if Precious would be in Miss Klein's fourth grade.

I heard someone call out, "Will!" and turned to see my Aunt Loma, hurrying to catch up with me. The way Loma was dressed you'd think she'd got Cold Sassy confused with New York City. Her curly red hair, cut short in the new style, was almost hidden under a gold-colored cloche hat. She had on a pale green silk dress, a short dress, way short enough to get talked about. Talk, talk, talk. Loma reveled in it. In Cold Sassy the ladies were just daring to show their ankles.

And that engagement ring! The diamond was big as a fat black-eyed pea! As if to keep her balance, she walked with her left hand held forward, wiggling her fingers, flashing the diamond in the sunshine.

"Hi, Will!" she said, a little out of breath.

"Hey, Aunt Loma."

"Hay is what horses eat, Southern boy," she said.

"And hi means you think Northerners are way up above us down here." I was teasing, but all that put-on Yankee accent irked me. Taking her hand, I bent down close to the diamond. "That's a nice piece of glass you got there, Aunt Loma."

14

"Glass, my foot. Don't show off your ignorance, Will." She laughed and took her hand back. I gave her a little hug and we walked on. She wiggled her ring finger at me again. "Are you impressed?"

"Well, yes, I admit I am."

"It's three and a half carats."

"Tell me about him," I said, "and tell me how come you're back in Cold Sassy so soon."

Before she could answer, I saw Miss Klein!

It's not too much to say that to me, at that moment, Sanna Klein looked like a bride, dressed head to foot in summer white except for the blue ribbons and blue silk roses on her white straw hat and a wide blue satin sash at her waist. She wore a thin cotton dress you could see through over an embroidered petticoat. The dress had long embroidered sleeves and a high collar. Her lips were the color of ripe raspberries and her hair was jet black, done up in a thick braid. She was the darkest white person I ever saw.

After Smiley's description, I had sort of pictured her as a refined Gypsy dancing-girl type, but there was no sparkle in these dark eyes. She looked anxious, like a little girl traveling alone and scared of losing her train ticket. She smiled nice and all, and stooped down to hug the little children. But it was easy to see that she wasn't having anywhere near as much fun as the folks who had come out to meet her.

Aunt Loma got to Miss Klein before I did. At thirty-one, Loma was still pretty, with eyes blue as Grandpa's and those short saucy curls of red hair peeping out from under her hat. But as always she talked catty, and talking catty with a Northern accent just made it worse. I'm sure she said what she did to Miss Klein just to call attention to herself. She talked real gushy. "I hear you have cousins in Germany, Miss Klein! I know you must be worried about them."

Papa's face turned red. Loma was questioning Miss Klein's patriotism, right out in public, which was the same as saying he shouldn't have hired her.

He spoke quickly. "Miss Klein, meet my sister-in-law, Mrs. Williams. She lives in New York City," he said, as if that explained everything.

"I'm very pleased to meet you, Mrs. Williams," Miss Klein said politely. Then, just as politely— but loud enough for those around her to hear— she said she guessed there were cousins somewhere in Germany, "but I really don't know them. My people came to this country in seventeen-twenty, back in the days when immigrants had to pledge loyalty to the Crown of England. When did your ancestors come, Mrs. Williams?" Loma looked confused and didn't try to answer. Then Miss Klein turned to Mrs. Means and little Ronald, waiting to be introduced.

At that exact moment an over-ripe slice of watermelon dropped out of the tree and landed on Miss Klein's shoulder, splattering her white dress with pink juice and dotting it with black seeds.

16

Everybody jumped back as if she had exploded; then all eyes turned upwards.

"Sampson, he done it!" yelled little Ada Foster, hopping around like a chicken with its head cut off. "Hit's Sampson Blakeslee, Miss Klein! See him? Up in the tree?" She pointed as two bare feet disappeared above a wide limb high overhead.

"Sampson, you come down from there!" Papa yelled.

The handsome, sun-browned face of nine-year-old Sampson appeared among the oak leaves. This was Miss Love's boy. The son Grandpa Blakeslee always wanted but didn't live to see get born. Half-brother to my mother and Aunt Loma.

My half-uncle.

Straddling the wide limb, Sampson grabbed a branch with one hand and leaned towards us so his innocence could be seen.

The band had stopped playing, a politician started giving a speech, and everybody under the tree was staring up at Sampson. "Gosh, Miss Klein, did it hit you?" he called down. Miss Klein was too angry to speak. Jerking off her hat, she picked furiously at bits of red watermelon nestled among the blue silk flowers.

"I am a-SHAMED of you, boy!" yelled Papa. Still looking up, he put his hand under the sticky wetness of Miss Klein's elbow to steady her.

"I didn't mean to, sir. That old watermelon, it just slid right . . ."

Little Ada was dancing again. "Sampson, here comes yore mama! I bet she's go'n git you good!"

17

"Naw, she ain't," mumbled Mr. Homer Boozer, speaking to everybody and nobody. With a hunk of watermelon heart in one hand and a salt shaker in the other, he had pushed through to see what the commotion was about. "Half the boy's trouble is Miss Love don't never git him good. Just gives him a talkin' to." Gesturing with his watermelon towards Sampson's perch in the tree, he said, "Ain't thet right, Will Tweedy? The Widder Blakeslee spares the rod and spiles the chil'."

What the child had spoilt was the vision of Miss Klein's loveliness. But he didn't need any hard words from me on top of what he was about to get, for here came Miss Love, yelling up the tree before she even got to it. "Simpson Rucker Blakeslee! What have you done now!" Then she saw Miss Klein, who had drooped with embarrassment, like a wet cat. "Good Lord, Sampson, what . . . ?"

"I didn't mean to, Mother." His voice sounded small and lonely in the sudden quiet under the tree.

Miss Love's hands were on her hips. "Why in the world did you have that watermelon up there in the first place?"

"I—I wanted to eat it in the tree. I hauled it up here! See?" He spoke proudly, holding out a zinc bucket with a long rope tied to the handle.

"You let that bucket down right now!" Miss Love shouted. "Before it falls on somebody!"

"Yes, ma'am."

In seconds the bucket was dangling in Miss

Klein's face. Miss Love grabbed it out of the air. "Now you get down from there yourself!" I looked up just in time to see Sampson swing to a lower limb, squat, and poise himself to jump to the ground.

Miss Klein gasped. "Oh, mercy, he'll break his neck!"

"Naw, he won't," said Mr. Boozer, taking a bite of his watermelon. "Thet boy's middle name is Circus. Wait'll you see him standin' on his mama's horse and hit a-gallopin'!"

WHUMP! Sampson landed on his feet, almost colliding with Aunt Loma.

"Smart aleck!" Loma snapped, her face flushing.

"Wasn't that a grand leap?" he asked her with a wide smile, as if expecting applause.

Miss Love was trying to dry off the teacher's arm with a lace handkerchief. "I'm just so sorry," she kept murmuring. Then she turned to Sampson. "Now I want to hear you apologize to Miss Klein," she ordered.

"I already did. Didn't I, Miss Klein?" With a bare foot he kicked aside the broken watermelon slice where yellow jackets were already crawling, and looked boldly at the wet dress. "Gosh, ma'am, I really am sorry."

Maybe he meant it, but there was the glimmer of a smirk on his face when he glanced around to see if everybody was looking at him. To old Mr. Boozer he said, "Did you watch me jump, sir?"

Just then Sampson saw and leaped on me,

wrapping his arms around my neck and his legs around my waist. "Uncle Will!" he said happily. "Did you see me jump?"

"Yes, I saw." Untwining him, I lowered him by his arms, and spoke sternly. "Now you get up that busted watermelon and put it in the barrel over yonder."

"Yes, sir, Uncle Will."

"And then go get Miss Klein one of those wet towels off of the sycamore stump."

While the boy picked up the mess with a great show of being busy, Papa made introductions. "Miss Klein, Miss Clack, Miss Hazelhurst, this is my son, Will Tweedy." He said my name proudly, as if I'd just made the honor roll. "Will, these fine young ladies are our new teachers." Then he noticed that Miss Klein was busy waving off yellow jackets. "Son," said Papa, "you better carry her on home."

"You can use my car," Miss Love offered.

"I'm too sticky," protested Miss Klein.

"I've got my motorsickle," I said. "Bein' sticky won't . . ."

"Oh, no, I couldn't!" The prospect seemed to horrify her. "I mean I haven't finished meeting people. I mean thank you but . . . o-o-oh!" She shrank from a yellow jacket hovering near her cheek.

"I've got the sidecar hitched on, Miss Klein."

Sampson had come back from the trash barrel. Waving the towel, he started hopping. "Can I ride, too, Uncle Will? Please, Uncle Will? Please?"

"Hush up beggin', Sampson. Here's the towel, Miss Klein. It might help." I wiped her face and hands and dabbed at the stickiness of the long sleeves, then handed the towel to Miss Love.

Miss Hazelhurst and Miss Clack and Papa turned back to the job at hand—greeting and meeting townspeople—and I took Miss Klein's arm. But she turned back to the boy. "I've got a thing or two to say first. Simpson Blakeslee?"

"Ma'am? You mean me?"

Miss Klein was already acquainted with Sampson of course, being as she was living at Miss Love's house. They were bound to have talked, since he talked to everybody. Talked friendly, I'm sure. But right now the teacher was fearsome to behold.

Using her hat to fan off yellow jackets, she grabbed Sampson by the hand and marched him away from the tree and the crowd. Miss Love looked at me. I nodded. Miss Klein didn't notice us following at a distance. When the teacher stopped, Sampson stood contrite and apprehensive before her. She plopped the hat back on her head. "You look here at me," she demanded, almost whispering, but that didn't hide her anger. "I said look at me. Not at the ground. That's better. Now, my roll-book says your name is Simpson Rucker Blakeslee, so in my classroom, you will be called Simpson."

"Yes, ma'am."

"Now, Simpson, I want to know if you think you're smart."

He looked surprised. After glancing back at his mother and me, he said respectfully, "Yes, ma'am. Everybody in town says I'm smart—like my daddy was."

"Can you name me the nations of the world?"

Hesitating, the boy glanced around again. "Uh, we haven't studied the nations yet, Miss Klein."

"Do you know nine times seven, Simpson?" She slapped at a yellow jacket on her arm. Killed him dead.

"Uh, no, ma'am. We haven't learned the nines." Poor Uncle Simpson. He dug his bare toes in the grass. "I'm s'posed to learn the nines this year, in fourth grade." Boldly: "You s'posed to teach them to me, ma'am."

Her voice softened. "You've had the sevens, Simpson. If seven times nine is sixty-three, what is nine times seven?"

He looked up, puzzled, then beamed. "Nine times seven is sixty-three?"

"That's good, Simpson. Now I want you to understand something else. I hope we'll be friends at home, but there are fifty-five names in my rollbook. That's a lot of children, and I'm supposed to teach all of you, and y'all are all going to learn. My classroom will not be yours or anybody else's playground."

"Yes, ma'am. I mean, no, ma'am. I mean, yes'm, I understand."

Loma had strolled over. She patted him on the cheek and said, "Simpson, sugar, I think you've just met your match."

He glared at her.

Stepping up behind him, I hung my arms around his shoulders and asked, "Miss Klein, ma'am, may we still call him Sampson after school?"

She couldn't help laughing, and Miss Love laughed, and Loma, and then Sampson did. He tugged at my arm. "I need to tell you somethin', Uncle Will."

"Well, OK, but make haste, son."

"I got to whisper it."

His mother shook her head. "Simpson, it's not polite to tell secrets in front of other people. You know that."

I winked at her. "Just this once, Step-Grand-ma?"

"Oh, Will, you . . . you . . ." Miss Love was blustering. "You're always undermining my dis-cipline."

"Yes'm." I smiled at her, shrugging my shoul-ders, and she stalked off, back to the party. Squat-ting down, I cupped my right ear forward with my hand. "All right, Uncle Sampson, the cave's open. Send in your secret." Miss Klein and Loma were watching, and I was showing off.

Sampson whispered in my ear. I tried to look disapproving. He whispered again. I grinned, nodded, and gave him a playful jab in the stom-ach. "OK, son, now go play."

When I stood up, Aunt Loma was right in front of me, her arms crossed. "You spoil him worse than Love does."

I tapped her diamond with a fingernail. "Looks to me like that Yankee spoils you."

"It's time somebody did," she snapped back.

A yellow jacket was buzzing around Miss Klein in circles. "Please, Mr. Tweedy, I think I'd better . . ."

"Will," said Aunt Loma, "I hope you don't really expect her to ride in that silly sidecar. She won't have a dab of dignity left."

"Are you willin', Miss Klein? If you'd rather not, I'll . . ."

"Anything, Mr. Tweedy. Oh, Lord, here's two more! No matter which way I turn, they're hanging in the air!"

"We'll walk around the crowd, through these woods, to get where I'm parked." With my hand on her elbow, I looked back and said, "Bye, Aunt Loma. See you later."

Three

THE HAR-R-RUMPH, HAR-R-RUMPH seemed deaf-
ening as we headed down the wagon road towards
the park entrance. Despite I didn't go fast, Miss
Klein was scared to death—braced herself in the
sidecar and shut her eyes tight.

At Miss Love's house we *varoomed* around to
the backyard, where I stopped under the big elm.
In the quiet after I shut off the engine, a cow lowed
somewhere far off and a rooster crowed. When
Miss Klein opened her eyes, she looked up to the
roof of leaves above us and murmured, "What a
beautiful tree!"

I told her it was my Grandpa Blakeslee's favorite. "He always said *el-lum* tree, like it had two
syllables, so naturally I said *el-lum,* too. Then a
botany professor over at the university set me
straight."

A mockingbird lit on a high branch and commenced his song. She watched him for a minute,
then lowered her gaze and smiled at me. "It wasn't
a bad ride," she said, taking off her hat. "Bumpy,
but not scary. Well, Mr. Tweedy, thank you." But
she made no move to go. Her black hair glinted
blue in a dapple of sunlight. A breeze stirred a
loose wisp of hair across a seed that had dried

25

on her cheek. She smelled like warm water-melon.

"You know somethin'?" I said. "Watermelon is very becomin'—to you, I mean. I don't think it would improve me any."

She smiled again. "Maybe you don't need improving."

"The U.S. Army says I do."

"What do you mean?"

"They won't let me join up unless I get fat. I'm six-foot-one and weigh about fifty pounds, which . . ."

She laughed. "Nobody's that skinny."

"Well, I guess a hundred pounds."

"That can't be. I weigh a hundred and twelve myself and I'm just five-three, and . . . oh, you're teasing!"

"Actually, a hundred and twenty-five according to the scales they use at Papa's store to weigh out cow feed and guano. Still, that doesn't suit the Army. Like I told the recruitin' officer, if I was a hog, it'd make sense to fatten me up for slaugh-ter. But as a soldier boy, the thinner I get, the harder I'll be to hit." I meant to sound light-hearted, but I couldn't laugh. My hands tightened on the handlebars. "Last week in Atlanta I saw a fraternity brother. He was in Army uniform with a corporal's stripes. I hadn't laid eyes on him in a year and we were good friends at the university, but I crossed the street hopin' he wouldn't see me."

I hadn't meant to say all that. Miss Klein looked

embarrassed for me. After an awkward silence, she said, "I really must go in, Mr. Tweedy."

I pretended not to hear her. Leaning back from the handlebars, I let my hands drop to my knees. "Over in Athens they say my work is important to the war."

"Then you must have a very responsible position."

"I'm what they call a county agent."

"A what?"

"The School of Agriculture thought it up two years ago, just before I graduated. They made me county agent for Clarke County." Miss Klein leaned forward, her hand on the handle of the sidecar's little door, but I kept talking. "I tell farmers how to farm."

She turned towards me again. "You're a farmer?"

"No, this is a salaried job. But it's the biggest joke I ever got into. Farmers aren't exactly thrilled over havin' a fool college boy claimin' to know better than they do. When the professor hired me, I said, 'Sir, even the hired hands will see I don't know what I'm doin'.' He said, 'If somebody has a problem you can't solve, don't admit it. Stall till you can find out what to do.' " I paused. "But you aren't interested in all this, Miss Klein. I better let you . . ."

"Oh, but I really am interested, Mr. Tweedy. I was born on a farm. My daddy was a farmer. My brother is, and . . ."

Surprised, I said, "I bet you miss it, don't you?

27

The farm, I mean. And the quiet, and the smell of fresh-cut hay and fresh-turned soil, and watchin' newborn lambs and calves frolic, and . . ."

"I don't miss any of that." Miss Klein shook her head. "I don't miss drawing well water, either. I will never ever live out in the country again. A man trying to make a decent living on the land? That's a lot bigger joke than what you do, Mr. Tweedy. Farming is nothing but hard work and high hopes, debt and disappointment."

"But I'll know all the new methods. Farmin' is a gamble, all right. Still, that's what keeps it excitin'."

"I hate excitement. That's just another word for worry."

"Farmin' lets a man work outdoors. I couldn't stand bein' cooped up in a store or office the rest of my life. Right now, though, I just want to enlist. Bein' a county agent won't mean pea-turkey to the fightin' men, the ones over here, or over there either." I itched to pluck that watermelon seed off her cheek. "Want me to give you a for-instance, Miss Klein? Yesterday I was out in the county advisin' an old fool named Duck Lassiter how to get one row of cotton picked. How's that go'n hep beat the Kaiser?"

She looked puzzled. "One row?"

"Old Duck plowed his field in a spiral, like a snail shell, and bragged that it was go'n be the world's longest gol-durn cotton row. His field hands hoed it, and they slopped the stalks with arsenic and molasses to kill the boll weevils, but they don't want to pick the cotton." I laughed. "Cotton pickers like to take a row apiece and move down a field together. If they have to space themselves out, that's lonesome pickin'. And it'll be heavy totin' and a lot of wasted time if they have to cut across the spiral to get to the cotton wagon. I told Duck he'd have to make a road across the spiral, but he said that'd mess up his row."

Miss Klein was really laughing. She didn't notice a yellow jacket closing in on her scent.

"Now tomorrow evenin', I'll be talkin' to a dozen or so farmers about crop rotation, which just might hep feed my frat brother. If the war lasts long enough." I couldn't resist any longer. I plucked the seed off her cheek and held it out to her. "A souvenir," I said.

Her smile was rueful. "I don't think I want it."

"Then I do," said I, and put it in my shirt pocket.

At that moment Miss Klein stood up, frantic, waving off the yellow jackets with her hat. Right quick I helped her out of the sidecar and followed her up the back steps. After Miss Klein dodged inside the screen door, I asked if I could take her to church the next Sunday night. "By then," I said through the screen, "I can tell you if I figured out how to get the world's longest row of cotton picked without messin' it up."

She hesitated. "I'm sorry, Mr. Tweedy. I'm going over to Jefferson Saturday. It'll be late when I get back Sunday. I'll . . . uh, I will be visiting my sweetheart's family."

She hesitated again, then blurted out, "I'll be meeting them for the first time, Mr. Tweedy, and I'm scared to death!"

Her perfume of watermelon drifted through the screen, and two yellow jackets crawled across it, looking for a way to get to her—like me. Trying to sound casual, I said, "You go'n marry this feller?"

"I'm . . . not sure." My spirits rose. She kind of smiled. "He did ask me one time if I could cook. That seemed encouraging."

"Can you? Cook?"

"I told him I could make real good mayonnaise and divinity candy. I don't think he was impressed."

"I am. Nothin' in the world better than divinity candy dipped in mayonnaise."

She half-laughed, traced her right index finger down the screen. "I just wish I knew where I stand with him. He writes me love letters and recites love sonnets, and he wants me to meet his family, and last time he was in Mitchellville, just before he left he said, 'If I asked you to marry me, would you?' He said it like teasing. There's only one answer to a sideways question like that. I said, 'Well, I might.' That made him mad, Mr. Tweedy! Heavens, did he expect me to say 'Oh, goody!' or beg him 'Please, ask me'? Now his mother has invited me to a family dinner party, and I don't know what that's supposed to mean. Am I being auditioned for a place in the family, or am I just invited because Hugh wants me there? I don't know how I'm supposed to act."

30

"You could practice on my folks," I offered. "I'll take you over home for supper tonight."

She laughed. A nervous little laugh. "I guess I just never have liked meeting people I don't know."

"You sound like my Grandpa Blakeslee. He used to say he didn't like to go anywhere he hadn't been. You really want to marry this feller, don't you?" A stupid question, but she answered it.

"I think I do. I feel so proud when I'm with him, Mr. Tweedy. Before him, I never even met anybody who went to Harvard. He remembers every name and date in history. He can quote whole acts of Shakespeare. And he . . . he actually enjoys me! When I said that to my Sister Maggie —that he seems to enjoy me—she said, 'Why wouldn't he? He does all the talking.' "

"He sounds like a friend of mine," I said. "Pink Predmore. Old Pink went to Harvard. Went there a nice feller, came out a snob with a silly accent."

Her reply was defensive. "Hugh isn't like that. He's . . ." She cut off the subject. "I don't know why I'm telling you this. And it's inconsiderate of me to keep you standing there talking through a screen door."

"I like talkin' through screen doors. But I expect you need to wash off, Miss Klein, and I got to go by home and see my sister. She's leavin' tomorrow for college." I had turned and was headed down the steps when I remembered something. "You want to hear Sampson's secret?"

31

"Why, Mr. Tweedy! You wouldn't tell a child's secret!"

"He said to. Said tell you he was aimin' at Loma with that watermelon. You met Loma, Miz Williams. She's his half-sister and my aunt, and neither one of us is crazy about her. He felt bad bout hittin' you, but I think he felt worse bout missin' her. You sure did shut Aunt Loma up, Miss Klein."

"What?"

"About those German ancestors, how they came over in the seventeen-hundreds."

"Would she be impressed if I told her one of them got a land grant from the King of England?"

"Yeah, that would impress Loma."

She laughed. "But then I'd have to un-impress her by admitting he couldn't write, and that he lost his land in a wrestling match."

"I think even Loma would rather have a German wrastler in the family than somebody like our Cudn Hortense, the wife of a Blakeslee cousin. She's traced her ancestry back to British royalty. Claims her parlor furniture came from Lord Baltimore, and she's got ribbons tied across the chair arms so nobody can sit in them. Cudn Hortense looks down on anybody whose name isn't English or French."

Miss Klein sighed. "There are a mighty lot of folks like her, Mr. Tweedy. With a four-year college degree I thought it would be easy to get a teaching job, but three towns turned me down. One school superintendent claimed the places were all filled, but a friend of mine who teaches there said they still had two openings. She thought the problem was my German name." Miss Klein was staring down at her hands. "Mama used to be so proud of our being German, because Germans are said to be smart. Since the war started, she never mentions it."

I wanted to see her laugh again. "They tell it on my Cudn T.D. how last year he refused to go to his daughter's weddin'. Said, 'I cain't bear to see Ethel git marritto a man from Texas named Ertzberger.' His wife, Cudn Huldah, said, 'T.D., how could you forgit that you marrit a Holtz-kaemper!' He said things were way different back then.

"Well, Miss Klein, I better get on over home. Like I said, my little sister's leavin' for college in the mornin'. I'll be seein' you soon, I hope?"

Four

MY SISTER, MARY TOY, was nineteen and a senior at Cox College in College Park, Georgia, near Atlanta. When I got home I found her in her room, packing for school. She'd come home early from the watermelon cutting.

Mama hadn't gone at all, despite Papa being president of the school board. She was in the kitchen, reaching into the warming oven above the big iron cookstove, taking out bowls of fried chicken, black-eyed peas, string beans, and a sweet potato soufflé. Mama never cooked at night on Sundays except maybe to slice tomatoes, since Queenie always cooked enough dinner to have it for supper. Still, there was always a rush to get it on the table early on account of Sunday night preaching.

"I cain't go to church with y'all tonight, Mama," I said. Lifting the thin linen cloth that kept flies off the bread, I picked up a cornstick. "I'll have to get on back to Athens. After dark it's slow goin' on a motorsickle."

"But you'll stay to supper, won't you, Will?" Mama didn't say it like an invite. More like an urgent plea. I realized she'd been crying.

"What's the matter, Mama?"

"I've got one of my sick headaches," she said, and burst into new tears. "Son, Loma's go'n go back to New York Wednesday mornin', and she's takin' . . . Will, she's takin' poor li'l . . ." When she got hold of herself, she looked towards the breakfast room door to be sure nobody was coming, and said in a low voice, "Will, the Yankee that Loma's engaged to, he's got a name so foreign I cain't pronounce it. And he's old! Will, what she came home for, she's go'n take Campbell Junior back up North with her!"

Campbell Junior had been staying with Mama and Papa for two years, ever since Aunt Loma set out on what she called her career. "Well," I reminded Mama, "you been sayin' the boy ought to be with his mother."

"But he's not go'n be with her! Will, that man she's engaged to? He's go'n pay for Campbell Junior at one of those military schools for rich boys. A boardin' school that's a hundred miles or more from New York City!"

"Good Lord! Loma don't know upside down from sideways! Campbell Junior cain't even hold his own with the boys here in Cold Sassy. Him in military school? He's never had a gun in his hands. Cain't stand thinkin' bout a bird or rabbit gettin' shot. Him in military school?"

Mama took it up. "They'll make fun of him for bein' fat and they'll mock his Southern accent, and . . . and I don't know what all." She looked around again at the door. Lowering her voice still more, she said, "If you ast me, he'll

35

die on the vine up there, or cry his eyes out, one. He's bright as a penny and makes good marks but . . ."

"But he don't know beans bout bein' a boy."

"He's such a little gentleman. They'll make fun of his manners."

Campbell Junior wasn't a little gentleman. He was a little lady. That was the trouble. He'd grown up around too many women. Papa treated him like his own, but Papa was always at the store or at a church meeting.

"Will, stay to supper and talk Loma out of it," Mama begged. "Campbell Junior is petrified."

I knew that anything I said would just make Aunt Loma more determined. "I'll try to come back Tuesday, Mama, and talk to him." I pulled out my pocket watch. "I really cain't stay long now, but since supper's ready I'll eat with y'all."

Mama splashed some water on her face, blew her nose, told me to bring the sweet potato soufflé, and picked up the platter of fried chicken. "What with the shame of his daddy shootin' himself dead and all," she muttered, "that poor boy's had more'n his share already."

The family gathered, and we hadn't sat down at the table good before Aunt Loma said in her put-on Northern accent, "You must have felt like a white knight this afternoon, Will, rescuing that poor maiden from those great big old mean yellow jackets."

Loma always did know how to get my goat.

When she was twelve and I was six, she decided to make me call her Aunt Loma. Mama, Papa, Granny, and even Grandpa had backed her up. They said she was a young lady now and I must show her proper respect.

Ever since I got grown, and especially after she got to be thirty, she'd been trying to make me go back to calling her just Loma. I could feel sorry for any woman worrying about getting old, even Aunt Loma. So I knew how to get back at her. Whenever I felt hateful, I'd stick my face in hers and say, "Ain't you my Aint Loma?"

That night around the supper table I said, "What I want to know, Aint Loma, is about this rich old Yankee you go'n marry. What's his name, and just how old is he? And how rich?"

"That's how rich!" Reaching across the table, Aunt Loma made a fist of her left hand and wagged that big old diamond ring at me.

Campbell Junior interrupted. "Cudn Will, I don't want to go up North," he whined, and bit glumly into a drumstick. I was his last hope. "Tell Mama I ain't go'n go to no military school."

"You'll like it once you get there," his mother said, not unkindly. "But you might as well quit saying 'ain't' right now. And start cutting up your chicken. New York people don't say 'ain't' and they don't eat chicken with their fingers."

"Not even fried chicken?"

"They don't have fried chicken. They flour it and brown it and then steam it awhile. That's what they call fried chicken."

Campbell Junior stared at her, unbelieving, and slowly lowered the drumstick to his plate.

"Never mind," Loma said. "Honey, you're going to have a daddy."

"I don't want a daddy. Uncle Hoyt is my daddy."

Smiling very sweetly at him, Loma said in exaggerated Southern, "Honey chile, you just go'n love Mr. Vitch."

"Mr. Vitch?" Papa repeated.

"The man I'm going to marry." She rattled off a twenty-syllable last name that I couldn't understand then and never could remember later. "Our friends call him Vitch. But when it's just us, I call him Mr. Rich Vitch. He likes that."

"Is he a Bolshevik?" asked Papa.

"Don't be silly, Brother Hoyt. Rich men aren't Bolsheviks."

"With a name like that he could be anything," said Papa.

Campbell Junior just sat there pushing his black-eyed peas into a mound with his fork and a cornstick.

"How," I asked, "did this man Itch make his money?"

Loma's face flushed. "I said Vitch. *Vitch.* I think he made it in the steel business. Or maybe coal. I'm not sure. But he told me he's doubled his money in the stock market."

I felt ornery enough to want to rake her a little. "You haven't said how old he is."

Loma hedged. "Wasn't Pa fifty-nine when he

38

married Miss Love? I'd say Mr. Vitch is a little older than that. Maybe two or three years older."

I started to ask if it was more like five years or ten or maybe twenty, but I chanced to look over at Mama. She couldn't stand it when conversation got tense at the table—or anywhere else, for that matter.

Mary Toy spoke up. "Aunt Loma whistled at church this morning, Will. It was just beautiful!"

Loma blushed with pleasure. As if suddenly realizing Mary Toy was somebody she cared about, she asked, "What are you majoring in, honey?"

"Latin."

"Latin? I majored in elocution and it's gotten me all the way to the New York stage. But, Lord, what in the world can you do with Latin?"

Papa, about to bite into the pulley bone, waved it in protest. "Mary Toy's go'n teach Latin, Loma. That's what."

For a few minutes everybody just ate. I found myself staring at my blue-eyed, auburn-haired sister. She was flowering at college. Her face was plain, like Mama's, but radiant in a special way. She and I liked each other.

I glanced then from Mama at one end of the table to Papa at the other, noticing with surprise, as if I hadn't been around lately, that Mama looked several years older than Miss Love, though they were the same age, and that Papa, at forty-eight, had gone from stocky to portly. Most prosperous middle-aged men got portly, as if it took a protruding stomach to show off a gold watch fob.

The store had survived the depression of 1914. When farmers made money, the store did too and the war had sent cotton prices soaring, easing Papa's worries. He'd started talking about buying the farm in Banks County from his father and giving it to me.

Papa still didn't have a sense of humor. People said if Mr. Hoyt heard something funny in the morning, it was night before he laughed. I knew he was a good man though, except for that one never-mentioned event that hung in the air at home. I wished he'd talk about it to me so I could tell him I didn't really hold it against him. Well, maybe he knew I didn't. We had got a lot closer since Grandpa Blakeslee died. When I was a boy I never noticed how Papa doted on me. I was too busy doting on Grandpa, despite Papa was always saying I made him proud.

What hung in the air right now was the family's unspoken objection to Mr. Vitch. Campbell Junior's fork screeched across his plate, Mama set her tea glass in its coaster, Mary Toy fiddled with her napkin ring. The loudness of these small sounds was finally interrupted by Loma's voice.

She didn't start off talking loud, just tight and bitter. "Y'all don't want Campbell Junior to get the education he deserves, do you? Here he's got a chance to go to a fine boarding school and you want to keep him stuck in P.C.—a backward town if I ever saw one."

Papa was indignant. Speaking as president of the school board, he said, "For Pete's sake, Loma, Campbell Junior cain't get a better education anywhere than right here. Mary Toy, pass the sugar. Chi'ren are lucky who grow up in a small town."

Loma snapped back at him, "You're the epitome of small town, Brother Hoyt. You think the city limits of P.C. are the boundary of the world. Even Atlanta"—she sputtered—"to you Atlanta is just the Southeastern Fair every fall. And you think New York is on the other side of the moon."

"I've been to New York City, you know. How you think we'd stock the store if I didn't go up there? But I tell you one thing, young lady. Anybody who'd deliberately go live in New York City is . . ."

"See what I mean? What this is all about tonight is y'all never did want me to go to New York, and now you don't want me to marry a Yankee." She glared around the table. "Y'all are so smug—you more than anybody, Will." Really gearing up, she had lapsed into Southern. "Why do y'all hate me? Why cain't . . . why cain't I live my life like I want to? Y'all are all like Pa. I had my big chance years ago, when that tourin' Shakespeare company asked me to join the troupe. But, oh no, Pa said, 'Loma, you ain't go'n be no actress, so hesh up. I ain't a-go'n let you do it.' I'll never forget the way he said it, like he was puttin' his foot down on me, and squashin' me. Then everybody in town had to have their say. 'Lord hep Loma if'n she ends up a actress.' I said someday I'll be doin'

41

command performances for King Edward the Seventh, and they said even if I did, I'd never live down the taint. Why does everybody hate me?"

"Now, Loma," I said. "Now, Loma, don't . . ."

"Don't you don't me, Will Tweedy! It's all y'all's fault I married Campbell Williams. Pa said, 'You ain't marryin' that fool, Loma. I ain't a-go'n let you.' Well, I showed Pa. But I'd have thought twice if he'd left me alone."

Campbell Junior's head hung down like a rose-bud that had withered before it could open. No-body said a word. As I'd just been reminded, if you talked back to Aunt Loma, it only fed the fire.

"Everybody said I couldn't make a livin' in New York City, but I did."

"Now, Loma," said Mama. "We just think you ought to marry your own kind."

"Mr. Vitch is my own kind. He cares about the finer things of life. And I'm go'n marry him. And I'm go'n keep on with my career, no matter what he or anybody else says. I found out there's not much future for an actress with a Southern accent who can only play Shakespeare and Abraham Lincoln's wife. But I'm not just any two-bit bo-hem'en. You'd know that if any of you had ever bothered to come see me perform. Y'all say you're too busy to come. Main thing, y'all are ashamed of my bein' an actress. You may like to know I've been offered a part in a real play! Mr. Vitch thinks I ought to quit the theater when we marry, but I've told him and told him . . ."

She stopped. Her face was steamy red. In a

frenzy, she raked her fingers through the short red curls, then clutched her forehead and threw her head back like in a New York melodrama. "I asked why y'all hate me. But I know why. Y'all are jealous. You'd like to be out of this hick town too, wouldn't you? Well, Campbell Junior's go'n be out of it, and have a chance to be somebody. He's not . . ."

"Loma Williams, shut up!" yelled Papa, banging his fist on the table.

I thought she'd start crying or light into Papa, one. But she didn't do either. Just pursed her lips and raised her chin—and shut us all out.

It was Mama who looked ready to break apart.

We all fell to eating again, or trying to. For once I couldn't think of a thing to say. But Mary Toy did.

With a forkful of string beans suspended halfway to her mouth, she grinned around the table as if Loma had just been chattering about somebody's mah-jongg party or the price of French perfume. "Let me tell the funniest thing!" said Mary Toy, then took time to chew her beans before she told it. "You know I went over to Athens last week? I went for a lecture by a famous woman Latin scholar. She read from a prepared speech. But all of a sudden she stopped, just stood there staring at her paper. Finally, shaking her head she said, 'This is certainly strange. Here's a word I never heard of. I can't imagine what it means, but it's in my handwriting! It's spelled H-E-R-E.' "

The faces around our supper table went blank.

43

Campbell Junior was the first to laugh. He never had been dull-witted.

"H-E-R-E," Mama murmured. "H-E-R-E." Then it dawned on her—and the rest of us. "That spells *here!* Just plain old HERE!"

"Hear, hear!" I said, and even Aunt Loma got off her high horse and laughed. All of us did.

Then Mary Toy changed the subject again. "On the train ride home," she said, looking at me, "I saw that red-headed Sorrows boy. You remember the Sorrowses, Will."

"Yeah, they moved to Commerce a few years ago. Julian Sorrows was in my class. We called him Julie."

"That's right. Julie. He's the one I saw. He told me he had enlisted in the Army. He seemed so proud."

I knew what Mary Toy was saying: why hadn't I enlisted yet. And I knew Mama and Papa were sitting there hoping I never would. Her question and their dread hung in the air. Even to my own family I was embarrassed to admit I got turned down just for being skinny. Mary Toy and Loma wouldn't believe it, and Mama and Papa would want to starve me to death.

I marveled how easy it had been to tell Sanna Klein.

Of course I was registered for the draft—one of 120,000 white boys registered in Georgia. "Did you know that more'n a hundred thousand Georgia Negroes are registered?" I asked casually. "If they keep callin' up our colored boys, Southern farmers sure will be hurtin' for wages hands. Already are hurtin' from so many colored families movin' up North, and now they're worried about the Army's draftin' jarheads."

"Jarheads?" asked Campbell Junior.

"I'm talkin' about mules, son. Last week the paper said the United States has already shipped a hundred thousand mules to France, and three hundred thousand horses. They pull artillery and ammunition wagons."

Papa was always uneasy with war talk, whereas Mary Toy was obsessed with it. She had a sweetheart, an engineering student at Georgia Tech in Atlanta. Now she said he'd written that aviators were being trained on the Tech campus, and that he wanted to apply to be one.

"That's what I'd like to do," I said. "Fly an air machine. I expect they want lightweight aviators." I glanced at Papa. When he didn't say anything, I added, "I expect aerial fightin' will get more and more important as the war goes on."

Mary Toy put in eagerly, "Remember what Grandpa Blakeslee said his granddaddy said? How someday people would ride through the air? Grandpa said folks thought the old man had lost his mind."

"I wish it was still just a prediction," said Mama. "Imagine, flyin' through the sky! The very idea scares me half to death."

Campbell Junior nodded. "Me too. I'd just bout soon fly, though, as go to a old military school full of Yankees."

Sitting beside him, I patted his knee, then pushed back my chair. "Son, I got to head on back to Athens. But Tuesday I'm go'n come to Cold Sassy, and I'm go'n take you to the drugstore and we'll get some ice cream. I'll buy you the big dish. Mama, I hate to eat and run, but I don't want to let the road get dark on me. Aint Loma, I'll see you Tuesday too. I'll kiss you good-bye then."

She always knew when I was teasing. "You don't exactly have to kiss me Tuesday, either," she said, smiling as I stood up. "But I hope you will." She wagged her left hand in my face again, and the diamond sparkled.

Five

I HAD ALREADY set up Tuesday to go see Mr. Ambrose Hall, whose one-horse farm was just south of Cold Sassy on the road to Commerce. To get there I took the early afternoon freight train from Athens, riding high in the cab with the engineer, Mr. Talkington. We'd been friends ever since I saved him from killing me on Blind Tillie Trestle when I was fourteen. I was fooling around up there on the trestle when his train came thundering onto the tracks, headed right towards me. I quick stretched myself out thin between the rails and the train ran over me, but I lived to tell it. All of which happened the same day Grandpa Blakeslee eloped with Miss Love. Now I rode with Mr. Talkington any time I couldn't wait for the passenger train to Cold Sassy.

I said good-bye to Mr. Talkington in Cold Sassy, borrowed Papa's Buick, drove out to see Mr. Ambrose, then back to Cold Sassy, where Campbell Junior was waiting for me on Papa's front steps.

When we got to the drugstore, Dr. Clarke, the pharmacist, was behind the counter. He piled an extra scoop on Campbell Junior's big-dish ice cream. "That ought to hold you from here to New

47

York City," he said, sliding it across the counter. "You want a big dish, Will?"

"Yessir. I got to fatten up."

"You been eatin' like a horse ever since you got legs, Will, but you still look like a crane. You'll use up this much ice cream just twitchin' your shoulders."

"I reckon I picked up that habit from my grand-daddy. He was a champion shoulder-twitcher."

"For a fact he was," said the druggist. "But, Will, if you want to gain weight, my advice is get married. I never knew a young man didn't gain after the weddin'. I was up twenty pounds in three months. Campbell Junior, how bout a Co-Cola?"

The boy looked at me. I nodded and said we'd both have a Coke.

Dr. Clarke put each Coca-Cola glass under the syrup spout, then under the carbonated water spout, stirred with a long spoon, chipped some ice off the big block, spooned it in, and handed over the drinks.

"No charge, Will. I mean for the boy's extra scoop and his Co-Cola. Campbell Junior, do yourself proud in that Yankee school, hear? And when you get back home, come tell me if they make Co-Colas up yonder as good as I do."

"Yessir. Thank you, sir. But maybe they don't drink Co-Colas up North, Dr. Clarke. Mama says they don't eat fried chicken."

"Everybody drinks Co-Colas, son. Even Yankees."

As we sat down at one of the little round tables,

white-topped on black iron legs, I nodded towards the ceiling fan. "Eat fast, Campbell Junior. The breeze feels mighty good, but it sure can melt ice cream."

While we ate, I told him about going to New York City with Papa on a buying trip for the store. I didn't tell him how scared I was, being only seven and having heard all my life how mean damn yankees were.

Campbell Junior got a little excited while I was raving on about the wonders of New York. But then he started talking about leaving home and all. "Miss Willa had a good-bye party for me today," he said sadly. "She made a cake for the whole class. She gave me the biggest piece, Cudn Will, and she ain't been my teacher but two days! I begged Mama to let me go to school in the mornin', just till time for the train, but she says I cain't."

When we got back to the house, I stood on the veranda with him, trying to think how to cheer him up. Then I remembered my buckeye. I pulled it out of my pants pocket and handed it to him. "For luck, son."

"Thank you, Cudn Will. Gosh, that makes forty-two!"

"Forty-two?"

"Wait a minute, can you?" He disappeared into the house and came back holding up a cloth tobacco sack. It bulged with buckeyes. "Everybody in my class brought me one today," he said proudly. "For luck in my new school."

"Well, that ought to do it, Campbell Junior. If you run short of money, you can sell some to those Yankee boys."

"I bet they never heard of a buckeye," he said.

We shook hands, man to man. But then I hugged him. Hard.

"You'll do fine, big boy. Just remember where you're from and who your folks are. Act proud."

He went inside, trying to be brave.

Aunt Loma was in the backyard out near Mama's flower pit, digging up a magnolia seedling. It was only a foot high, but it had five or six big waxy green leaves.

Lighting a cigar, I watched a minute, then asked, "What you doin', Aunt Loma?"

"I'm gettin' me a magnolia tree." She didn't sound Yankee at all. Her short red hair, damp with sweat, had shrunk into tight curls.

"You go'n carry it on the train?"

"In my lap all the way, if I have to."

I took the trowel out of her hands. "Let me do that. You need a bigger pot."

"I cain't hold too big a pot," she protested.

"But if it's too little a pot you won't have enough dirt to nourish the tree. I'll get one out of the flower pit. And we need some good black dirt instead of this red clay."

She stood there watching, rubbing her hands together to get off the dirt, while I dug up the seedling and potted it with black dirt from out by the cowshed. "Don't let it dry out," I said, watering it from the rain barrel, "and give it plenty of light. Do you have a window facin' south?"

"How do you tell south?"

I explained as simply as I knew how. "If sun comes in a window in the mornin', that's the east side of the buildin'. If it's sunny in the afternoon, that's the west side. If it doesn't come in at all, that's north. The best exposure is southern. Come winter, sunlight will flood into a south window." I didn't say how dumb it was for anybody to be thirty-one years old and not know such, though I was tempted. "I hope you don't expect to show off this li'l old thing. It won't impress anybody."

Brushing dirt off the pot with my hands, I looked at Aunt Loma. She was wiping her eyes. "I'm not takin' it to impress anybody," she said, her lip quivering. "I'm takin' it for myself. It . . . I need somethin' to remind me of home."

I handed her the seedling. "Mama has a scrap left over from that new oilcloth on the kitchen table. Tie some around the pot, why don't you? So it won't get your dress dirty. Well, good-bye, Aunt Loma." I put my arms around both of them —her and the baby magnolia. "Look after this good, hear, and look after your boy. And you look after yourself."

"You too, Will. Do you still see Trulu?"

"No," I said firmly.

"Just asking. You're too good for her anyway. Well, good-bye, Will."

51

"You haven't said when you're gettin' married."

"Some time next month. In New York, of course. Not here."

"Mama will have a conniption fit."

"It can't be helped." Her tone was formal, defensive.

"I don't know as I can get off work long enough to make the trip."

"It won't be a family kind of wedding," she said quickly. "Just the two of us, and a justice of the peace. And Campbell Junior, of course, and two of our friends for witnesses."

I was about to say nobody in our family had ever got hitched in a courthouse when she added, "Pa and Miss Love did it that way, remember." Raising her chin, she said again, "Good-bye, Will," and started up the back steps with her magnolia tree.

Campbell Junior wasn't the only one trying to act brave.

"Aunt Loma?" I called after her. "Uh, take the oilcloth off when you get there, hear? The roots'll rot if it cain't drain."

She nodded.

I called again. "Don't worry if the leaves fall off. That won't mean it's dead."

Though it wasn't anywhere near train time, I didn't want to hang around. I'd had about all the sad good-byes I could take. I decided to amble on up to Miss Love's. Check over the animals. See who was home.

On the way I met Sampson. "What you got there, son?" I asked.

"A present for Campbell Junior." He proudly held up a big contraption of nailed-together wood scraps. "See, sir, he can mash this and that and that, and then turn this magic wand down towards Georgia and wish himself right back home. If he does everything right, the wish will come true. I invented it!"

After inspecting and admiring and not saying it had about as much chance of going to New York as Campbell Junior had of staying here, I asked Sampson if he thought Miss Klein was a good teacher.

He said she sure was strict.

I asked if Miss Klein and Miss Clack and Miss Hazelhurst had got home yet.

"No, sir. All the teachers stayed in after school. They had to go to the principal's office," he said, spinning a loosely nailed stick on his invention. "I don't think they've been bad. They just had to go meet."

"Yeah, well, son, I'm on my way to your house. It's time to inspect the livestock." Every so often I'd stop by to check over Papa's cow, Grandpa's old mule, Miss Love's gelding, known as Mr. Beautiful, and Sampson's pony, Miss H, named by him when he was four and learning the alphabet. "You still puttin' that salve on H's leg?" I asked.

The boy hedged. "Uh, most of the time Loomis does it, Uncle Will. Mother pays him to feed and

53

water, so I just asked him to doctor H's leg, too, while he's at it."

"It's not your place to tell Loomis what to do."

"He said he'd be glad to. Just glad to."

"Well, you're old enough now to do all the stable work. You're not even feedin' and curryin' the pony?"

"Why should I, Uncle Will? I don't ride her anymore. She's got so little, and all she wants to do is walk or trot. Hey, just let me run give this to Campbell Junior. I'll be right back. I want to show you my new circus trick on Mr. Beautiful!"

"You're gettin' too big for your britches, but you're not big enough for that tall horse. Stay off of him, Sampson."

His face reddened. "Mother lets me. I don't have to mind you."

"And I don't have to fool with a smart aleck named Simpson." I turned to walk away. He grabbed my arm.

"Please don't call me Simpson, Uncle Will. Cause of Miss Klein, everybody at school calls me Simpleton now. Please, Uncle Will? I was just mad at you. I didn't mean it, sir."

I looked at him hard. "Try being a friend to Campbell Junior this afternoon, Sampson. He's in bad need of one right now."

Six

WHEN I GOT back to Miss Love's house after checking the animals, I was naturally hoping Sanna Klein would be there. She wasn't, and it occurred to me that even if she came in before I had to leave, she probably wouldn't be by herself. So I sat down at the kitchen table and wrote her a note, using my office stationery with the letterhead *Cooperative Extension Service, Georgia State College of Agriculture, Athens, Georgia.*

> Dear Miss Klein,
> I would still like to see you Sunday night provided you get in from Jefferson early enough. I plan on being in Cold Sassy anyway, so you don't need to let me know ahead. I'll come down to Miss Love's right after supper to see if you're back yet, and we can go to church. I often spend Sunday night with my folks and ride the early freight train back to Athens next morning.
> Please excuse the eccentric appearance of this paper. It's been folded up in my pants pocket.
> Hoyt Willis Tweedy

Miss Love kept envelopes on top of her desk. I wrote "To Miss Klein" on one and dropped the letter in the teachers' mail basket on the hall table by the stairs. I couldn't help noticing Miss Klein had a letter there from Mrs. Henry K. Jolley in Mitchellville, and two more in long business envelopes with the embossed return address *Blankenship, Crowe, and Blankenship, Attorneys-at-Law, Jefferson, Georgia.* In a bold scrawl above the print was written "Hugh A. Blankenship, Jr."

I knew about the legal firm of Blankenship and Crowe. I used to go over to Jefferson sometimes for court week with Pink Predmore and his law-yer-daddy, and if it was a trial that amounted to anything, you could count on Mr. Blankenship or Mr. Crowe representing one side or the other. I was discouraged for a second or two but tossed my note in the basket anyway.

I blame everything that's happened between Sanna and me on the sight of that name scrawled so bold and confident, as if he and his daddy's firm had legal rights to her. Before that moment I'd only been smitten by Sanna Klein's beauty. Suddenly I was determined to marry her.

That's what I was thinking as I headed for the front door, but I stopped in my tracks when I re-alized that the veranda was occupied. I recognized the voice of Miss Alice Ann Boozer. "Did you know Loma Blakeslee Williams come in on the train last week from New York City?"

"Everybody this side the cemetery knows it,"

said a voice I couldn't quite place. "Why you think I wouldn't know a thing like that?"

"Cause you been gone, Miz Jones," said Miss Alice Ann.

Of course. The other lady was the wife of the Reverend Brother Belie Jones.

I knew I ought to go speak to them, but not being in much of a mood for woman talk, I tiptoed over to Miss Love's wing chair by the window and sat down with a magazine. But I couldn't read with those voices floating right in. I heard Miss Alice Ann ask Mrs. Jones how was her sister.

"Sister's really on the down-go," said the preacher's wife. "But I couldn't just stay on there till Kingdom Come. Like I told her, Brother Jones needs lookin' after too. So yesterd'y I hired her a colored girl and took the train home."

"Where is it she lives? I never can remember."

"A little coal-minin' town—Brilliant, in Alabama."

"Funny name."

I could hear rocking chairs just going to town out there. Then one stopped and Miss Alice Ann spoke again. "When's Miss Love go'n git here?"

"Any minute now. I phoned down at the store, and she said meet her here, she'd be on terreckly. I've got my good fall hat in this hatbox. She's go'n make it over. I'm sure glad you happened along to keep me comp'ny."

With the chairs going *rockity-rockity-rockity,* I didn't have to be out there to see Mrs. Jones, a tall stout lady in her sixties with swimmy eyes and

57

a red face, probably fanning herself with a piece of cardboard, or Miss Alice Ann, so fat she didn't have a lap and so short her little feet barely touched the floor.

Years ago Miss Alice Ann had caught me kissing Lightfoot McLendon in the cemetery and told it all over town. I hated her back then, but now she was just an old lady. Suddenly she said, "I bet you ain't heard about Loma Williams splashin' her bare chest with cold well water, Miz Jones. I mean BARE chest! Done it out on the Tweedys' back porch!"

"My land!"

"And she was wearin' her shirtwaist tucked into some long baggy purple pants! I seen a movin' pitcher show one time with some ha-reem women dancin' in thin baggy pants. That's all right for heathen women, I reckon, but it don't speak well of a Christian lady to wear such."

"No, it don't."

"Anyhow, Queenie said Loma splashed water on herself a while and then buttoned up that shirt-waist and commenced to stretch. This-a-way and that-a-way, up, down, and sideways. Queenie told Miz Predmore she got skeered Miss Loma'd had a stroke, she went to breathin' so hard! Time she got done she was downright raspin'—like a peach seed had got stuck in her th'oat!" Sitting inside by the open window, I nearly laughed out loud. Mama hadn't told me all this.

"Loma told Queenie how in New York City she stands in front of a open window to splash herself

58

—even when hit's a-snowin'. Said you sho do feel good when you git th'ew."

"It don't take a genius to know why you'd feel good to git th'ew," said Mrs. Jones, "but it'd take a fool to think it up in the first place. All I got to say, folks sure do turn strange when they go live in New York City."

"I reckon you know Loma's done got herself engaged to one a-them Yankees. Shoo, now. Git away!" she yelled all of a sudden. "I think God invented yellow jackets just to drive folks off of their porches. Specially in hot muggy weather like we been havin'. Shoo, shoo! Git! Shoo! What Loma ought to do, she ought to come on back to P.C. where she belongs."

"I don't know as she belongs down here any-more," Mrs. Jones put in. "A woman who'd smoke and wear pants? And make her livin' on a vaudeville stage?"

Almost in hugging distance of the conversation, I wanted in the worst way to go join in. But I knew if I went out there, they'd just go to talking about the weather.

"Of course she don't admit she works in vaude-ville," Miss Alice Ann was saying. "Loma calls it a the-ater. But lately she's been doin' manne-quin work, too!"

"No!"

"Yes'm! She told somebody that's how she met this man that she's a-go'n marry. Her and some other ladies was modelin' Gossard corsets one mornin', s'posed to be just lady buyers in the auditorium, but halfway th'ew, somebody spied a man hidin' under a seat off to the side, and hit was him! Loma told it herself. She thinks it's funny."

I sure thought it was funny. But not one hee-hee or ha-ha came from the preacher's wife. "I bet he got hustled out in a hurry," she said with disgust.

"I speck he did. But Loma said he come back-stage later and ast her to go eat with him, and Lord if she didn't have any better sense'n to do it! He took her to one a-them fancy rest'rants. I reckon with him bein' so old, and hit daylight and a nice place, Loma figured he couldn't do her no harm."

So that's how Aunt Loma got her diamond.

"Too bad she didn't stay here and marry Herbert Sloan back when he ast her to. Li'l Herbert, I mean. Not his daddy. But they say Loma said Li'l Herbert was pussy-footy—and besides, she couldn't stand the name Herbert, and anyhow she wouldn't marry anybody short as him if his name was Valentino."

Mrs. Jones snorted. "I bet if Loma had of known Li'l Herbert would inherit that pile of money, he'd of looked two feet taller. All I got to say is anybody mean enough to say a thing like that about such a sweet little man deserves to marry a Yankee. I never could understand how she's had so many men chasin' after her. I got to admit it, though, she's helt on to her looks."

"Maybe so. But not her brains," said Miss Alice Ann.

"You know what she's come home for? To git Campbell Junior and—"

The big clock in the hall struck. Mrs. Jones said, "I wonder what's helt Miss Love up. I got to git on home."

Miss Alice Ann said she needed to get on, too. I heard the chairs rock free, knew the ladies had stood up, and decided to go out there and say howdy.

Just as I was about to open the screen door, I heard the preacher's wife say, "I didn't get to the watermelon cuttin'. Did you? Did you meet the new teachers?" She lowered her voice to a whisper. "They say one of'm is real foreign-lookin'."

"That's Miss Klein," Miss Alice Ann whispered back.

"C-L-I-N-E?" Miss Jones whispered. "That's an Irish name. We don't need any Irish Catholics in Progressive City."

"Hit ain't spelt C-L-I-N-E. Hit's spelt K-L-E-I-N."

I heard them sink back down into the rockers.

"Must be she's a Jew girl."

"Sh-h-h, Miz Jones. Might be she's to home."

"Only Jew we ever had here was Mr. Izzie Lieberman, who had the furniture store," Mrs. Jones whispered. "They say he drank hot tea out of a tall glass. But everybody liked him."

"Miss Klein ain't no Jewess. She went to the Methodist church with Miss Love Sunday."

"Well, she must be some kind of hyphenated American," said the preacher's wife.

"What you mean, hyph'nated?"

"Oh, there's Irish-Americans and German-Americans, and British-Americans, and Italian-Americans and—well, hyphenated is what the politicians call all those." The chairs commenced rocking.

"Wonder why we don't say Indian-Americans instead of American Indians," Miss Alice Ann mused. "Maybe because they got here first. What are we, Miz Jones? American-Americans.

"Think, Miss Alice Ann. The hyphenateds aren't us. They're the immigrants. Like those Irish Catholics. They came over to this country starvin'. A potato famine drove'm here, and they ought to be thankin' the hands that fed them. But no, they're sidin' with the Kaiser in the war."

"Why come?"

"Cause Ireland hates England. Always has. I read how up North a Irish-American will get yellow paint slapped on their house if they don't buy Liberty Bonds. German-Americans too, of course. I can see why German-Americans are protestin' us gettin' in the war—after all, we're fightin' their brothers and cousins. Still, if Miss Klein's got kinfolks in the German Army, it don't make sense to pay her forty dollars a month to teach school in Progressive City. Not with our boys over there in France gettin' gassed by the Kaiser and dyin' and all."

For a minute or two neither lady spoke. Then Miss Alice Ann said, "I'm thinkin' on Mr. Izzie. Wonderin' why he went back to Germany."

"They say he went back to get marrit."

"Wonder is he fightin' in the Kaiser's army?"

"I doubt it. The Kaiser don't like Jews."

"You know, Miz Jones, ever since Mr. Izzie left to go back to Germany, they ain't been any dark-skinned white folks in this town—not less'n you count that Armenian in the graveyard. Remember him? Come here sellin' per-fume soap and died on us, and weren't nothin' to do but bury him?"

"Law, I'd clean forgot about him!" exclaimed Mrs. Jones. "Remember the big fuss about whether he ought to be buried in the cemetery? Somebody had heard that Armenians are Christians, but nobody knew for certain."

Miss Alice Ann sighed. "LeGrand Tribble donated his extra lot, remember? Said weren't nobody left in his fam'ly to put there, or to get mad at him for invitin' a stranger in, either one. And Brother Jones sure give that man a nice graveside ceremony, Miz Jones."

"He thought it was the right thing. I mean in case he was a Christian."

"Mr. Boozer said the reason all us ladies insisted on it, we liked his soap and he had them foreign good looks." A moment of silence for the dead, and she added, "I don't see as he'll ever git a marker, though. Who'd pay for it?"

They stood up again, and I was halfway to the door when Mrs. Jones said, "Oh, I meant to ast you. What about Will Tweedy?" I drew back as they moved towards the steps. "Did he join the Army while I was gone?"

63

"Not as I know of."

"I just don't see how he's managed to stay out. Nothin's wrong with him."

Miss Alice Ann said the trouble was my daddy. "Mr. Hoyt just goes to pieces when anybody asts has Will joined up. Claims Will is a heap more use to the war on the home front than if he was a-totin' a gun."

Mrs. Jones had just one question. "What could be more use to the war than him doin' his patriotic duty?"

I wanted to stalk out there and take up for myself and Papa too, but what could I say? "I've always been crazy about that boy," added the preacher's wife, "but even before I left to go see about Sister, folks were sayin' looks like Will's a slacker. I don't think Mr. Hoyt ought to carry on so. He ain't the only daddy that cain't bear to think of his boy in foreign trenches."

I retreated. Sneaked down the hall, out the back door and down the steps, and wandered into what used to be Granny Blakeslee's rose garden.

For the first time in my life I hated Cold Sassy and all it stood for. Call it Progressive City or Branch Water, I didn't care. "I don't belong here anymore," I muttered to the rose bushes among the tangled expanse of jimson weed, honeysuckle, trumpet vine, and Johnson grass. I took a cigar and a match out of my shirt pocket, scratched the match across a rock, lit up, and stood there puffing smoke and staring— at nothing. I was suddenly overwhelmed by a great homesickness for Granny Blakeslee and Grandpa.

Granny had died when I was fourteen. Grandpa and I were out here cutting roses at daybreak on the morning of her funeral. I remembered how he had straightened up, indicating the dewy splendor of color around us with the stub of his left arm, and said, "Miss Mattie Lou shore was a fool about roses. Did you know, boy, she's got over sixty different kinds?" Later, as he was lining the open grave pit with roses, tears had spilled down on his cheeks.

That was June the fourteenth, 1906. Three weeks later, Grandpa Blakeslee told my mother and Aunt Loma he aimed to marry Miss Love Simpson, the young milliner at his store. He said Miss Mattie Lou was dead as she'd ever be and he needed him a housekeeper, and a wife would just be cheaper than hiring a colored woman. That afternoon he took Miss Love over to Jefferson in his mule-drawn buggy. They got married at the courthouse.

When Grandpa died the next May, I overheard Miss Alice Ann Boozer say, "It serves him right, after the way he done Miss Mattie Lou. Married that Yankee woman and didn't live a year." Cold Sassy eventually accepted the fact of the marriage. But even now, ten years later, nobody ever let anybody forget it.

Her first summer as a widow, Miss Love told me she intended to keep up Miss Mattie Lou's rose garden. But her talent was making hats and money, not growing roses. After Sampson was born, in February 1908, the sixty varieties were on their own—or, as we say in the South, "own their own."

I could have waited for Miss Sanna Klein another fifteen minutes and still made the train, but could I really compete with a Harvard lawyer named Blankenship who could quote Shakespeare? I didn't even like Shakespeare. I might have if the teachers hadn't made us read all those footnotes. I could do a pretty good job quoting "To a Daffodil" or "To a Mouse"— *Wee, sleekit, cow'rin, hm'rous beastie, o what a panic's in thy breastie*—but that's hardly a love sonnet.

If this Hugh Junior was so smart, why wasn't he in the Army? I bet his daddy was busy pulling strings to get him a cushy lawyer job in Washington.

I left Granny's garden and cut through a gap in the hedge to the backyard of the house next door, where Miss Effie Belle Tate and Mr. Bubba used to live. Their niece, Miss Hyta Mae Brown, had a few boarders and ran a public dining room. Miss Love's three teachers took all their meals over there.

The smell of vegetable soup drifted from the kitchen window as I walked by. One of the cooks, Evaline, came out to the side of the back porch and poured her soapy dish water on the fig bush. "Evenin', Mist' Will!" she called. "Dish water sho' do make figs grow. You wont som'a my good ole soup and cawnbread, son? Come on in de kitchen, I dish you up some. Hit'll put meat on dem bones you got for laigs."

"That's hard to pass up, Evaline, but I got to catch a train." I walked as far as Miss Hyta Mae's pigeon cote before I turned towards South Main, far enough to avoid being seen from Miss Love's veranda.

If I passed anybody on the sidewalk, if any children were playing in their yards, if any lady waved at me from her porch, I didn't notice. Walking fast, puffing furiously on the cigar, I kept repeating the name Progressive City, over and over. At the depot, I stared at the sign as if it had been put up only that morning. For ten years it had declared this was PROGRESSIVE CITY to train passengers, and for ten years I'd kept reading it COLD SASSY.

Well, no more. All of a sudden the name Cold Sassy was as dead as Grandpa and Granny, and my old dog T.R., and Miss Effie Belle and Mr. Bubba. Growing up, I'd been made to feel like I was the town's great hope for the future. Everybody proud of me, ready to make allowances. Now this was Progressive City, and I was just somebody who used to live here. My home town had gone on without me in the six years I'd been in Athens. And I had gone on without it, except for family.

The truth was, I had outgrown Progressive City. I wondered why I never understood that before.

The next day I saw the house in Mitchellville where Sanna Klein's sister lived, and where Sanna had grown up.

Seven

THERE'S NO DIRECT railroad line to Mitchellville. You go there by train; then somebody has to meet you five miles away at the depot in 1888, Georgia, a town named for the year it got incorporated. When my train pulled in, old Mr. Charlie Cadenhead was already there, waiting in a battered Model-T Ford.

Mr. Charlie ran a dairy farm just south of Mitchellville and had done considerable cross-breeding of cattle. And Professor Harris, who ran the county agent program, wanted the dairy-man's figures regarding increase or decrease in milk production.

Mr. Charlie was a short, white-haired, peculiar-shaped man. Had a big square head, thick neck, massive chest, bulging stomach, small hips, short arms, and short thin legs. He had on a blue denim shirt, a big straw hat, and overalls, and he smelled of chewing tobacco and hay.

Soon as he found out my home town was Progressive City, he said, "Y'all got a new teacher this year, Miss Sanna Klein. She's the prettiest little thang I ever seen. You met her yet?"

"Yessir."

He didn't give me time to say more. Spitting

69

out the window as we bounced on a rough dirt road with nothing but woods and farmland to either side, he shouted above the motor's racket, "I tell you what, Mr. Tweedy. When I was fifteen year younger and not marrit, little Sanna wouldn't never have even got to P.C. I said so to her, on the steps of the post office, day before she left here. She just smiled and patted my arm." Mr. Charlie honked at two boys walking on the road, and waved as we passed, leaving them in a wake of dust. "I told her, 'I reckon you heard how teachers don't last more'n a year in that town.' Just teasin', you know, but Miss Sanna thought I meant they git fired. I told her, 'No'm, they git marrit.' She cain't blush, Mr. Tweedy, on account of she's got that dark complexion. But she looked mighty flustered, sayin' marriage was the fartherest thang from her mind. I said, 'Yes'm, but everbody knows a town's got to keep gittin' in good new bloodlines if it's go'n keep a-growin'—just like me with my dairy herd.' "

We were on the little wagon road that led up to his farmhouse, and Mr. Charlie turned to give me a wide grin and a wink. "Are you a single man, Mr. Tweedy?"

"Look out, sir!" I shouted. A big white hen, frantic and squawking, was back-and-forthing across the road not knowing which way to go. But when she decided the only way to go was up, she nearly hit the windshield in a panic of squawks and flailing wings.

Mr. Charlie stuck his head out the window and

shouted back at her, "You dang dummy!" Then he turned to me and grumped, "That one's ready for the pot. Too old to lay aiggs, but she's Miss Emma's pet."

I saw the herd, copied Mr. Charlie's figures, helped him and Miss Emma eat a big dinner, and asked her if she'd give me the recipe for her whipped cream and chocolate pie for my mama —"that is, if you don't keep it secret."

Driving back through Mitchellville, Mr. Charlie went down a side street and slowed almost to a stop in front of a large white frame house. "That's where little Miss Sanna Klein growed up," he explained. "Come here when she was a little girl to live with the Henry Jolleys. Miss Maggie is her older sister. Mr. Henry's mayor of Mitchellville and has got his hands in just about every business around here. Owns the bank and sawmill and a little factory makin' shuttles out of dogwood for textile mills, and a furniture factory. That one's turnin' out rifle butts now for the U.S. Army. The mayor owns considerable land, too. Buys it cheap on the courthouse square whenever his bank forecloses on somebody. They's some that faults him, with good reason, but he shore done right by little Sanna, sendin' her th'ew four year at college like she was his blood kin. Well, you got a train to ketch."

Going on through town, Mr. Charlie waved towards a building and said that was Mayor Jolley's bank.

"The mayor is sump'm to see. Must weigh four

71

hundret pounds. Everthin' bout him is big, cept he ain't tall. His whole face and head is fat—fat ears, fat lips, and his eyelids so swole up with fat you cain't hardly see his eyes. His face is always red, mainly cause he's bad to drank. That's his main fault. He thinks bootleggers are man's best friend. They say he told the sheriff to let them stills alone long as the boys don't hurt nobody. They pay him back in free moonshine.

"Now, Mitchellville ain't a place to think well of folks drankin' licker, but he's so friendly-like and heps so many folks, they just keep a-votin' for him. Course it heps a politician if he's got plenty of money and spreads it around. Like on Sarady mornin' . . . well, ever Friday night he and his drinkin' cronies play cards in Miss Maggie's parlor, which she don't like, but on Sarady mornin' he goes up town, after a little nip to cure his hangover, full of jokes and generosity. He's really funny when he's had a little to drank. The deadbeats lay in wait for him. Always got hard-luck stories, and he's always ready for 'em with a pocketful of bills. I mean, he's ready for them and they ready for him.

"He's always had a soft heart for young folks. But it ain't just Miss Sanna he's hepped go to school. Many a boy with folks havin' hard times —well, who ain't these days—he heps'em finish high school. I heard about a family on hard times, their boy got the promise of a job in the freight yards in Atlanta, but they couldn't scrape up enough train fare to get him there. He ast the mayor to lend him ten dollars for his ticket and to see him through the first week. He said Mr. Jolley give him twelve and said, 'You don't owe it back. Just go make sump'm of yourself.'

"You never saw anybody want chi'ren bad as the Jolleys. They always used to be takin' in somebody—orphans and nieces and nephews and all like that. Then Miss Maggie, she adopted her a little baby boy they call Lonzo. His mama died when he was born and nobody thought the baby could live and the daddy said she could take him if she wanted him. Well, that baby warn't no bigger'n a fryin'-size chicken. Miss Maggie brought him home on the train on a pillow, and wadn't nothin' but her wantin' that baby so bad kept him alive. Bout a year later they finally had a little girl of their own. Annie Laurie started at Shorter College last week, and Lonzo is a junior at Mercer. And Miss Sanna, well now, she's gone, too."

I looked at that big white house and tried to imagine Sanna Klein as a little girl, maybe sleeping upstairs while the mayor of Mitchellville got drunk and played cards in the parlor below. I had no idea, then, that I'd soon be spending a night in that house myself.

Eight

AT THE TIME I met Sanna, I'd been a county agent for two years.

Part of the job was treating sick livestock. Since farmers didn't trust college boys or book learning either one, they never sent for me till an animal was about dead.

Tell the truth, I didn't know all that much about veterinary medicine. The way I got by, I'd examine a sick cow and say to the farmer, "You called me too late. But I'll try to save her." That way, if she died it was his fault. If she lived, I was the greatest doctor in the world. The Ag School furnished me just one medicine, and no matter what the disease, I drenched with it. Drenching means you put the liquid medicine in a bottle, pull the animal's head way up, and pour the stuff down its throat. My first week as a county agent I found out you can't drench a hog. A hog will choke if you try to make him swallow with his head up. They never taught me that at the university.

Eventually I was doing everything from breeding and midwifing cows to castrating bulls, horses, and hogs. Most of them lived.

Manufacturers would send fertilizer or cow feed to the Ag School so we could give out samples to farmers. A lot of politics was involved. The college wanted the commissioners to support its new county agent program, so in actual fact it was the custom for free shipments of fertilizer or other products to go right to the commissioners for their own fields. We'd invite other farmers in the area to come see it poured on, and later to see the results.

Of course part of my job was talking. What Clarke County farmers didn't know from experience, they were supposed to learn from me, based on work being done at the agricultural experiment stations. I'd hold night meetings at schoolhouses for these strong men with rough hands and leathered faces, who came in the same overalls, denim shirts, and mud-caked brogans they'd worn in the fields all day. I'd tell them how to feed out their hogs and cattle to get more meat in a shorter time, when and what variety of corn to plant for the best yield, why they ought to quit pulling fodder for cattle when the corn is still green. "As all y'all know, the kernels are bigger if you let the ears mature," I explained. "And in the long run you'll produce more animal feed. We've proved it."

Naturally I talked about ways to head off the boll weevil. "Plant your cotton early, fertilize it good, and cultivate once a week so your crop will grow faster. Destroy the old cotton stalks this winter, and get rid of weeds and rubbish."

Because of the boll weevil, the 1917 cotton crop in south Georgia was off by more than three-fourths. In northeast Georgia half the cotton was damaged. That was reason enough to urge farmers to start diversifying. Go to hogs, beef cattle, more grain crops, field peas, white potatoes, watermelons, turnips, sugar cane. Some cotton farmers didn't even raise enough hay or corn for their own livestock feed, much less to have any to sell. With no cash crops, they had to let their cotton go on the market as soon as it got ginned and baled, regardless of price.

Farm labor was becoming a serious problem. In the past year and a half, sixty to seventy thousand Negroes had left Georgia and moved to cities like Cincinnati and Philadelphia. Once I made the mistake of trying to sympathize. "With so many colored folks leavin' and so many enlistin' in the Army or gettin' drafted, y'all are kind of up against it."

Angry voices rumbled in the room. "That shore is the truth!" yelled one man, his face flushing red. "How them colored think we can run a farm without no hep?"

"It makes me madder'n hell," said another, "the way they sneak off in the night. Anybody sneaks off, they know they doin' wrong. If we find out a nigger's plottin' to leave, Mr. Tweedy, we git us up a posse and go to the depot with guns."

"Yeah," said another. "Yeah, them colored boys git the message real quick. Real quick. They see us a-comin', they know they go'n miss that train."

A giant-size farmer, laughing, added, "And them that do git away, what's go'n happen to'm up North? They ath't go'n know nobody. Ain't go'n have no pickled pig feet or hambone or fat-back, ain't go'n have no collards, no turnip salat. And come winter, they go'n freeze to death."

A short stocky man stood up. "Well, now, how I look at it, are we Christians or ain't we? They got a right to go if'n . . ."

"Set down, Worth Haley! We talkin' bout crops rottin' in the fields. We talkin' bout plowin' for spring plantin'. A whole fam'ly of cotton pickers left out from my place the night I paid'm off, and never a thank-you to nobody for all that's been done for 'em."

"The State Department of Agriculture," I said, talking loud, "is lookin' into ways of addressin' this problem. They're encouragin' white mill hands to try share-croppin', or hire out for field work. Most used to live in the mountains, and—"

"Mr. Tweedy, I'd a long sight rather have colored hands and tenants than sour-lookin' whites," retorted the red-faced man. "Last year a sorry no-count white sharecropper on my farm shot his wife in the chicken yard and then kilt hisself in the hog pen. That goes to show what kind of trash they was. I'd of lost half a-their crop if I hadn't set my own farmhands to pickin' the dead man's cotton."

There aren't any better people in the world than farmers. But these men felt betrayed. The colored could leave, but they couldn't. I didn't bring up that subject again anywhere.

I spoke often to meetings of farm wives, telling

77

them how to store corn for the family by brining, urging them to dry more fruits and vegetables. "And y'all put Leghorns in your hen houses. They're the best layers."

One night a gray-headed lady in a dress made out of feed sacks got up and told how to get rid of flies. She said, "Spray lavender water. Put it in one a-them glass atomizers, you know like perfume comes in? I spray it all over my kitchen and dinin' room. They say flies jest cain't stand it, the smell, I mean. My husband says he cain't stand it either, and I ain't sure it heps, but the *Progressive Farmer* magazine said so. What you think, Mr. Tweedy?"

"Since your husband don't like lavender water, try using blue tablecloths. Flies really hate the color blue." They knew I was joking. "Or try to get you some screens for the windows."

"I know a lady got screens," said the woman, "and she is forever chasin' after flies with a swatter. You git screens, them flies cain't git out."

That just about covers my experience with county agenting. On October 2, 1917, I got fired.

In actual fact I was asked to take up a state job with the Agricultural Extension Service.

In the new job I traveled over the whole state, helping farmers and students learn how to build barns and silos and chicken houses, put in drainage ditches, and so forth.

One of my first assignments was at Young Harris College in Towns County. Boys studying agriculture had put up framing for a cow barn, and their professor wanted me to come cut the pattern for a gambrel roof—which I didn't know how to do. I found blueprints for a dairy barn but not for any gambrel roof. So I went out to Banks County to see old Mr. Luthie Fletcher, a carpenter. He used to take me fishing on the Hudson River when I was a boy. I said to him, "Mr. Luthie, let's go up to the mountains next Monday. I got to mark off timbers for a barn roof, but if you hep me, we can get in some fishin'."

I didn't tell him I'd never designed a gambrel roof. I put the emphasis on time to fish.

We got to Young Harris real early Monday morning and I handed him a pencil and said, "Now, Mr. Luthie, I'll look over my blueprints while you mark off timbers for a pattern. Do it light, and then I'll mark over them again while the students watch." Mr. Luthie grinned at me. He knew what I was up to. But he marked the timbers light, and when the boys arrived, I'd ask one to bring me a plank and I'd go over the marks, and pretty soon me and Mr. Luthie were off fishing.

When we got back to Young Harris, those students had cut and mounted the timbers and were ready to nail on the tin. Prettiest thing you ever saw. The president of the college wrote me a letter saying it all fit just perfect.

People wanted blueprints for everything, houses and privies, barns and chicken houses. The president of the Central of Georgia Railroad had a farm at Orchard Hill and he wanted a concrete silo. I'd never even seen one. Silos had always been made out of wood. I didn't know what I'd do, but I just happened to see an ad in the paper for a company in Atlanta that had started selling steel forms for concrete silos. I got to Atlanta early the next morning and presented myself as a representative of the University of Georgia's Agricultural School.

"We're doin' a demonstration project at Orchard Hill for the president of the Central of Georgia Railroad," I said, "and I think it would be the best advertisement in the world for y'all if you'd build it with your new form."

The day they started on it we had a crowd of farmers over there. The steel form was like a doughnut with a big hole. They'd pour in the concrete, let it set up, then raise the form and pour in some more. They did that over and over, clear to the top.

If that silo is still standing, it's got my name on it. I scratched it in the concrete. I thought about adding Sanna's name to mine, but I didn't do it, even though I had already asked her to marry me. But all that came later.

Nine

I SPENT THE week after the watermelon cutting hoping that Miss Sanna Klein would get cold feet and not go to Jefferson, in which case she'd have to attend Sunday school and preaching in P.C., as is expected of teachers. In that case, I meant to be waiting when she and Miss Love and Sampson came in from the Methodist service. I took the train to P.C. Sunday morning and walked up to Miss Love's house. Sunday school hadn't let out yet, much less church, so I sat down on the porch swing, lit a cigar, and opened the *Atlanta Journal* wide.

I had sense enough to know Miss Klein had probably spent last night with the Blankenships. But even if she had, at least I had an excuse to spend the morning enjoying the newspaper instead of wiggling and shoulder twitching through a long Presbyterian sermon with my folks.

Fools in love get fool hopes. My idea was if Miss Klein hadn't gone to Jefferson, I could save her from an afternoon of misery in her room alone. A few hours with me would surely seem better than nothing. I'd thought of taking her to ride, maybe out to my Grandpa Tweedy's farm in Banks County. I knew I could use Papa's car, since kinfolks were coming for Sunday dinner and would sit visiting all afternoon.

Concentrating on the newspaper wasn't easy, nervous as I was and distracted by hope and cooking smells from Miss Hyta Mae's boarding house next door and a squirrel in the fig tree who kept barking at a cat. Finally my eyes lit on an item that interested me:

The Rev. Mr. Jared Elder, age 70, has dug his own grave in Silver Shoal Community and lined the sides with Portland Cement. He is in good health, so expects to wait a few years before occupying the home he has prepared for his body. But he brags that when the final hour comes, his neighbors will not have to be summoned to dig a hole. Mr. Elder did a good job, but it does not look inviting.

I tore that out, and also a little boxed-off story about base pay for soldiers in different countries. I already knew American privates were drawing thirty-three dollars a month, but I never imagined that French privates got only a dollar-fifty, a soldier of the same grade in Russia thirty-two cents, and in Germany sixty-five cents. It said the British Army was paying seven dollars and sixty cents a month plus extra for service in France. Japanese privates earned eight dollars a year.

Then I noticed a little item I'd almost missed:

Miss Trulu Philpot, formerly of Athens, will be

honored as Miss Liberty Bond at a gala in the nation's capital on Saturday night, October 3, to raise money for the War Effort. This is 'The Event' of Washington's social season.

According to Miss Philpot's mother, Mrs. Cason R. Philpot, her daughter's 'court' will include her escort, Captain Horace Luck, a U.S. Army aviator who leaves soon for France, and some of his fellow aviators.

Miss Philpot is staying with her maternal aunt and is one of this year's most sought-after debutantes in Washington.

Lord, I was tired of Trulu intruding on everything I did.

Trulu Philpot was a modern girl with hypnotic blue eyes and golden hair. Before Sanna, I never looked twice at a dark-haired girl. If you only dated blondes, I figured, you were sure to marry a blonde. I'd loved blondes ever since Lightfoot's hair shone like an angel's in the sunlight as she bent over me on Blind Tillie Trestle the day the train ran over me. Tru was a vamp and flirted with everybody, but I was the only one she fell in love with, and we got engaged. It had been announced and everything.

Tru's grandfather was a major general in the War Between the States and he was the man who built the white-columned mansion in Athens where Trulu and her family lived. That impressed Papa and Mama, and they were even more impressed when I said the whole Philpot family made the grand tour of Europe and Russia in 1910.

They were less impressed when they met her. She'd just got her blond hair cut short—that was some time before Loma cut hers—and though Tru didn't smoke that day, Mama smelled it on her clothes. "I'm sure she's just sweet as she can be," said Mama later, "but I don't know, Will. I'm just not used to these modrun ladies. She don't seem like somebody who'd be happy on a farm."

"Oh, we've talked a lot about that," I said. "I don't reckon she'll be sweepin' the yard or feedin' the chickens, but she'll keep friends comin' out for weekends inthe country. I doubt she'll be bored." I guess Mama and Papa had the same unspoken thoughts I did. When I got ready to quit my job in Athens and move to Banks County, Tru's daddy would put money into my farm. After all, she was his only child.

A flea had more common sense than I did around Tru. All my life I'd dreamed of taking over Grandpa Tweedy's farm, but Trulu Philpot got me to promise I'd keep my job in Athens. "We can use the farm for house parties," she said. "Everybody loves to go to the country."

I didn't tell Mama and Papa she was a great dancer. I'd never even told them what a great dancer I was. They thought dancing was a sin, like playing cards. Everything was a sin if you did it on Sunday except church, Bible reading, big Sunday dinners, and swapping gossip. What Sunday afternoons were for was visiting kinfolks and neighbors. I couldn't tell them I didn't believe in sin anymore, or that Trulu had hold of me, body and soul, or that I was "wild" about her. Trulu was wild in the most literal sense of the word *wild*. She got expelled from the normal school in Athens. She didn't plan to be a teacher anyhow.

I closed the newspaper in disgust, checked my pocket watch, and settled down to wait for a girl who was everything Trulu was not.

I didn't have to wait long. Minutes later a big fancy touring car slowed to a stop in front of the house. I watched as the driver, a middle-aged man, escorted Sanna up the steps, set her grip down, and said gruffly, "I'm sorry it turned out this way, Miss Klein. Maybe next time things will . . ." His voice trailed off.

Neither one smiled. She thanked him for bringing her home, said good-bye, and watched till he drove off. Then she started for the door.

The face she turned towards me was a portrait of fatigue and misery. Circles dark as bruises made a mask around dull black eyes. "Why, Mr. Tweedy, I . . . I didn't expect . . ."

I asked did she have a good time.

"Yes, thank you," she murmured. "I had a v-very nice t-t-time." Her lower lip quivered on the last words and her eyes brimmed with tears.

"What happened? Is he sick or something?"

She didn't answer. Just opened the screen door and hurried in. I followed her, bringing the grip. "You forgot this," I called as she rushed for the

85

stairs. "What's happened, Miss Klein?" I asked again, like it was any of my business.

"I . . . he . . . I . . . I t-took a b-b-bath!" she wailed, and sank down on the bottom step, sobbing. The long navy blue skirt of her travel suit hid high-buttoned shoes. Her hands hid her face. Whenever Mama or Loma used to tune up like that around Grandpa Blakeslee, he'd say, "Iffen they's one thang I cain't stand, it's a woman cryin'. So hesh up!" Even when I was real young, I could see that such talk didn't turn off any faucets. Soon as Miss Klein's sobbing let up enough for her to hear me, I asked by way of changing the subject if the Blankenships lived in a big old Victorian house set way back on the street on the outskirts. "Tan-colored? Gold trim, brown shutters?"

With new tears running down her cheeks, she nodded. I had passed that house many a time. Papa thought it was built soon after the War Between the States by a rich man from Philadelphia. It had three stories, a tall turret on one side, gingerbread doodads on porches and balconies, and stained glass panels in the front door. I was torn between curiosity about Miss Klein's awful bath and the hope that I could get her calmed down enough to tell me about it.

"Did the family pass?" I asked suddenly.

"W-what?" She looked up at me from her seat on the bottom step, kind of dazed.

"I mean, do you approve of this feller's folks? Are they good enough for you?"

"Oh, they're very"—she searched for the right word—"very n-n-nice." Miss Klein wiped her eyes with a handkerchief and drew a deep, steadying breath. I could see then that she needed to talk worse than she needed to cry, so I asked her about the bath. And sure enough, it was pretty awful.

As Sanna told it, Mrs. Blankenship had come hurrying up from the back hall before she got in the house good, arms outstretched in greeting and with a big smile. "So this is Miss Klein! May I call you Sanna? I'm so glad you could come, dear." Then Hugh introduced their "maid," Missouri, who showed Sanna upstairs to the company room where she would sleep.

Not saying a word, Missouri opened what looked like a small closet door, but inside was a lavatory. The bathtub was in one corner of the bedroom behind a Chinese screen. "It was the shortest, fattest little tub you ever saw," Miss Klein told me.

"Missouri's silence was getting on my nerves, so I said, 'What a funny little tub!' Without even looking at me, she answered back, 'De drain, it ain't been workin' right here lately. Miz Blankenship, she keep aimin' to call Mr. Amos, but she ain't did it yet.'

"Mr. Tweedy, Missouri had on a white uniform and Hugh had introduced her as 'our maid.' But she treated me as if she knew I'd never known anybody whose help wore a white uniform and was called a maid. And I haven't."

"Me neither," I lied. At Trulu's home in Athens they had three Negro servants who wore white uniforms and got called maid. And, according to Mama, Aunt Loma claimed Mr. Vitch had a whole bunch of maids—white maids who wore black uniforms.

"She treated me as if she knew I wasn't used to formal dinner parties." A tiny flash of anger stilled her tears for a minute.

"Who is?" I asked, trying to make light of it. "Most folks I know never even heard of a dinner party." That was true. Everybody in Cold Sassy used the good tablecloths and the good china, silver, and goblets on Sunday, and usually invited kinfolks or the preacher's family or neighbors. Mama was always saying she "owed" somebody a meal, and if Mama's watermelon pickle or sweet tomato sauce or fried eggplant was their favorite, you could count on that being on the table along with eight or ten more dishes, hot yeast rolls, and everything good you ever thought of eating. But it was just called Sunday dinner, not dinner party. If you had a party at night, it was a barbecue or fish fry.

The truth was, I almost got used to fancy dinner parties when I was engaged to Trulu, and now I confessed to one of them.

"You want to hear about it, Miss Klein? Well, I'll tell you about mine if you'll tell me about yours," I said, leaning back against the wall. "This rich family in Athens, see, they needed an extra man to balance out the table. The hostess . . .

uh, I was told it would be a black tie affair. I didn't have one, and didn't know it meant wear a tux either, till I got there. The hostess said never mind, so I didn't. No point letting a little thing like that spoil your dinner. They had Negro men waiters who didn't just wear uniforms, they wore white gloves to serve the food. And I don't mean they just brought everything to the table for us to pass around. They served it from behind you. Here would come this meat on a silver tray or a bowl of vegetables, and a waiter would stick it between you and the next person and you had to take what they forked over. Well . . ."

Miss Klein was staring up at me, almost forgetting her own troubles for a moment. "Well," I continued, "I don't remember what all we ate, but when we got through with the main meal and the homemade ice cream, the waiter they called the butler reached between two folks and picked up the ice swan and started serving it. I don't know why he started with me, but I took a bunch of grapes. Then he offered it to the lady next to me and she ran her fingers over the swan's back and then wiped them real dainty on her napkin. It was quiet around the table like everybody thought I ought to put the grapes back. I'd heard of finger bowls, but I'd never seen anybody use one, much less an ice swan."

I could tell by Miss Klein's face that she thought I'd never get asked back again to that house. "How awful! You must have felt like crawling under the table."

"No, I just said to the butler, 'Hey, ah, how bout bringin' that back? I don't want to miss anything!' And everybody just laughed. That was the first time everybody at the table had laughed. Before, they all were just talking quiet to who they were sittin' next to."

Miss Klein actually smiled. Almost laughed. "I'd have been mortified to death, Mr. Tweedy. I wish I could be like that."

I propped an elbow on the newel post and smiled down at her. "You want to tell me what your dinner party was like? Who all came?" I was trying to prime the pump, keep her talking.

"Oh, his parents, of course. Mr. Blankenship, he's not handsome like Hugh, but he's lean and strong-looking. His sister and her doctor-husband were there. Neither one of them said much. I guess I didn't say much either." Miss Klein spoke carefully, as if assuming I really wanted to know. "And his grandmother. She was dressed like a genteel old lady, but she talked country. I liked her. Mr. Crowe was there, the law partner, a tight-looking little man with a pencil mustache. Mrs. Crowe was nice, but talked through her nose. And Judge Fuss of the circuit court was there. He was big and fat, from sitting so much, I guess. Oh, and Hugh's Aunt Trudy from Virginia."

Everybody had gathered in the parlor, a room full of Victorian furniture, ornately carved tables with marble tops, big electric lamps with globe shades, fringed velvet pillows on the sofa, and dark draperies. Framed photographs and water-color country scenes covered the walls. Figurines and vases of peacock feathers or silk roses and books were crowded on the mantel, the tables, and the top of the big, heavily carved upright grand piano.

As I listened I realized that taking a bath had the worst consequences for Miss Klein but it wasn't her only mistake. The first one was when Missouri came around with a tray full of little glasses of sherry wine and offered it to Miss Klein. Instead of just murmuring no thank you, she said, too loud, "I don't drink." Hugh shot her a disapproving glance.

The elegant deaf grandmother, who hadn't heard the I-don't-drink remark, said in a loud country voice, "Ain't it been a hot day?"

"Ain't it been hot all week?" echoed Judge Fuss. "If y'all think it's hot settin' on the screen porch, you ought a-been in my courtroom this week. Packed with everybody and his cousin and hotter'n hell. Excuse me, ladies, but it was. But maybe the court ain't any hotter'n your classroom, Miss Klein, less'n you ain't got but ten pupils."

She said, "I have fifty-five pupils," and gratefully took a bite of her little cucumber sandwich.

Judge Fuss, who was sitting next to her, leaned close and said, "I taught school. After two weeks of it I vowed if I could just get through that year I'd never set foot in a classroom again. That's when I decided to go to law school. Law school was easy after that year."

After some more conversation, Hugh and his daddy got up and recited "The Jabberwocky" together. It was an amazing feat. They took turns with each verse, till close to the end they joined together and got faster and faster and faster.

Then Mrs. Blankenship, who had studied music in New York, played a long, heavy piece on the big piano.

The concert finally crescendoed to a stop, and before the smacks of applause died down, Missouri pushed the twin sliding doors apart and called out, "Y'all come on to supper . . . uh, I, whut I mean to say, DINNER IS SERVE!"

Considering it was already first dark, and the dining room lit only with candles and a circle of tiny electric bulbs in the huge crystal chandelier, it's no wonder Miss Klein was nervous at dinner. In the soft flickering light, she wasn't sure till she tasted it whether Missouri had served her rice or creamed corn.

"None of it was as splendid as the dinner party you went to must have been, Mr. Tweedy, but it was at least as grand as Sister Maggie's Thanksgiving dinner and Christmas dinner and Easter dinner put together. Everything just so glittery and beautiful. Vases of flowers everywhere. And cut-glass goblets and heavy scrolled silverware reflecting the light."

The centerpiece was red roses in a large silver bowl, and the china was gold-and-white Spode.

Suddenly Miss Love's big hall clock bonged the noon hour, echoing in the stairwell. We listened to the twelve strikes. Then, as the last one died away, Miss Klein blew her nose and stood up. Reaching for her leather grip, she mounted a few stairs. Paused. Leaned wearily against the wall. "I'm so t-tired, Mr. Tweedy. I didn't sleep last night after . . . I was . . . oh, it was all just awful! I c-can't . . ."

I interrupted before she could move on up-stairs or go to crying again. "You mean . . . your bath?"

"It . . . wasn't the bath." She took a deep breath, let it out in a long shaky sigh. "It was what h-happened afterwards. Mr. Tweedy, at dinner I was actually having a good time. They are nice people, and the table conversation . . . well, it wasn't high-brow the way I expected—I mean, with Hugh being so intellectual and all." There had been a lot of talk about the war news, until Mrs. Blanken-ship said she'd rather hear the men talk politics than war, and Miss Klein was asked questions like where was she born and where did she go to col-lege. Then the lawyers swapped stories about col-ored folks and country hicks they'd dealt with in their practice.

Maybe the people didn't act highbrow, but the food sounded mighty la-di-dah to me. No field peas or turnip salad and cornbread on that table. Green tomato pickles, a bowl of sliced fresh to-matoes with raw onion, and a congealed fruit salad on lettuce were on the table, but, as at Trulu's family dinner parties, the food was served to each guest from behind by Missouri and the cook, who had taken off her kitchen apron and put on a clean white maid's uniform.

Miss Klein told me the menu like a fourth-grader reciting the names of United States Presidents: first, a shallow bowl of creamed onion soup, followed by smothered chicken, smoked ham slices, rice, baked dressing that was chock-full of Apalachicola oysters, chicken gravy, fried eggplant, a sweet potato soufflé, and a big silver vase-shaped pot of hot yeast rolls.

By the time the eating and talking were in full swing, Miss Klein was thinking she could get used to all this. Then she was startled by the sight of a drop of water that splatted down onto a red rose in the centerpiece. A few petals danced, then danced again, then again. For a minute Miss Klein just stared, puzzled, and finally looked up. The ceiling plaster was wet!

She nudged Hugh, and he glanced at the ceiling, but just said *sh-h-h-h*. He wanted to hear Judge Fuss tell about his first legal client, a chicken thief called Two Fingers.

But the judge never got to say what happened at Two Fingers's trial. He stopped in midsentence, staring up as those first drops became a stream. The dim electric lights flickered, went out! Before anybody could duck or dodge, the crystal chandelier crashed down with a mess of wet plaster. Women screamed and men cursed, and the colored women in their white uniforms flew in. Missouri looked up and shouted, "Lawd a mercy, de bed gwine come down nex'!"

Miss Klein, sobbing anew, said, "It was j-just the biggest m-m-mess you ever saw, Mr. Tweedy!" The candles on the sideboard and buffet gave enough light to show plaster and food all over the lace tablecloth, roses scattered, cut-glass goblets and china plates broken. Everything was crushed, and the chandelier sprawled over the table like a big dead octopus.

Judge Fuss's shoulders were drenched with water and crumbled plaster. A piece of oyster clung to Mr. Crowe's vest. One arm of the chandelier dripped gravy. A green tomato pickle was impaled on the jagged glass of a broken electric light bulb. Miss Klein discovered she had wet congealed salad in her lap.

Mr. Blankenship jumped up and shouted at his wife, "That fool tub! How come you didn't call Mr. Amos like I told you to!"

Hugh grabbed Miss Klein's shoulder and said, "Sanna! Did you take a bath?" Then he dashed upstairs behind his daddy.

Miss Klein was too shocked to speak.

Missouri shook her fist at the ceiling. "I'se been a-tellin' you, Miz 'Ships, dem faucets and dem drainpipes, dey ain' nothin' but RUST. An' all dat fine china busted!" She waved her arms towards the table. "Lawd hep us. Whut we go'n do, Ma 'Ships?"

As if rising from a stupor, Mrs. Blankenship got up and said, "We're going to clean it up."

Sanna was weeping by then. "It's all m-my f-fault! I took a bath!"

"No, it's mine. I just kept putting off calling Mr. Amos. Sanna, see if you can help Aunt Trudy wipe the soufflé off her neck."

I could tell that Sanna Klein was reliving all this now, after reliving it all the time she should have been sleeping the night before. "And you do see, Mr. Tweedy," she wailed, "why no matter how much Mrs. Blankenship tried to comfort me, it was all—all—m-my f-f-fault! I just f-felt so hot and d-dusty after the ride over! I hated to p-put on my nice dress f-for the p-party when I was so sweaty—I mean, perspiring so much. I . . . ."

She had completely run out of steam.

My way of comforting probably wasn't like Mrs. Blankenship's. I said, "It strikes me as how this would make a fine scene in a movie film, Miss Klein. Comedy or tragedy, either one."

She didn't say anything. Just kept crying.

"Gosh, Miss Klein," I said finally, "from now on you'd better watch out."

"Wh-what?" she spoke from the middle of a sob.

"I mean, you may be in real danger. One day you're under a tree and a watermelon drops out of it and hits you, and a week later a chandelier crashes down onto a dinner table and splashes you with congealed salad!"

A moment of stunned silence on her part, then as I started laughing, Miss Klein's mouth turned up at the corners. But not for long. "I wish I could see something funny about the rest of last night." She looked at me and went to laughing again. As the big clock bonged for twelve-thirty, I heard a clatter of voices and high heels on the front porch.

"Must be Miss Love and them, Miss Klein, comin' in from church."

"Oh, my," she whispered, distressed. "I don't . . . can you just tell Miss Love I'm back, Mr. Tweedy?" And she reached out and touched my hand, "and thank you." With that, she grabbed her bag and disappeared up the stairs.

During Sanna Klein's miserable recital of broken glass and gravy stains I had begun to feel as if this were something we were in together. But walking home for dinner with my folks, I kept puzzling. None of what Miss Klein told me explained why she'd come back so early in the day, or why it was the daddy who brought her home. Why not the sweetheart?

She couldn't have flunked out of the fancy family. If so, Mr. Blankenship wouldn't have sounded so kind and sad, saying he wished things had turned out different.

What did it all mean? It was months before I found out.

Cudn Milford and his wife, Cudn Zena, had arrived by buggy, in time to go to church with Mama and Papa. When I get home they were on the front porch with Papa. They lived in Pocatelago Community, better known as Poky, which was eight miles from P.C. All Poky amounted to was a large general store at the crossroads and farms all around. One of those farms was where Grandpa Blakeslee grew up.

Cudn Zena's face was lop-sided from a stroke. Her right eye and cheek drooped and the right side of her mouth, which made her *f*'s come out like *h*'s. But that didn't stop her from talking.

"My, don't you look hine, Will!" she said as I came up the steps. "Spittin' image of Cudn Rucker, ain't he, Mr. Milhord. But, son, you need some weight on you. Skinniest, long-leggedest thang I ever seen. Come 'ere and hug this old lady!"

"How you been doin', Cudn Zena," I asked, reaching down to her in a bear hug.

"Well, my hace ain't too good, but the rest of me is as good as common, thank you, thank you." Cudn Zena always was a talker, once she got started, and right then she got started telling Papa and me her latest hope for a cure. "Y'all know Porter Springs, don't you, up in the mountains near Dahlonega? Other day I got to rememberin' my Uncle Alva, how he was so afflicted with the rheumatism, he dragged his heet around like an alligator. And he got well at Porter Springs. Told me he stayed three days in a boardin' house up thar and drank two gallons a day of that mineral water, and when he come home, he could walk just hine and go about his worldly bizness."

Cudn Milford butted in. "She wants me to take her up yonder, but I cain't afford it. Miss Zena, I'm willin' if you're willin' to sleep in a tent."

"I got my aigg money," she replied from the good side of her mouth.

"Maybe he likes you the way you are," I said cheerfully.

"Well, I don't. Lookin' like a clown don't matter much, but my eye hurts. Hit cain't blink. I have to keep my hand over it like this and tie a rag across it at night. Uncle Alva told me bout lots of sick holks he met up there, stayin' in them little cottages or the boardin' house or the ho-tel and drankin' the water. Just miracles. One man had piles in the worst way, and he spent hive days on the spring water and his piles was healed. A lady who'd had laig sores for seven years got cured in a two-week period. Now, listen to this, Hoyt—a man from White County had the dropsy? You know, somethin' wrong with his heart and him swole up all over? Uncle Alva said the man at the ho-tel said the man come up there swole up all over like he'd bust if you stuck a pin in him. Weighed three hundret pound if he weighed a ounce. And drankin' that water made him start'. In just three weeks he was down to a hundret and thirty. The ho-tel man swore on a Bible that time he was ready to leave, this man could run, wrestle, lift thangs like anybody else! I don't know if Porter Springs is the hancy summer resort it used to be back then, but there's still places to stay, I know that."

A tear rolled down her cheek from the drooped eye. But she wiped it off, and though the right side of her face drooped in despair, a smile of hope brightened the good side. About then Mama called us in to dinner. Once we'd passed all the food and got to eating good, Cudn Zena started talking about my Grandpa Blakeslee.

"Remember that old log cabin your daddy was born in?" she asked Mama. "You know, up on that woody clay hill between Poky and Erastus? Well, we went over there to see it—I reckon it was a year ago January, wadn't it, Mr. Milford?"

He nodded and said the cabin had plumb rotted down.

"Vines growin' betwist and between the logs," said Cudn Zena. "Them vines had just pulled it apart."

Everybody was sad to hear that, but then we had a good time swapping stories about Grandpa Blakeslee. The Poky folks told some I'd never heard before. Like for instance when Grandpa was about twelve years old and stayed out possum hunting on Saturday night and went to sleep on the bench next morning at church. "The preacher noticed," said Cudn Zena, "and right in the middle of his sermon he said real loud, 'Rucker Blakeslee, I'm askin' you to pray.' Remember Aunt Lula Pritchett? Well, Aunt Lula, she punched Rucker and said, 'Git up and pray, son.'" Grandpa, stumbling to his feet, said *Lordmakeus-thankfulfortheseandallourmanyblessin's.* Amen. Then he sat down and went back to sleep.

I told about the Halloween night Grandpa pushed over the privy at the Cold Sassy depot, knowing the Yankee president of the railroad was in there, and how the man offered a fifty-dollar reward to anybody who'd tell who did it. Nobody would. Mama and Queenie were clearing off the table by then, ready to bring in Cudn Zena's pecan pie.

I sat there wishing Mary Toy and Aunt Loma and Campbell Junior were still here. The table seemed suddenly lonesome without them.

And without Granny and Grandpa . . .

I didn't look forward to an afternoon hearing about who all in the family was sick, so when Mr. Talmadge from Athens stopped by in his automobile to see Papa and offered me a ride back, I took him up on it.

That night I spent an hour writing a five-sentence letter to Sanna Klein:

Dear Miss Klein,
I'm sitting here in my rented room eating sardines and crackers whereas I had hoped to be with you. If it's in order, I would like to take you to church next Sunday night. Please let me know if that is OK. I hope you don't have a "previous." You already seem like an old acquaintance.
                                         Hoyt Willis Tweedy

Ten

MORE THAN SEVENTEEN years passed between the September night I wrote that letter and the Monday night last November when I read it again, in a dingy one-room cabin at the Rest-Easy Motor Court near Shellman, Georgia.

In desperation I had taken a cotton-buying job as one of four field men in a new farmers' co-operative. When I started traveling in south Georgia for forty-five dollars a month, all I had in the world was a wife, four children, a milk cow, a bird dog, a worn-out Model-A Ford, and an expense account for gas plus two dollars and fifty cents a day for food and lodging.

If I happened to be talking to a farmer anywhere near noon, I could count on his wife inviting me to dinner. If I slept in the car two nights, I could save enough expense money to buy gas and get home to Progressive City for a weekend. If it wasn't a hot night, sleeping in the car was real pleasant. Plenty of fresh air, no roaches, and not many more mosquitoes than in a cheap hotel room.

In the car I had to sleep folded up, but that wasn't much worse than sleeping at the Rest-Easy Motor Court, where the mattress was thin and the springs as rusty and sagging as my spirits.

I was lonely, tired to the bone, too restless to sleep. My shoulders kept twitching, and my eyes were red and sore from driving all day on dusty roads.

I wished I hadn't gone home for the weekend —home now being an upstairs apartment in P.C., rented from a silent old man and a sharp-tongued old lady who didn't like children fussing and banging doors. I wasn't used to that anymore myself. The children made me nervous as heck, Sanna was a witch, and the dog was whining and limping from a thorn in his foot that had begun to fester.

I got the thorn out and soaked Pup's foot in Epsom salts water, but there was no balm for the anger that was festering in Sanna.

I didn't blame her. Responsibility for the children was a heavy weight to bear alone. They had always gone to school and church in P.C., so they already had friends there. But my losing the farm and our new house had broken Sanna's heart and my pride. Change of any kind was hard on Sanna, but she always said she was never happier than out there in the country having babies—four born in less than five years—with me coming in for meals, helping any way I could. It was hard on her when I had to quit farming and start traveling. It was a lot worse when she was looking after four rowdy children by herself—trying to sound brave but worrying by herself, sleeping by herself, trying to make my little salary last till the end of the month and feeling disliked by my mama.

But good Lord, it wasn't easy on me either. I

was really by myself. The first time I had to leave her for south Georgia, neither Sanna nor I slept the night before, and at four A.M. I said, "There's no point waitin' for the clock to ring. I'm gettin' up." Sanna had packed my bags the night before. She fixed me a good breakfast, and by first light I was raring to be off.

"Do you want to look in on the children?" Sanna asked.

"I'll never leave if I do," I said. We went hand in hand down the stairs, tiptoeing so as not to wake anybody.

I kissed Sanna good-bye, but we kept clinging to each other. Leaving her and the children was like having my arms and legs torn off. My heart ached. I held her head to my chest and stroked her hair. Then with a deep sigh, trying to make my voice cheerful, I said, "I'll be back this weekend, hon. Or at least by the next weekend. It won't seem so long."

"It will to me," she said. "Will, I hate living in P.C. when we owe everybody in town. What if something happens to one of the children? What if . . ."

"Mama and Papa are just three blocks away, and Miss Love says she'll help you. All you got to do is ask."

Taking her hands in mine, I kissed them. I got past the screen door then, but couldn't walk away. Her on one side of the screen, me on the other, and we were both crying. We both knew things would never be the same again.

They haven't been.

But by the time the Model-A hit the city limits of Progressive City, my spirits rose like a balloon. Ahead lay new places, new people, new challenges. I had a job, by gosh, and it had a future. "God help me, I'm go'n make a livin' for my fam'ly! Dear God, I got to get my self respect back."

With my foot heavy on the gas pedal, the car picked up speed and I let out a yell. "Boy howdy, God!" I hadn't said boy howdy in years. I hadn't *felt* like saying boy howdy in years.

I had quit farming in 1928, when the banks foreclosed. Before we knew what hit us, we'd lost the farm and were renting rooms in town. When I first went to work for a former county agent who organized a Georgia cotton cooperative, I had to travel, but I could make it home most nights. That venture failed, but Mr. Downes formed a new cooperative, and I agreed to take south Georgia as my territory. Sanna said I should have insisted on the northeast territory. I told her I'd never get ahead if I made demands, but I guess I was wrong. The northeast went to a man whose wife refused ever to move. Sanna always resented that.

Long before the end of the cotton season in south Georgia, I'd stopped trying to get home every single weekend. I was working eighteen hours a day and sometimes couldn't get off before two o'clock Saturday afternoon. Heading for home, I'd be so excited about seeing Sanna I wouldn't stop for supper, just maybe get a Co-

Cola and a moon pie when I stopped for gas. If I didn't have a blow-out and the roads weren't slick, I'd get in around ten at night, worn out and hungry for supper. I did try for every other weekend, but the longer we lived apart, the more my life in south Georgia seemed to be the real thing, and my family in Progressive City a little remote. When I'd let myself worry about home, I couldn't do my job. When I did go home, after a night with Sanna and seeing that she and the children were all right, and how the money was holding out, then it seemed like I might as well just go on back. I'd leave right after Sunday dinner, which we always had at Mama and Papa's house. That made Sanna anxious, because she knew they didn't approve of the way she was raising the children. On Monday I'd start the week already worn out.

Part of my job was to buy cotton, but the most important part was to try to sell the farmers on the advantages of belonging to a cooperative, instead of selling to middlemen who tried to buy cheap and could hold the bales in warehouses till the price went up and then sell high to the mills. It cost an individual farmer a lot to warehouse his cotton crop. "You go with the co-ops," I told them, "and whatever profit gets made will come back to you, according to how much cotton you sell through us. And when spring comes we'll sell you seed and fertillzer, and whatever else you need, at a discount, and at the end of the year whatever we've made above expenses goes back to you." To show how we kept down operating expenses, I always managed to get in how much the wives of us field men fussed about how low our salaries were. And that was the truth. Sanna couldn't see that we'd lose the farmers' trust if we drove big cars or stayed in high-priced hotels. I kept reminding her I'd have more time at home when the fall cotton session wound down.

I found the letters just before I left on Sunday, when I was looking through drawers for a screwdriver to tighten a doorknob for Sanna, but I didn't try to read any till I got to Shellman the next night. The only light in the little room was a bulb hanging from the ceiling on a long cord. I turned the pillows to the foot of the bed and untied the faded blue ribbon. I think what I was hoping for was some understanding of the difference between what Sanna and I had in the beginning and this mixed-up mess we were in now. Part of it, of course, was being separated, but that wasn't all.

Sanna had them sorted according to postmark date. Her letters and mine. I reckon she kept every letter I ever wrote her, which is not exactly surprising. She can't throw away an old grocery list, much less the dentist bill from 1929 that we still haven't paid and may never be able to.

Before Sanna, the only letters I ever tried to keep were from Trulu Philpot. A week after our engagement was announced in the newspaper, I called it off. That great love affair ended at a house party in the mountains. We all went out to pick blackberries and were scattered along the road-side when a thunderstorm came up. I ran under a bridge to get out of the rain, and there was Trulu, kissing one of my fraternity brothers. Right then and there I demanded my ring back. It like to killed me.

There's nobody quite as mad as an old flame when she gives you back your letters and your picture and demands hers, and you have to admit you never saved them. When Trulu asked me for her letters, I got some satisfaction out of telling her I'd been using them to get fires going in my fireplace. It wasn't so, but I said it. Then for spite I passed them around the Sigma Chi house for the boys to read and laugh at. It was a mean thing to do, but I did it.

That happened a year before I met Sanna. I'd be excited, opening a letter from Trulu, but I don't remember ever reading one twice. From the beginning I knew it was different, how I felt about Sanna, because I'd keep reading her words over and over till the next letter came.

They haven't lost any of their magic, but not many are here in the collection. I know I tried to keep all Sanna's letters, but I'm sure many got left behind in hotel rooms—lost from pure care-lessness.

Now, holding Sanna's packet of letters, I grieve for all those she wrote that aren't here.

My second letter to Sanna was written after our first "date"—the evening service at church.

Wednesday, September 19, 1917

Dear Sanna,
I hope you don't mind if I call you Sanna.
I've known you a long time now—two whole
weeks and three days.

This is circus day in Athens. Everybody
from everywhere is in the big tent, including
the people I'm supposed to work with, so I'm
sitting at my desk with nothing to do but
write up reports. It was like a light came on in
here when I decided to write to you instead.

I certainly did enjoy that long-drawn-out
sermon Sunday night, and our chat after we
carried the others home. I hope you don't
mind the way I filled up Papa's car with
friends. The more people, see, the closer I
can sit to you. Too bad our number keeps
diminishing. If this war keeps up and everybody but me gets to go, I'll be looking after
all you girls by myself. Call it a slacker's par-
adise. I'm equal to it and I'd take pleasure
in doing my duty. But I wouldn't take pride
in it.

This is some busy week. I've already been
everywhere except Mitchellville and would
have gone there if you could have gone with
me.

Had a telegram yesterday from my Aunt
Loma in New York (you met her at the watermelon cutting) saying she had tied the
knot. Her new husband is rich and old and

a Yankee, and most likely a Republican. Mama is real upset about it. Miss Alice Ann Boozer (have you met her?) says, "Anythang that's outlandish, Loma has did it." I think marrying a Yankee takes the cake when it comes to outlandish.

I like the way "Dear Sanna" looks on paper. I've been practicing the way it sounds. I never heard the name Sanna before. Were you named for a grandmother or somebody?

May I impose on you for a date Saturday night? Please write that it's OK.

> Sincerely,
> Will T.

Sanna's answer is the next letter in the stack. Reading my name on the envelope, I feel again the same rush of excitement I always did when an envelope came addressed in her handwriting. Now as then, I can picture her sitting down to write at the oak table in her upstairs room at Miss Love's house. Her long black hair is braided for the night. The drapey silk shade on the lamp casts a soft glow on her dark skin, and her small lovely hand is graceful as she dips the pen into the ink bottle.

Dear Will T.,
Your letter was in the mail basket when I got in from school today. I'm pleased to say I have no plans for Saturday night.

No, I didn't mind "the crowd." They were all so nice to me. I'm a rather shy person, but they were easy to be with, and you saw to it that I and everybody else had a good time.

This was a hard day. I had to paddle two boys. With fifty-five fourth-graders I don't have an easy job, but I am not discouraged. The main problem is the animosity between town children and mill children. We didn't have that in Mitchellville, though poor farm children are looked down on there—people say they're "from over the river."

Your Uncle Sampson is trying very hard to be good, but he still talks instead of listening, and he distracts the class. He's always plotting mischief. But he is bright and charming and at home we are good friends. Little Precious Roach is a delight. I hope she doesn't come to hate her name the way I used to hate mine.

You asked how I happen to be called Sanna.

My mother, named Flora, gave flower names to all six children ahead of me. The first three were grown and married before I was born—Blossom, Lily Maude, and Magnolia. Magnolia, called Maggie, raised me from the time I was ten years old. After them came Zinnia, Violet, and Joe Pye. (I'm sure you know the big dusky-pink Joe Pye weed that grows by the roadside. When Joe

Pye was a boy, everybody called him "Weed" and he never minded. I'd have hated it.)

There was another boy, born before me. He died of pneumonia at six months so I never knew him. His name was Welcome Peter George Klein. Mrs. Herndon, our neighbor across the road, says that when he was born she asked Mama, "Miss Flora, how come you named him Welcome Peter George? You ain't near run out of flowers yet. Not even boy flowers." She says Mama told her, "One name sounds good as another when you get to be forty years old. I reckon I'm just tired of gardenin'. From here on out I'll just reach up and pick me one out of the air."

Mama was forty-three when I was born. She picked my name out of the air. It made me feel different in the family, and at school, too.

Little Sophronia came four years later, and Mama named her for a childhood friend at Brick Store Community in Newton County where she grew up. Poor Sophie was what the country people speak of as "illy formed." Her head was too big, and she never sat up by herself or talked. I have only one memory of her, lying on a blue blanket near the hearth like a limp doll, watching the logs flicker. Sophie lived only eighteen months.

When Mama was forty-seven, she had Carrie, called Tattie, and made a pet out of her. Mrs. Herndon says Tattie was the first child Mama had time to spoil.

Ever since my papa died, when I was thirteen and I went to live with Sister Maggie and Brother Hen in Mitchellville, their house has seemed more like home than the farm does.

I have papers to grade so I will close by saying I look forward to Saturday night. You forgot to tell me what time.

Sincerely,
Sanna K.

Eleven

AT THE TIME, all I really knew about Sister Maggie and her husband, Mr. Henry Jolley, was the gossip I'd heard from Mr. Charlie in Mitchellville. But Sanna had told me how much they had done for her. Mayor Jolley had sent her through Shorter, a Baptist college for girls in Rome, Georgia, from which she graduated in 1915 with a degree in mathematics. Then she'd lived with them and taught fourth grade for two years in Mitchellville before coming to P.C.

"But I got so restless," she'd told me as we sat on Miss Love's porch swing after church Sunday night. "Most of my friends were married and gone, and I wanted to make a new life for myself. One Sunday a missionary who was home from Africa talked at our church, hoping to recruit young people to the mission field, and I wanted to go. A college friend of mine had married a missionary and they went to China. Every time I had a letter from her, I'd say I'm going to be a missionary someday. Imagine, teaching heathen people about the love of Jesus Christ, and teaching them to read! All the time the man was talking about Africa, I felt God was calling me, telling me to go there. Even showing

me the way. How to apply, where to get training."

"But you didn't do it," I said.

Sanna gave a helpless little shrug. "Sister Maggie wouldn't hear of it. She kept saying, 'You'll
just end up an old maid in the jungle. With you
being so particular, I can't imagine you living in
a dirty hut in a village full of savages. They don't
have any dentists or doctors in Africa. You'll get
leprosy and jungle fever and I don't know what
all.' Sister Maggie told me about a young missionary lady who got all her teeth pulled on a visit
home so she wouldn't have to worry about tooth-
aches in Africa. Will, I'm ashamed to admit it,
but after Sister Maggie said that, God's call got
weaker."

I told Sanna I was glad she didn't end up in
the jungle, since I wouldn't be there.

"I felt so guilty. Jesus said, 'Go ye into all the
world' but Sister Maggie kept saying, 'Don't go,
don't rot your life away after all the advantages
we've given you.' I couldn't bring myself to go,
with her so opposed. It seemed unappreciative.
But I've always regretted it."

I knew what it was like to have somebody pushing and pulling at you. "Grandpa Blakeslee always
expected me to come into his store business," I
told her. "He had a fit when I said I wanted to
be a farmer."

"I can see why," she said, wrinkling her nose
as if she'd had a whiff of pigpen.

"Grandpa died when I was fifteen, so it never

115

came to a head. The choice, I mean. But if Grandpa had lived and kept aggravatin' me about the store, I'd have just got more hard-headed. I'm that much like him."

She smiled. "Well, I'd hate to see you get old behind a mule, Will. This way you aren't exactly wasting your degree, and you get paid every month."

"I aim to farm someday." I said it real firm. "Soon as the war's over, Papa's go'n buy the land and the home place from his daddy out in Banks County and give it to me. I'll take you out there one day, Sanna, to see Grandpa Tweedy. He's the world's laziest man. He married a widow woman named Miz Jones, and that's what he still calls her. Too lazy to change it. He used to sit on the porch all day swattin' flies, and he had a pet hen to peck up the dead ones. Now the hen's dead, so he just sits there."

"I think you like him," she said with a laugh.

"I hated him when I was a boy. But I don't have to mind him now."

Sanna hadn't mentioned Hugh again. You don't help somebody forget anybody if you keep bringing up the subject, so I didn't, and pretty soon I forgot about him myself. But I did ask Miss Love one day if Sanna was getting much mail from Jefferson.

"No," she said. "Sanna told me she wouldn't be seeing the young man anymore. I never thought that would be the end of it, but I guess it was."

Miss Love took the opportunity to tell me how nice Sanna was, how she kept her room neat as a pin and her clothes immaculate. "She reminds me of Mrs. Villy, a woman I knew in Baltimore. After every rain Mrs. Villy got out a stepladder and wiped off the outside of all her windows. I really like Sanna," Miss Love continued. "She never complains about anything, which is more than I can say about the others, especially Issie. Issie says her mattress is too hard, it's hot up there, she wishes she didn't have to go next door for meals, and she fusses about Sanna hogging the bathroom. Sanna can spend an hour in the tub, it's true, and she's forever washing her hands. I didn't expect girls to be spilling over into my bathroom when I rented those rooms, but I've told them they can if they have to."

That was the closest Miss Love ever came to criticizing Sanna. Mostly she kept trying to sell her to me, as if she was selling a hat or a car at the store. Any time she wasn't bragging about how neat Sanna kept her room, she was saying what beautiful taste she had in clothes. "Her Sister Maggie makes most of them, you know. Sanna says when she was learning to sew, if a seam was the least bit crooked, her sister made her take it out and stitch it again. Now she makes herself do that. I think it's admirable, don't you, Will?"

"It sounds tedious to me."

"I mean, to try that hard, and be conscientious enough to take the time."

One afternoon Miss Love said that when she

117

got home from the store, Sanna was in the parlor playing the piano. "Sanna played very competently, but when she saw me, she quit."

Later, when I asked Sanna to play me a piece, she wouldn't. Her lovely eyes were cast down and she was picking at her thumb with a fingernail. "Will, I've never told—well, my piano teacher at Shorter asked me once if I'd heard much music as a child. I said no, and she said she thought not. She thought I played mechanically, said I worried so much about getting the right notes, I couldn't play with feeling. I've never had much confidence since then—about my music. If anybody's listening, I just can't play."

We were sitting together on Miss Love's loveseat in the parlor.

"Me neither," I said. "Not if somebody's listenin', or if they aren't. I count it as one of my blessings, Sanna. I'm crazy about dance music, especially the way Miss Love plays it, but the most miserable six weeks of my life was that time Papa traded twenty pounds of cornmeal for a clarinet. Folks were always bringin' in things like that to the store. One time a troupe of midget clowns got financially strapped here and talked him into swappin' some tobacco and canned goods for a clown costume. He brought it home for Mary Toy to play dress-up in."

"But what about the clarinet?"

I shifted a little on the loveseat. In her direction. "A man came to town sellin' band instruments and givin' lessons, and we had the clarinet, so

Mama made me take them. Practicin' was about as prickly and borin' as pickin' up sweetgum balls. I told my teacher I hated practicin'. He said, 'Just play a little while and then walk around the house and then practice some more.' The piece I learned on was 'Abide With Me.' It got so I couldn't abide 'Abide With Me,' much less the clarinet. One day I traded it to Pink Predmore for a pair of skates. Mama fussed, but I think it was a relief to her and everybody."

By now we were somehow sitting right close on the loveseat, and she was looking up at me, saying how much more fun life would be if she were more like me, taking things as they come and not being scared to fail.

"Oh, I don't take kindly to failin', as they say in the country." I eased my arm across the back of the loveseat behind her, getting set to casually touch her shoulder. "But if one thing won't work, I try another. It's a challenge," I said softly. Our eyes met. The raspberry lips parted slightly. I could feel her warm breath. My arm was around her. "Like for instance," I whispered, "I've tried a dozen times to kiss you, and you . . ."

She pushed me away firmly and stood up. "It's late, Will. I think you'd better go."

I got up, stood looking down at her, moved a step closer. Slowly, slowly, I bent forward.

She moved a step back. "I thought you were different from other men, Will. Why do you keep . . ."

"I love you, Sanna. I love you."

119

"Nobody can really be in love this fast."

"I can. I am."

"Then quit trying to force yourself on me. Please, Will." She was very upset.

"I don't want to force anything. I just . . ."

"Good night, Will." She gave me a quivery little smile.

I followed her to the parlor door and watched as she ran quickly up the stairs.

Twelve

Editor's note: *During the fall of 1917, with Will constantly on the road, he and Sanna fell in love through their letters. In the first draft of the manuscript, Olive Ann Burns told much of the story through these letters, but in her revision she intended to replace some of them with scenes in which Sanna and Will learned about each other face to face.*

In the following letters Will declares his love for Sanna and makes plans to accompany her to Thanksgiving dinner in Mitchellville.

October 31, 1917

My dear Sanna,
I bet you haven't written me one line, but I'm going to Macon tomorrow just to find out.

I left Athens Monday, got to Camilla at ten on Tuesday, built a barn, and came on to Vidalia. We had a food-conservation meeting tonight at which Yours Truly presided and told all he knew in two minutes. We'll hold another tomorrow morning at the schoolhouse to try to get the kids to save waste paper and eat a little less of the foods needed by the Army and Navy for my boyhood pals and fraternity brothers in uniform.

I'll leave here tomorrow afternoon for Macon to get my precious letter from you, be there thirty minutes, go on to Tifton, hold meetings, go on from there to Barnesville, hold meetings, then back to Athens and then P.C. Saturday evening, when I hope to find you without a date. That's my program for the week and I'll complete it or bust.

Vidalia is a quaint little south Georgia town, with the same old moon that rides above your room at Miss Love's house. It's a beautiful night, almost perfect, but not perfect because you're not with me. I didn't really know how much I could miss you until I came way off down here.

Sanna, I know you think I'm the biggest fool in the world, but I can't help saying I love you. I knew it almost from the moment I saw Sampson's watermelon explode on your shoulder. I've tried to hold back, Lord knows. I can tell it makes you uneasy. But it's hard to have self-control when I love you so much. You'll pardon me saying all this, won't you, Sanna? Please at least consider me a true friend who's always ready and willing to help you any way I can. Ask me to do anything that will be of help to you or give you pleasure. I will do it. You are the sweetest, truest, best person I have ever known.

It's after one o'clock, so be good and don't forget—

Will T.

Sunday, November 18, 1917

Dear Sanna,

Little ole girl, I like to talk to you, I love to think of you and be with you. I don't ask for all your time or thoughts. I just want a little of your love, though I'm not worthy of even your friendship.

I'm trying to live a better life from knowing you, and because I love you so and want to be worthy of you. Girl, you don't know how much difference you have made in me. There are things I would have done did I not know you. When thoughts come that shouldn't be in my mind, I picture your own dear self—your happy smile, your beautiful sparkling black eyes—and your image drives temptation away.

This is one dark gloomy day. Even the clouds sigh for you. When autumn leaves were in color I loved hearing you exclaim, "Oh, look at the beautiful trees!" You have brought so much sunshine into my life that this morning I noticed for the first time how dead with winter everything looks. By spring, when the maple tree outside my office window dangles its transparent yellow-green winged fruit, lit by sunlight, I hope love for me will have begun to light up your heart . . .

Sanna, please thank your sister for the kind invitation to stay over for Thanksgiving dinner. I'll try to make Mama and Papa see how important this is to me. If it's freezing cold or raining and you have to go on the train, I'll come to Mitchellville to get you on Sunday, weather permitting. Otherwise, I'll meet your train in Athens and ride with you to Progressive City.

Back when I was in high school, Sanna, I had a girl in any direction—Jefferson, Franklin Springs, Wilson's Chapel, Royston. I'd hitch up old Jack, Grandpa Blakeslee's mule, and leave in the morning to reach Royston by five in the afternoon. At eight or nine o'clock I'd start back. It took all night to get back, but of course the mule knew the way home. I could just turn old Jack's reins loose, go to sleep, and wake up at Grandpa's stable. Us boys and our dogs had a lot of night life in those days. We were always slipping out to go possum or coon hunting.

Right now I'd better get to work.

As ever,
Will

In reply to my letter she wrote:

Dear Will,
I am indeed grateful for your offer to carry me to Mitchellville the day before Thanksgiv-

ing. Of course I realize you can't drive through the country if it's freezing cold or the roads are muddy and slick. I know it will disappoint your parents for you not to be at home, so I will certainly understand if you can't.

Will, I see why every girl in P.C. has been in love with you at one time or another (or so I am told) and probably half the girls in Athens. You're so anxious to please, you make people laugh and have a good time, you put yourself out for everybody, young or old. You are wonderful to Simpson. You are something of a flirt, of course, but everybody knows it's partly just your way of being friendly. I wish I could be the way you are with strangers. In two minutes it's as if they're old acquaintances.

As I've told you, I really enjoy the food at the boarding house, but now I'm not sure I can keep eating there—not since I found out the monkey can get in the kitchen.

Yesterday I finally had a real visit with Miss Hyta. She had asked me to come by for coffee after school, and we sat talking at one end of that long dining table. I've wondered about her Greek name. She said her father was a Greek scholar and it was his idea to call her Hyta. I said I'd heard she was a direct descendant of George Washington. "Who told you that?" she snapped. I said Will Tweedy, and she said, "You tell

Will to get his facts straight. Everybody knows George Washington had no children, so a statement like that impugns his character." She said President Washington was her great-great-great-uncle. His sister Betty married Fielding Lewis and they had eight children, and one of those was her grandfather's father.

So, Will, you are now set straight.

I am impressed that she is also kin to the King of England and Chief Justice John Marshall, but I liked her better after she said her mama always told her a family tree should be like a potato vine, with the best part underground. "Of course I'm proud to be descended from the Washington family, but nobody else cares about that except the D.A.R. I'm more interested in the United Daughters of the Confederacy than the D.A.R."

I begged Miss Hyta to come talk to my class about George Washington, but she says everybody already knows about her and him. She offered to come talk about the women's suffrage movement or the Women's Christian Temperance Union, but warned me that certain men in Progressive City would want me fired if she did either one.

I was about to ask her about living in the Panama Canal Zone when one of the cooks rushed in and said, "Lawdy, Miss Hyta, come quick! Yo monkey loose in de kitchen!

He done made a gran' mess wid my cus-
tard!"

You'd told me about the monkey, but I
thought he stayed in a cage in the barn. It
gives me the creeps just thinking about him.
I can't even stand a dog in the house.

With best regards,
Sanna

I was crazy about Hyta Mae Brown. I think I
halfway fell in love with her when she came to
Cold Sassy in 1910. I was eighteen then, and I guess
she was about ten years older. Not pretty or anything, but there was something quick and special
about her, almost electric, and she had sad eyes.

I'd never known a lady before who said exactly
what she thought about anything and everything,
as if she had nothing to lose anymore. Her mouth
was usually going ninety-to-nothing, but you
never learned much about her except the George
Washington stuff and her life in the Canal Zone.
Her mother was dead, and she had gone to Panama to keep house for her daddy. That was in
1904. The French had given up on digging the
canal because of yellow fever and malaria, and her
daddy, a civil engineer, went there to help clear
out the swamps where mosquitoes bred. There
were no schools. Miss Hyta tutored a bunch of
American children in the French cottage where
they lived. She liked telling how termites ate up
the floors every two or three years and government carpenters replaced them free.

Other than such as that you never heard Miss Hyta talk about herself. Nothing personal, I mean. Frolic Flournoy, the postmaster in P.C., said she mailed a letter every Monday to a man in the Canal Zone named Mr. G. Leeds Wildman, and letters came from him to her, sometimes two or three at a time, but nobody dared ask her who he was, and she never mentioned him.

As I explained to Sanna, Miss Hyta was still an outsider in Progressive City, her and the squirrel monkey both, despite they'd been here seven years. Miss Hyta's daddy had died of malaria and she came to P.C. to live with Miss Effie Belle Tate and Mr. Bubba, her mother's sister and brother. Mr. Bubba died the next year at age 105, and that's when Miss Effie Belle started renting out rooms.

One paying guest I remember was an old lady named Mrs. Merkle. If she was going somewhere, even for just an hour, she'd take a spool of black thread and run it from the knob of her hall door to the bedposts and through drawer pulls on the dresser, all around the room to her closet door. The thread was never broken. One time four old maids were rooming there, Miss Rachel, Miss Jessie, Miss Grace, and Miss Bessie. Miss Grace had stock in the Coca-Cola Company and lived on her dividends. When she got too old to go down for meals, Miss Hyta or Miss Effie Belle took her a tray upstairs three times a day with no extra pay for it. Miss Grace kept saying she'd leave Miss Effie Belle her Coca-Cola stock, but when she died her will said it was to go to the American Red Cross.

After she died and Miss Bessie went to live with her sister, Miss Hyta and Miss Effie Belle decided to fix up two apartments, meaning a tiny stove and sink were installed. Mrs. Eubanks lived in one of them. She put coffee grounds and water in a pan and hard-boiled an egg in it while the coffee brewed. We always hoped she washed the egg good first. She also sprinkled psilum seeds on her oatmeal. Psilum, which she called persilum, was for her colon. She's the only woman I ever heard talk about her colon. "The seeds swell up in the digestive track," she said. "They keep me reg'lar."

I once had to go get a dead rat out of the closet for Mrs. Eubanks.

A retired Baptist preacher and his wife lived in the other apartment, upstairs. The lady was crazy. One day she got tired of washing dishes and just threw the dishpan out the window, soapy water and dishes included. The dishes were English Wedgwood brought from the Canal Zone.

After that, Miss Effie Belle changed the apartments back to rooms and decided to start a boarding house. On account of Miss Hyta's monkey, it wasn't easy to hire help or get customers. But good food soon outweighed the zoo, and people from all over town got to coming there for dinner. When Miss Effie Belle died in 1914, Miss Hyta inherited the house and business.

Which is why she and Sanna were talking in the dining room that day after school.

Thirteen

THE WEDNESDAY BEFORE Thanksgiving turned out rainy and cold, which meant driving to Mitchellville was out of the question. However, by then it had been decided that, rain or shine, I would be eating my turkey with the Jolleys. Sanna was to leave P.C. Wednesday afternoon and I would join her at the station in Athens, where she had to change trains.

The Athens depot was an anthill of goings and comings. University students, old folks, and families were all trying to get somewhere for Thanksgiving. I watched one tattered poor-white family running single file across the tracks, scared they'd missed their train. The daddy was first, followed by the mama and a string of stairstep younguns. The littlest one, struggling to keep up, kept yelling, "Wait for baby, dod-dammit! Wait for baby!"

Sanna and I managed to get seats together in the passenger car. "Just think," I said, "I've got you all to myself!"

She laughed. "Look around, Will. We aren't exactly alone."

The seats were all full. The conductor was taking up tickets. "Don't see a soul," I said, and touched her cheek.

Moments later, a stout farm woman wearing a big toothless smile and a man's old wool overcoat lumbered down the aisle, aimed right at us. Above the *whoosh* of steam and grinding of wheels as the train pulled out of the station, she shouted, "Lawd, if it ain't li'l Sanna Maria Klein!"

"Why, it's Mrs. Herndon!" Sanna exclaimed. She rose quickly, held out her arms. They hugged like long-lost relatives. "Oh, I'm so glad to see you! It's been years!"

I stood up too, of course.

"Lemme look at you, Sanna Maria!" Holding on to a seat, Mrs. Herndon stepped back a little. "Lawd, if you ain't done growed up and got ladyfied! But I'd know you for one a-them Klein girls anywheres. All y'all got yore mama's looks—blackheaded, and that brunette skin and them black eyes. Who's your mister?"

"Oh, I'm sorry." Sanna put her hand on my arm and introduced me. "Mrs. Herndon, this is Mr. Tweedy."

"Hidy-do, sir."

"Mrs. Herndon lives down the road a piece from Mama," Sanna explained. To Mrs. Herndon she said, "We're, uh, on our way to . . . to Mitchellville. For Thanksgiving."

"You ought to be a-goin' home for Thanksgivin', Sanna Maria."

"How's Mama?"

"Good as common, I reckon. But she complains she don't see you much since yore daddy died."

"Well, it's hard to get there and—I mean, I stay so busy . . ."

"Hit grieves her, Sanna Maria. She thinks you done got shamed of the fam'ly."

I could tell that Sanna was flustered. She said, "You know that's not so."

"I know it and you know it. But she don't."

It was an awkward moment. I said, "Take my seat, Miz Herndon, so y'all can visit."

"Thank you, sir, but I got a seat of my own, and it looks like I better go on back to it." The passenger car started rocking. She turned and staggered up the aisle.

Sanna called after her, "Tell Mama you saw me, hear? And give my best to Li'l George and them when you get home."

Without looking back she shouted, "Yes'm, I'll do that."

As we settled into our seats again, I wondered about Sanna and her mama. Had Sanna thought about going to the farm for Thanksgiving? "You're twitching your shoulders, Will. What's bothering you?"

"Nothin'. Just thinkin' about Miz Herndon." I smiled at her. "You know, right now you remind me of a chicken that just got its head pecked by a brood hen."

She didn't like that. There was a long silence between us, underlaid by train sounds and sprinkled with coughs and chatter from other passengers. Somebody going to the next car opened the end

132

door, letting in a blast of cold damp air and loud clickety-clacks.

"Hey, Sanna Maria Klein." I leaned my head close to hers. "You never did tell me how your mama picked that name out of the air."

She didn't answer. Just sat watching trees move backwards past the train window. Then, rifling through her handbag, she pulled out a little mirror, surveyed her face, tucked a loose strand of black hair under her red hat. I tried again. "I don't know why, but Sanna Maria sounds kind of familiar."

She had gone back to staring out the window. Still not looking at me, she said, "Do you remember the names of Columbus's ships?"

"What's that got to do with it?"

"Just tell me the names of Columbus's ships."

"Okay, they were the *Nina,* the *Pinta,* and the *Sanna Maria.* " I pronounced the last one without the *t,* the way I'd always said and heard it. Light dawned as the train car rocked in a sudden buffet of rain and wind. "You mean . . . ?"

With a little sigh, she said, "I'm afraid so. I was born on Columbus Day, and Mama was still trying to decide on a name when Lily Maude came home from school, singsonging, 'The-Nina-the-Pinta-and-the-Sanna-Maria.' She went on like that all afternoon—'the-Nina-the-Pinta-the-Sanna-Maria'—and Mama started thinking that Nina or Sanna Maria, either one, would make a pretty name for the baby. Me."

Sanna still wasn't looking at me. She was staring

133

through the rain that now sheeted the train windows. "I've hated my name ever since Columbus Day in the first grade."

"I don't see . . ."

"The teacher wrote the names of the ships on the blackboard and made us recite them out loud over and over, just the way Lily Maude had done. 'The-Nina-the-Pinta-and-the-Sanna-Maria.' I remember Miss Dot slapping out the beat with a yardstick."

Trees kept sailing backwards, followed by more trees and cotton fields and an occasional lonely unpainted farmhouse, but Sanna didn't see them. She was looking inside herself. "You may not believe it, Will, but I was a very shy child. It took a lot of nerve, but that day I halfway raised my hand, and Miss Dot nodded. I stood up and proudly announced, 'Today is my birthday. I'm six years old. I was named for Columbus's ship!' I thought Miss Dot would say how nice. What she said was, 'In that case, your name's not spelled right.' She turned to the blackboard and underlined the *Santa* part of *Santa Maria* and told me to copy it thirty times. All the children laughed. This was a one-room school, Will—first through seventh grades—and everybody laughed. Even my brother, Joe Pye. Even Lily Maude."

The train slowed as we passed a small community of wood frame houses, then screeched and hissed to a stop across the road from a little store and a small church named Hard Creek Baptist. When the door opened to let an old man get off, cold air swept through the car and set us shivering. We were moving again before Sanna said, "From that day, I never opened my mouth in class unless I got called on. If I didn't speak, I couldn't say anything stupid and get laughed at. Will, there's a little girl in my class now, shyest child you ever saw. She makes perfect grades on her papers, but if I call on her, she can't say a word. I've quit calling on her."

She looked up at me with a little smile that turned off as quickly as it had turned on. "I copied *Santa Maria* thirty times, but that night I got out the family Bible and found the names. Of course the only one I could read was mine: Sanna Maria Klein. That's how Mama had written it, so that was my name—no matter what Miss Dot said."

I ached for the shy little girl she'd been. I longed to take her in my arms, soothe her with tender kisses, stroke her hair. But we were on a train, and she wouldn't have let me touch her anyhow. So I just asked what did her mother say about it.

"I didn't tell Mama," said Sanna. "None of us ever went to Mama about anything. We went to Papa. That night he wrote a note for me to take Miss Dot, saying he wanted the spelling to stay the way it was. That didn't stop the children, though. For weeks they taunted me. I hated them and I hated my name. When I went to live with Sister Maggie, I asked her to please just call me Sanna, and that's been my name ever since. I guess I'll always be Sanna Maria to Mama and Mrs. Herndon and everybody else in Mount Sinai Community—the same way Progressive City is still Cold Sassy to Miss Love and Doc Slaughter —and you."

"Not to me. Not anymore. Anyway, at least you've got one thing to be thankful for, Sanna."

She looked up at me, puzzled.

"What if you'd been born on Christmas Day? You might have been named Santa Claus and called Sannie Claus."

"Don't make fun of me, Will."

"I love you, Sanna. If your name was Issie or Pocahontas or King George, I'd still love you." I put my hand on hers and she let it stay—for about two seconds.

"You want to hear my mother's name, Will? Mama had a great-uncle, Wilhelm Barnhart, and when she was born he declared her a special child. 'Like one born with a caul over her face,' he said, and claimed the right to name her. What he came up with was Flora Plantena Lemma Sadai Zetta Susannah Greta Margarethe Utilly Meety Keesy Barnhart. It's all there in the Barnhart family Bible. When Mama was little she'd have to recite all her names for preachers and visiting relatives, and she enjoyed the attention. She was just called Flora. Being Flora was why she got so interested in flower names . . ." She sighed again.

"You think your mother will come for Thanksgiving dinner?" As soon as I asked, I knew I should have kept my mouth shut.

136

"She never comes to Mitchellville," Sanna said bitterly. Then, brightening, she added, "Will, you don't know what it means to me that you'll finally get to meet my people—I mean the ones who've made all the difference in my life. I wouldn't be anything if it weren't for Sister Maggie and Brother Henry.

"From my first day in school I wanted to be a teacher. Mount Sinai only had seven grades and wasn't much of a school, but Mitchellville had a high school. So Sister Maggie asked Papa if he'd let me spend the school year with them and go home for holidays and summer vacations, and he said yes.

"I'd been promoted to sixth grade, but I had to take tests in Mitchellville, and as soon as I saw the math test I knew I couldn't pass it and asked to stay back. I had a wonderful girlhood in Mitchellville. Sister Maggie taught me to sew and paid for piano lessons and had parties for me and saw that I had nice friends.

"And then Brother Henry sent me to college. Paid all my expenses, and me just his sister-in-law. I wasn't even theirs, the way Annie Laurie and Lonzo are."

At that moment the engineer blew the whistle, and with much screeching and grinding of wheels, the train stopped and the woman who had been sitting across the aisle from us hurried to the door.

It took Mrs. Herndon less than a minute to seize the opportunity. She landed in the vacated seat with a lapful of boxes, sacks, and bundles. Leaning across the aisle, she tapped Sanna on the shoulder. "How's Maggie? She feelin' all right?"

Sanna's answer was brief. "Yes'm, except she's been sneezing ever since August."

"Her and yore mama both. Once they git a-goin', they can sneeze their heads off. I seen Miss Flora just fore I left to go visit Helen'n'em in Commerce. Hit were on a Tuesday. No, Wednesday. No, hit was a Tuesday, cause that was the day Mr. Paul Pur-due tuck a wagonload of corn to the gristmill. You remember Mr. Pur-due. When I went in, Miss Flora was sneezin' like hit was pepper up her nose. Eyes a-runnin', nose a-runnin', her face broke out red all over and hit a-itchin'. Said she'd been sweepin'. Sweepin' always gits her goin'." The train slowed to plod up a steep grade. "I shore do hope hit don't stall," said Mrs. Herndon. "When I rid this thang to Commerce, hit hit a artermobile at a crossin'. Didn't nobody git hurt, but we waited the longest kind a-time. Well, I cain't git over you bein' so fancy, Sanna Maria. You still little-bitty, though. Ain't tall like Maggie and Blossom."

"No, ma'am, I'm not."

The train picked up speed again. A baby started crying. A child's voice wailed, "Papa, I'm cold." There was loud laughter from a group of soldiers at the front of the car. Sanna took a book out of her handbag, but Mrs. Herndon wasn't about to be cut off. Placing her feet in the aisle, she leaned forward the better to see me, and said, "Mr.

Tweedy, ain't Sanna Maria just the prettiest thang you ever seen? You ought've seed her when she was a baby. Law, I remember one day, I reckon she warn't no more'n eight month old, and her sisters brought in a big dishpan full of black-berries, fresh-picked and shiny, with lots of red'ns to make the jelly firm up right." The book was still open but I knew Sanna was listening. "Honey, you got so excited. Kicked yore li'l ole legs and bounced in Miss Flora's lap a-pointin' to them red berries and just a-crowin'! You was tryin' to say, 'See? See?' What come out was 'Tee? Tee?' Hit 'as the first time you'd tried to talk. Miss Flora, she was real proud."

Sanna, delighted, said she'd never heard that story before.

Mrs. Herndon knew how to keep an audience once she got hold of it. "I recollect another time," she said. "It was a Sunday afternoon, and Miss Flora was still dressed up cause the preacher was there, him and his wife both. Miss Flora was a beautiful lady then, Sanna Maria, not all wore out like now. She had on the prettiest dressin' sac, lots of lace on it. I can see her now, a-holdin' on to yore li'l dress to hep you balance. You was just larnin' to walk."

Sanna had planted her feet in the aisle too, almost touching Mrs. Herndon's, but their con-versation was interrupted by a shiny-faced young soldier standing in the aisle. "Excuse me, ladies, I got to get by." The doughboy looked pressed and proud in his new uniform. You'd have thought he was a general, they made way for him so quick. In my Sunday suit, I felt like a fool.

After he passed, I leaned around Sanna and asked Mrs. Herndon if she was going home for Thanksgiving.

"I reckon. Though I ain't shore where home's at no more."

Sanna looked surprised. "Didn't you stay on at the farm after, uh . . ."

"You mean after Big George walked out on me? Yes'm. But I couldn't keep thangs goin' by myself. So when Bertie Ruth and her husband offered to move in and take over, I said, 'Hep yoreself, and welcome.' Sanna Maria, you remember Bertie Ruth. She married a man old as her daddy. Dance O'Neill, that's his name. I knowed Mr. O'Neill was in the loggin' business, but hit shore did surprise me when he went to loggin' my woods stead of farmin' my land. Pretty soon their oldest boy, he moved in with his bride. Said he 'as go'n grow him some cotton. Said hit'd be all the same to me whether he farmed hit or I let the fields lie fallow, and I couldn't argue with that. And then Katie, she come with her husband—he works for the railroad—and pretty soon t'warn't my house.

"They wouldn't let me do nothin' cept rock babies. I couldn't wring a chicken or pick a chicken, neither one. Hit makes me proud, the way they treated me so nice, but like I told Bertie Ruth, I can rest in the grave. Hit 'as like I was just comp'ny. So three or more weeks ago I went

140

to see Helen over in Commerce. Sanna Maria, you remember Helen."

"Oh, yes, we used to study together. She was really smart, Mrs. Herndon."

"She still is. Works her head off. Her and her husband, Richard, they both do twelve-hour shifts in the mill, and they was mighty proud to see me, I tell you. They let me do all the cookin' and the washin' and the cleanin', and by me bein' thar, the oldest chi'ren could go to school reg'lar cause I could hep to see after the li'l uns. Helen's got eight chi'ren already, Sanna Maria, and another'n on the way that looks like twins. Well, that li'l ole sorry mill house felt a lot more like home than my farm, but I did get right tarred a-not restin'. So when Bertie Ruth wrote and begged me to come spend Thanksgivin', I was right ready to."

"So you go'n stay on at Mount Sinai?" I asked.

"I don't know. I been a-livin' in that house nigh on fifty year, but, well, we'll see."

The train jerked and a box on Mrs. Herndon's lap toppled into the aisle. Reaching for it, she said, "I got some shuttles in here. Broke ones. They tho'm out at the mill, and so Helen, she brings'm home for the babies to play with. I'm takin' these here to Bertie Ruth's crowd, and I'll give some to the colored chi'ren."

"How many does Bertie Ruth have?" Sanna asked.

"Fifteen. Ain't none of her girls had to get marrit, but they's a few boys I call speckled. I mean they ain't bad but they ain't good either.

141

Out of that many, they cain't all turn out good."
She laughed. "Want to hear sump'm awful, Sanna
Maria? Bertie Ruth, she wrote me last week a
colored hand on old Baldwin's place up and ran
off in the night. His wife, she said he'd deserted
her and the chi'ren, but one a-her boys, the uppity
one—he's go'n git hisself shot if he don' be careful —he said his daddy had gone to Cincinnati.
Said his daddy could make a decent livin' up
North and was a-go'n send for the whole fam'ly
later. Mr. Baldwin got so mad he might-near
turned'm all out right then and thar, but he
thought twice. Knowed he'd be in a pickle if they
left fore hog killin'. The way them colored ack
here lately, I'm bout ready to move up North
myself, just to git away from'm."

Sanna bristled. "You can't blame them. Jesus
said—"

"Jesus didn't say nothin' bout farm hands
leavin' their white folks in the lurch. Jesus said
do unto others as you would have them do unto
you." Staring straight ahead, Mrs. Herndon was
quiet for a while. Then she said again, "I still think
you ought to be goin' home for Thanksgivin',
Sanna Maria. You go see Maggie'n'em all

Sanna didn't answer. She just opened her book
again. Ten minutes later the train steamed into
the depot at Greensboro. It looked like the whole
town had come to meet somebody. Families
waved and hollered when they spotted the passenger they were waiting for, especially if it was
a college student or a man in uniform. It wasn't

hard to locate Mr. Henry Jolley. A huge man, much taller than I was, and built like a hog. Big head, fat face and lips, and small eyes squinting through folds of fat. No neck you could see, ham-sized arms, big fat hands, massive chest, and a stomach that led the rest of him.

"Sanna! Here, girl!" he called, waving a big cigar.

Her face brightened, and, forgetting me, she ran towards him, arms outstretched.

Even as he hugged her to him, I could tell he was drunk.

Fourteeen

BESIDE MAYOR JOLLEY'S bigness, Sanna's small-
ness struck me. Her head barely came to his chest
as he folded her into a tight hug. That's when her
glowing smile faded to dismay and embarrassment, then anger. He smelled of whiskey, and he
staggered against her as she tried to guide him
away from the depot's crush of people. When she
introduced us, his fat lips stretched into a silly
grin. He was holding his cigar in the hand he extended, and that just made him giggle. He leaned
on Sanna as we hurried on towards his new seven-
passenger touring car in the cold mist of late afternoon.

It was easy to picture us freezing to death in
a ditch or stuck in the mud or worse, so I said
I'd sure like to get the feel of the steering wheel
if he didn't mind my driving. "By all means, Mr.
Tweedy," he said, and was asleep in the back seat
before we reached the road to Mitchellville. Supper was a mix of good hot food and imitation gai-
ety, a lame attempt by everybody to cover up the
fact that the big man at the head of the table was
besotted. He belched loudly, flirted with Sarah,
his daughter Annie Laurie's friend from Shorter
College, fussed at Lonzo about his grades in front

of the two boys he had brought home from Mercer, and asked Mrs. Jolley where in hell did she get that sausage. "You know I like hot sausage," he said, "and this lye hominy, I don't see one piece of red pepper in it."

"Well, the girls are here," said Mrs. Jolley, a tall, plump, matronly woman with dark eyes like Sanna's. Her brown hair was plaited and wound around her head. "You know, Mr. Jolley, they don't like hot sausage, and—"

"You could have cooked some of both." He glared at her. Nobody spoke while the lye hominy was being passed, and the stewed tomatoes and butter beans.

Sanna asked Annie Laurie and Sarah if teachers she'd had were still at Shorter. And she told about the time it was announced that senior girls could have the privilege of not going to supper on Sunday night. "A friend and I thought you should take advantage of any special privilege, so we didn't go to supper and then about nine o'clock we were starving. We went around to every room hoping that somebody had something to eat and finally a girl gave us a five-cent package of crackers. We didn't ever skip Sunday night supper again."

Mr. Jolley couldn't reach his food if he sat straight in front of the table. He had to sit sideways to keep that big stomach out in front and his right hand close to the nearest plate. Everybody was pointedly ignoring him, so I said, "When I was at the University of Georgia, we had pressing clubs. You had to join and it cost a dollar a month.

I joined one month and my friend Frank would join the next and somebody else the next. We'd all send our clothes in on one membership."

Mr. Jolley got on Lonzo about his grades again, and I looked at the mayor and said, "When I was leavin' for college, old Loomis Toy, who worked for us, brought my trunk up there to the depot in a wheelbarrow and my daddy came to see me off. That day Papa told me he didn't know anything bout college and never heard of one until he was grown, but he said, 'I understand there is a lot more to college than what you get out of books and I want you to get it all.' Maybe Lonzo's just tryin' to get it all, sir."

Tall like her mother, Annie Laurie was a plump girl with mischievous eyes. Sanna asked her if she'd been invited yet to the president's house as she had. "Dr. Van Hoose was a sweet man," she said. "He and his wife had a pretty house down the hill from the college and they'd invite a few girls to their home for Sunday dinner sometimes."

I noticed that every time Mr. Jolley tried to say something, Mrs. Jolley said something else. She seemed furious at him for getting drunk. When supper was over and the girls had cleared the table, Mrs. Jolley brought in a coconut pie. Mr. Jolley stared at Annie Laurie and said, "Sugar, you've put on weight."

Sanna said, "All girls do that their freshman year, Brother Hen."

"Maybe you'd better let me eat your piece of pie, honey," he said.

146

"If you want to talk about weight, Papa, I think you've put on some too. How bout letting me eat *your* pie?"

His face turned red, and suddenly he got up and left the room. There was an embarrassed silence. Finally Mrs. Jolley said, "I hope y'all will excuse him. He hasn't been himself lately."

At that moment he came back in. Flailing a hacksaw in the air, Mayor Jolley pushed his chair aside with his foot and said, "I'm sick and tired of sittin' sideways to eat." With everybody watching, eyes wide and mouths open, he proceeded to cut out a half-moon at his place at the mahogany table. When he was almost through, his wife covered her face with her hands and started to cry. He ignored her.

"All right, now," he said as the cut-out piece clattered to the floor. "A table had ought to fit the man that provisions it." He sat down, pulled his chair up, and his stomach fitted the hole perfectly. He pulled his pie and a cup of coffee to the right of his stomach, ate the pie, sucked up the coffee, and lit a cigar, wearing a triumphant smile.

After supper, while Miss Maggie and the girls were washing, drying, and putting away dishes and setting out plate scrapings for the dog, Mr. Henry and the boys and I smoked in the parlor.

Mr. Henry was in charge, and seemed to have sobered up a little, but he was still belligerent. "I understand you studied agriculture at the university," he said to me, puffing to get his cigar started again.

147

"Yessir."

"Would you like to manage one of my farms over in Twiggs County? Or maybe you are about to get drafted. You trying to get in the Army or trying to stay out?"

"Tryin' to get in, sir." I almost told him I was too skinny, but in the presence of his bulk, I lacked the nerve.

"Well, if you get rejected, my offer stands. It's mighty hard to get good overseers."

I thanked him, but told him about the Tweedy farm in Banks County that I wanted to farm when the war was over.

Later, after Brother Hen and Sister Maggie had said good night, Sanna came into the parlor. We could hear loud talk from their bedroom—mean talk.

As we stood together in front of the fire, Sanna suddenly began to cry. I put my arms around her, and she rested her head on my chest as sobs racked her body. I kissed her forehead but had the good sense not to try for more. She never raised her face to mine, just sobbed. Finally I put my arm around her and guided her to the couch that was drawn up near the fire.

"How could he do this to Sister Maggie?" she said, with the tears still running down her cheeks. "As long as I can remember he got drunk on weekends, but never like this. He's never done anything like this. She's so humiliated, so ashamed. And she's heartbroken at the mess he's made of her dining table. She's always been so proud of the dining room suite.

"Right now I just hate him. He—I guess there haven't been many Friday nights he didn't get drunk, but not on weekdays and not when our friends were here. I just can't understand how he could be the mayor, sworn to uphold Georgia law, and we've got this Prohibition Act and he thinks nothing of violating it.

"To him the bootleggers are man's best friend. He's told the sheriff to let them alone as long as they don't hurt anybody, so the moonshiners come in the night and leave jars of moonshine behind the sacks of cow feed in the milk shed. 'As long as it doesn't hurt anybody.' It just about kills Sister Maggie, and Annie Laurie and Lonzo and I have lived with it all our lives here. He's such a good, kind, wonderful man when he's sober, but a drink of whiskey makes him mean as he can be. Sister Maggie's never complained, she's never even admitted to us that he drinks, as if we wouldn't know it if she didn't say so."

Sanna told me about Mr. Jolley's Friday night card games with his drinking cronies. She said her sister was helpless to put an end to them.

One night Sister Maggie got so mad she screamed at him, "No more card games here! I'm putting my foot down!" The next morning, she was groaning in pain as she limped to the break-fast table. "She told Annie Laurie and me that she dropped a heavy picture frame on her foot the night before, but we knew better. That's what she

149

told everybody in town. When Sister Maggie realized that Brother Hen was either pretending not to know that he'd stepped on her foot and broken it, or that he really didn't remember, she told him the same story she'd told everybody else.

"But Annie Laurie had heard the whole thing the night before.

"I don't know what Sister Maggie will tell everybody at Thanksgiving dinner about what he did tonight. Of course, when he realizes how much he's upset her, he'll be sorry and he'll offer to buy her a new table. He can't buy what this one means to her, though. It was our grandmother's table." Sanna was quiet for a moment, staring into the flames.

Then she said, "Annie Laurie and I have always vowed we would never marry a man who would even take a drink. Sister Maggie says if a man has habits you can't live with, and he doesn't love you enough to change before the wedding, don't expect him to change later. She had to learn that the hard way. I've learned it the hard way too. Will, I didn't really tell you what happened that night with Hugh in Jefferson, did I? You remember what I told you about the tub running over and the mess the dinner party became, and I told you that I wished the rest of what had happened was as funny? Hugh got mad with me that night, Will, and I was mad with him, and he got drunk. He stayed up drinking after everybody went to bed, and I didn't sleep a wink either. In the middle of the night I smelled smoke and ran out to the hall, and his mother and father were already rushing towards the parlor with blankets and buckets of water. Hugh had gone to sleep smoking a cigarette and the upholstery had caught fire. He and his father had an awful row when it was all over and I wasn't supposed to know any of it. Hugh didn't come down to breakfast the next morning and everybody was upset—the way it's going to be here in the morning—and when Mr. Blankenship offered to bring me on back home—he said Hugh was sick—well, you were there when I arrived.

"I vowed never to marry a man who drinks, and I'm not going to."

I was driven to confess. "Sanna, there's a lot of drinkin' goes on at frat houses. One night I took a drink and I guess I took another and another, but I started feelin' sick and went to my room. Some time in the night I woke up in a pool of vomit. I couldn't believe it. I'd thrown up all that stinkin' stuff and was too drunk even to wake up."

She went pale and her face tensed. Before she could say anything, I said, "I tried to drink a few times since then, Sanna. I've found out that one drink makes me sick. Every time. I can't even finish a drink, in fact. So now I have a good excuse not to. I just tell people it makes me sick, and then I don't feel so awkward, or like, because I'm not drinkin', I'm passin' judgment on what other people are doin'. So you see, that's not anything you have to worry about with me, now or ever. I can't drink and I know it, and all my friends know it."

Mr. Henry had very little to say at breakfast and looked awful, fitted into his semicircle at the table. He was gone most of the morning to get his two cousins from his farm near Mitchellville. The boys went over to see a friend of Lonzo's, and the girls helped in the kitchen.

I met Maybelle, the cook, a sweet, dignified brown-colored woman with scant hair and no teeth. I could tell she had been crying. Later, when I was reading in the parlor, I could hear Sanna and Maybelle through the open doors of the dining room. They were at the buffet, taking out silver and linens for the table. Maybelle said, "Miss Sanna, ever'body in town go'n be laughin' at us. Dey go'n ax me do it be so, did Mr. Henry cut up Miss Maggie's table, but I ain' go'n tell nobody nuthin'. I des go'n make lak I don' hear, or I go'n say, 'What Mist' Henry do or doan do ain' none my bizness.' But I go'n be shamed, Miss Sanna, and po' Miss Maggie, she go'n be mighty shamed."

The rain had stopped, and the day was cold and darkly overcast. But the dinner Miss Maggie served that afternoon was splendid. The turkey was a huge tom, and the dressing was the best I think I ever ate, baked and browned crisp, but what I was most thankful for at that dinner was the good cheer. It was as if a quick rain had cleared out the strain and anger at Mr. Henry that had spoiled the air ever since I arrived. I'm sure it began as just courtesy, with everyone trying not to bring hard feelings to the festivities, but the festivities took over as soon as Mr. Henry got back with the two old cousins. I remember how happy the young people were, and how the strained looks on Sanna's and Miss Maggie's faces lifted, and how even Mr. Henry joined in. His morning-after misery seemed to have eased, and he was the jovial, twinkled-eyed fat man I had expected him to be. He sat in the curve of that whacked-out semicircle as casually as if the table had been designed and built that way.

I'm sure we talked about the war—everybody did in those days—and I remember the old ladies talked about their ailments. Everybody talked about past Thanksgivings, and I did my best to liven things up anywhere I could. Mr. Henry's two old cousins, Cudn Em and Cudn Abby, both had heavy mustaches, and Cudn Em had a humped back. Sanna said later they never went anywhere except to see close relatives because they were so embarrassed about their mustaches. I asked her why they didn't just shave, but she said they thought that's the way the Lord meant for them to look and to change it would be a sin.

Cudn Em was especially taken with sin. She had a Bible covered in faded red calico that she kept in her lap. The hump on her back reminded me of a man who came through Cold Sassy once selling blankets. He carried them on his back the way Cudn Em carried her hump. Sanna said Cudn Em felt the Lord was punishing her with the bent back for some sin. She never could figure out what the sin was, but she'd got the notion that if she kept opening the Bible, closed her eyes, then looked where her finger landed on a page, it might give her a clue about her sin. I liked her. Her head was bent so far forward she couldn't hold it up, but every now and then she'd look at me sideways with a shy little smile.

Another guest, Mrs. Faunt, was a neighbor whose husband had died on the Fourth of July. The Jolleys invited her for dinner when they heard she would be alone for Thanksgiving. She had an ear trumpet, which she aimed in the direction of whoever was speaking. She was a beautiful old lady in a navy blue wool dress, with a heavy shawl around her shoulders. Her face was powdered, her thick gray hair piled fashionably atop her head. She was the one who started the liveliest conversation of the day, about storms. The lightning we'd had the day before was unusual, and Mrs. Faunt said she was scared to death.

"That lightnin' yesterday brings to mind the time we was all settin' on the porch after dinner," she said. "That was in the summertime, and all-a sudden it come up a storm, a real bad one, with lightnin' flashin' and thunder thunderin' somethin' awful. We all went inside, and the dogs and cats tried to get in the house too, but Mama said, 'Don't let them animals come in! They'll draw the lightnin'!' We had a big old rooster named Uncle Lenox and that rooster flew up on the porch to get out of the rain, but Mama went out and shooed him off. Then he flew up on the iron gate and Mama told Lem to go make him get down. 'He'll draw lightnin',' but Lem said, 'Roosters ain't animals, they birds. And birds don't draw no lightnin'.' He said he could prove it, and he yelled out the door, 'All right, rooster, draw. Draw! I say draw that lightnin', Uncle Lenox!' And bless patty, down come a single bolt and down fell Uncle Lenox! We had him for supper that night."

Maybelle was passing her big yeast rolls. "I heerd that a white man got hit by lightnin'," she said, "and he turnt black. But I doan know as he stayed black."

Cudn Abby, hiding her mustache with her hand, said, "I had a teacher got hit one time and from then on her neck was twisted to one side. Good thing lightnin' never strikes twice in the same place." She laughed. "If Miss Mable had got hit in the neck again, she'd a-been lookin' backwards the rest of her life."

"Well, it can strike twice," said Mr. Henry. "Miss Maggie will back me up on it. The Quillians over on Fourth Street, their chimney got struck by lightnin' fifteen years ago and it happened again just a short while back, sometime last year."

"That's right," said Miss Maggie. "They say brick and ashes fell down all over Mrs. Quillian's living room furniture."

I got in on that. "One night we had an electrical storm so bad," I said, with the last of my turkey poised on my fork, "that next morning our neighbor came to the back door with a long coil of pine

155

bark in his hand. 'I think this belongs to y'all,' he told Mama. Lightnin' had struck the big tree that straddles the fence between our house and his. I kind of collect stories about weather, so I remember."

Sanna went with us that evening when Mr. Henry drove me to the depot in Greensboro. It was black dark when I got home, and there was a Western Union telegram under my door.

Received at 7:50 p.m.—Air F430
                              New York, New York
                              11/28/17
Mr. H. W. Tweedy
c/o Mayfield Boarding House
Athens, Georgia
ARRIVING MORNING TRAIN SATURDAY WITH
CAMPBELL JUNIOR STOP BEG YOU BREAK
NEWS TO FAMILY STOP LOMA

Fifteen

THERE WAS NO way to break news like that gently to Mama and Papa. With the office closed, I had planned on spending Friday and Saturday with them in P.C., so I just took the telegram with me and said, "Mama, looks like you don't have to worry about Campbell Junior up there with the Yankees anymore."

"Will, do you think this means Loma's gettin' a divorce? What . . ."

"Maybe it's the old man that's gettin' a divorce. But if you notice, she didn't say anything about divorce. Maybe she'll just do like lots of people and come home for a while and then they'll make up and off she'll go again, specially if he waves some money in her direction. You know what they say. A dollar is the fastest flyin' machine yet known."

Mama always was one to worry about what everybody would think, but I believe it was Aunt Loma she was worrying about while we waited at the depot for the train to come in on Saturday.

They arrived, just like the telegram said they would. Campbell Junior looked like he had grown an inch since September and lost some of that fat. You never saw a boy so happy to be home.

Aunt Loma had dark circles under her eyes, and her clothes looked like she'd slept in them all night, which she had. The only thing looked good about her was the fur coat she was wearing, and that diamond flashing in the sunlight. Within a day or so I learned that what was troubling Loma was something clean clothes and a good night's sleep couldn't put right. Loma was depressed. Whenever Mama saw her coming, she'd go lie down on the black leather daybed. "I can just take Loma better if I'm layin' down," she told me.

To Mama and Papa and the rest of the town she had nothing much to say. But Loma needed to talk, and by her second day home she'd realized I was probably the closest friend she had. "Will, I guess you think I was crazy in the first place, but I didn't marry him just for his money. I mean, I married him a lot for his money, but I was really very fond of him." Loma got herself a glass of tap water and sat down at the kitchen table with a dramatic sigh.

"He claimed he was a Russian count. He had a wife and four children, and when he was still young they all died in a typhoid epidemic. He came to America in eighteen eighty-nine with twelve dollars in gold coins in his pocket and got a job in a New York factory.

"If you remember," she said bitterly, "Pa never knew I existed from the time you were born. You had two daddies, your grandpa and your pa. I never had any. Vitch didn't treat me like a daughter. It was more like I was a princess. He even

158

called me Princess, and I found myself acting like one. When he'd have a party and I was his hostess, I'd pretend I was really a princess, kind of like stage acting, and it gave me a feeling of pride in myself. I liked that."

Mama was taking a nap upstairs and Daddy was out visiting with Campbell Junior, showing off all the changes in town. It occurred to me that if I just kept quiet, Loma would tell me everything. I set some of Mama's leftover Thanksgiving pie out on the table, got out two forks and plates, and settled down to listen.

"He never came to see me without bringing a gift, perfume or earrings," Loma said dreamily. "Once he brought me a little lap dog. I made him take that back. I just couldn't look after a little dog like that in an apartment when I was gone so much.

"He came to every performance I was in. I guess you heard about him being at my performance when I was modeling corsets. That's when we met." She laughed. "He was so gallant and his foreign accent made him seem glamorous. He had all this money he'd made in America. And he talked all the time about the castle he grew up in, and the toys he'd had, and the servants, and the literary parties his parents put on. I just was too . . . he . . . it was just a world I used to read about and couldn't believe existed. I'm not sure it ever did, even for Vitch.

"He'd kiss my hand when we met and he acted so proud of me. When he talked about us marrying, he said he'd build a mansion for me away from the noise and grime of New York City."

I tried to picture Loma living in a mansion, bossing servants around.

"I respected him and I felt he respected me. It wasn't like with Camp. I knew I couldn't step all over Vitch the way I did Camp. Oh, Will, I was so disgusted by Camp, and then after he died I was so ashamed of the way I'd treated him." Loma blushed, and I knew she was wondering if she should go on. But she was in too deep to stop now. I nodded to her, and then pretended to study my pie.

"But, Will, from the first night after I married Vitch, I knew . . . I couldn't stand . . . I mean, he was like a coal miner or somebody. Good Lord, Will, you've got a degree in agriculture. You must know all about animal husbandry. I don't know why it's so hard for me to tell you. Well, let's say that my rich, gallant Mr. Vitch's idea of husbandry was very animal."

Loma said after the second night she was so repulsed and so mad, she told Vitch never to set foot in her room again. He got mean. "He said he'd take my name out of his will. He finally admitted that the main reason he wanted to marry me instead of just courting the rest of his life was because he wanted heirs. The next night I locked my bedroom door and he got a key and unlocked it. I didn't have to fight him off then. He was so cold and calm. He said, 'You will not leave this room until you grant me my rights.' And he took

160

my key and left and locked the door behind him."

For a week he sent the maid in with Loma's meals. Even though the maid was afraid she'd lose her job if she didn't lock the door behind her, at last she felt so sorry for Loma, she did leave the door open. Loma packed a bag and was sneaking down the steps when Vitch saw her and forced her back to her room. The next day there were gardeners working outside near her window. She called to them that she was being kept prisoner and asked them to bring her a ladder. She threw a diamond pin down to them, then put the rest of her jewelry in a drawstring bag that she tied around her waist, stuffed a few clothes in a small satchel, climbed down the ladder, and got away in a taxi.

She sent a telegram to the headmaster at Campbell Junior's school, saying she had to take him out early for the holidays because of illness in the family. She met his train in New York after hocking her gold pins in a pawnshop so she could buy their train tickets to Cold Sassy.

I never doubted Loma would find a way to get back at Mr. Vitch. She was so vindictive that Grandpa once said if he wanted to make a raid on Hell, he would make Loma his first lieutenant.

Editor's note: *Although Olive Ann worked on several scenes that were to appear later in the novel, the chronological narrative ends here. We know from her notes for the rest of this chapter that the following Sunday was going to be a beautiful day and that Will was going to borrow his papa's car to pick up Sanna in Mitchellville and drive her back to Cold Sassy.*

From Olive Ann Burns's Chapter Notes:

On the way home Sanna is going to tell Will more about the situation in Mitchellville—in fact, this may be when she tells him some of the stuff that I have her telling him the night before. May somehow get around to her telling him about the day Papa got hooked by the bull. Want as fast as possible for him to learn more about her and her family, but there are things she won't tell him until she knows they are going to marry and she knows she has got to tell him about her family.

Feed in some of the information about Loma and her husband in letters home—the braggy things she can write home about so that her returning home is totally unexpected. That way she won't have so much to tell Will, and it will keep Loma alive in the minds of the reader if there are little dribbles of it from the time she comes home to get Campbell Junior to go back North with her. Now Loma is left high and dry in New York, as far as the reader is concerned, except for the letter saying that she has just gotten married.

Note: Actually I think what I'm going to do is have Loma say nothing about why she's home. Just say she's homesick and wanted to come home and Campbell Junior wanted to come back there to school and she's obviously very upset, though she tells everybody else in town. . . . Want her to have time after arriving to get the word out around town that she's just homesick, and then the Sunday paper (maybe of Thanksgiving weekend or the following), the headlines in the Atlanta newspaper, pick up a story in great detail from New York telling all the gory details about this rich man, and his wife having to escape from him by climbing down a ladder and being helped by two gardeners and how she claims she was locked in her room. Saw this story in a paper about 1895 —have notes on this with more details—look up and concentrate on getting details—in 1917 same kind of yellow journalism, though in a local weekly they would not—they would protect the people —let this be a shock to Cold Sassy, not only the details but her name given and her home town, where according to the paper her husband suspects she may have gone.

Note: When Loma left to go to New York City, she knew she would have to finance herself because she couldn't be sure of getting enough work in the entertainment field. Loma has her house rented. Will asks if she's going to live there. "You could pretend you're a widow. I heard about a widow who painted her house black the week after her husband died." She sold her interest in the store to Hoyt. Miss Love and Sampson own half the store and Hoyt owns the other half and runs the store, which he would love to do anyway, so when she's back she has these jewels but she's not going to be there long, so she rents rooms at Miss Hyta Mae's boarding house for herself and Camp

—maybe at this point Camp's room and the room she had used before she went to New York—maybe Mama has rented it to a teacher or someone. In those days people were always renting rooms, so it may not be available for her to come back to and she doesn't want to either, because she doesn't think she'll be there long—and this will get Miss Hyta Mae back into the reader's mind. I want her to be a running character through the book, because she's interesting. I don't know what wonderful or awful things will be happening to her, but I think when Will is through with the Army and comes back to farm, it will be the Depression, and I think Miss Hyta Mae and Miss Love and Will's mother will all be calling on him to do the kinds of things that need doing around the house that a woman can't do or thinks she can't do, and that's going to be a bone of contention with Sanna because maybe he needs to fix fences on the farm and instead he goes over to do little things for all these women who depend on him.

Notes

SANNA—A PERFECTIONIST and a worrier. Obsessed with idea of finding happiness, and for her, happiness means being first with somebody, having her own home, being loved by a perfect man and perfect, loving children. She will never have to have second place there, will be secure, life will be happily ever after, no more misery or problems. She never feels secure with new people or in new situations—doesn't want change—and revels in the way Will is easy with people and never fazed by the unexpected. In fact, the harder things are, the more he is excited and challenged. She thought all troubles would be over if she found the right man. Marries Will—hard time of war months—pregnant, etc.

The theme of Sanna is disillusionment—her life is the pursuit of happiness and perfection, but she finds happiness and perfection impossible to obtain—her idea of happiness is constant joy, no changes.

Will's idea of life is to be challenged. Loves trying anything new, loves change, is impatient with Sanna. Living is a matter of making things work if you can, seeing if you can make things work.

At end of book he is leaving home, happy and excited to have a job, to be able to hope to support his family. Hates leaving Sanna and children, but he's not just off to Dawson, he's off on a new adventure.

Soon after arriving in Cold Sassy and causing trouble with Sanna, Loma has a car accident and breaks her back. [Editor's note: *Although there are no written notes on this, Olive Ann said that she wanted Loma to undergo a personality change through her suffering, to be able to walk again and pay all her medical bills, and then to settle down in Cold Sassy and teach elocution.*]

Perhaps Miss Love's father, sick and dying, age 70 to 75, comes to P.C. for her to look after, and she does it. He has to be waited on, bedridden. Sanna helps her.

Sampson falls in love with Precious, child of Lightfoot and Hosie Roach. Used to getting his way, marries her at end of book despite family feelings.

Loma tells Sanna, "It's just common, like po' white trash, the way you get pregnant every year. Just *common*. I can't imagine anybody smart as you think you are not knowing how to keep from getting that way. You've embarrassed the whole family."

SANNA: Well, I've got three things to say to *you*. Number one, you're crude and mean and your side of my family has just as much to do with it as I do. Will, I mean. Number two, it's *our* business, not any of yours. I never wanted a baby every year—I'm *tired.* But it's none of your business. And if you want to talk about embarrassing the family, look in the mirror. You think everybody is proud of your smoking and drinking cocktails and getting a *divorce?*

LOMA: I'll smoke and drink and get a divorce any time I want to.

SANNA: And Will and I will have babies if we want to. One thing I know, I'll never have to get a divorce.

LOMA: Don't you know the talk in town? How often Will goes by to see Carrie Summers?

The book will be the story of Sanna and Will, and Sanna and Loma, and Sanna and Miss Love and the boy Sampson, Sanna and the Depression, Sanna and her perfectionism and anxiety and obsessiveness and possessiveness.

It will show Loma doggedly determined not only to walk again, but to repay all medical bills.

It will show Sanna caught in yet another situation where she feels second—except with the children. She centers her life on them. So does Will, so this is their togetherness. Their separateness comes from his being pulled between his family and Sanna, and conflicts over money.

Miss Love is a sort of catalyst. She says things like "I put a dimmer light at my mirror. I don't like wrinkles."

She tells Sanna: "Be kind to Will."

Sanna tells her: "I read some psychology books

in college. Everything that's supposed to warp a child happened to me."

Miss Love: "Everything that could warp a child happened to me, too. But understanding that doesn't help. It's interesting, but it doesn't help. I figure that what you do with your life now is all that counts. I try not to look back."

About Papa's affair:

Mama and Papa had been praying for another baby for years, and hadn't had any, but when I was twenty and Mary Toy fourteen and Mama was forty-two . . . She was so happy. After it came out about Papa and that young woman, it was like she hated her own baby. She didn't make any clothes for it, and even before she started showing, she quit going anywhere, not even to church or missionary circle, and she never smiled or hardly ate. She didn't talk about Papa, of course. But she was too shamed to face anybody, and angry to the core.

Miss Mabry went back home and married an old man who'd been after her, and nobody would have known the scandal if Miss Mabry hadn't got so upset she told his best friend. After Mama heard the baby was a healthy boy, she cleaned a big closet. Lifting and reaching up to high shelves. She thought the reaching did it. That night the pains started and the baby was born dead, the cord around his neck. She never forgave herself. If she'd wanted to punish Papa, she did it. Punished all of us. I'd have loved having a little brother.

There are the family scandals that hurt so— Papa's baby; Papa dies, had life insurance for the other woman.

Then Brother Henry writes letter so Will marries Sanna even though he realizes it as a mistake, and he tries to be a good husband. (Papa got a special delivery letter from Brother Henry saying if I put off the wedding again, he would send the sheriff after me to put me in jail and sue me for breach of promise.) He will never hurt her, he vows to her and himself. At first he transfers his love from Trulu to Sanna. Only after he is engaged does he realize she doesn't provoke the wild passion Trulu did. He's sorry he acted in haste, but knows he couldn't have trusted Trulu.

Talking to Sanna after Jefferson, he doesn't tell her that the grand party was celebrating his engagement to Trulu. He sat to Mrs. Philpot's right —there was an orchestra (give its name).

Loma divorces finally, comes home after Will and Sanna's marriage, miserable—accuses Sanna of being snobbish, above everybody else. Sanna judging Loma for divorce and smoking and drinking.

Loma says awful things to Sanna. When Loma breaks her back, Sanna has to ride in ambulance with her.

Will thinks he won Sanna. Really it's that she broke up with Hugh—drinking, near-rape. Will learns this after engaged. Hugh becomes politician, runs for government. Sanna doesn't know about Brother Henry's letter, believes Army duties caused two postponements of wedding.

Will is proud of Sanna, feels great tenderness and appreciation of Sanna, enjoys being with her. Kind of girl he'd always hoped to marry. He is also challenged by her being hard to get—first kiss is dynamic. After he proposes, he meets Sanna's family—prejudiced—loses that feeling on next date. Always remembers Trulu, how she made him feel, how he still yearns for her. He sees her in Athens and is bitter: knew he couldn't trust her, knew she was no good, but wishes . . . All through the years he longs for her.

She marries an aviator; he is killed in air crash in WWI. Will goes to see her when she invites him. This is after he quits farming, maybe 1929—her father has lost his money.

In Dawson, Will rents room and takes meals with couple who have no children. She fascinates him. Husband mean. "I never did anythin', but I'm sure the attraction was mutual. Of course I didn't dare let her husband know." But Sanna came down with him for a week and she knew. Didn't say anything, but Will knew she knew.

Trulu, who has married again (first husband killed in war) and lives in Milledgeville, no money, comes back into his life (like Norma). Will hides behind Sanna's skirts—can't divorce and hurt her.

Sanna finds out, breaks it up, decides divorce better than living like that, but if the affair ends she will be happier in an imperfect marriage than most divorcees.

Old man decided he was going to die, no use bothering to eat. Turned on his side, facing wall. Two days later, when he hadn't died, he decided to eat again. Got well.

Old lady had such tender feet, hospital attendants investigated—doctor had told her twenty-five years before to stay in bed. She never asked if she could get up, he never told her to, and now she really couldn't.

It's not hard to forgive a person after he's no longer a threat.—Sanna

Story of two people who marry, love, respect, appreciate, but are not *in love*.

Toward end of book (maybe *at* the end) Will goes home for weekend. Sanna has settled his "affair," which he insists to her and to readers was just bad judgment, not really an affair. She says: "I'm sorry you married me. You would be much happier with a modern woman. It disappoints you that I don't drive, I don't wear tailored clothes, and I don't wear jewelry or make-up. I don't get permanent waves, my skin breaks out, and I itch and scratch. I don't dance. I watch you dancing with other women at parties and see how much you enjoy dancing. A lot of what I don't do is because we can't afford it. I don't have dinner parties because it costs money, but mostly, I guess, because I go to pieces worrying about whether the food will taste good and will it be enough and we don't have fine china and lace tablecloths, and because by the time I do all the housework and look after the children, I'm worn out. But I know some women could do all I do and have time and energy to entertain. I don't really care about all that, but I'd like to because you enjoy people so. I wish I didn't worry about time or dirt or money. I wish I weren't anxious all the time, afraid of what tomorrow will bring.

"I'm mostly sorry I can't approve of everything you say or do. I can't say I'm glad you paid thirty-five dollars for a pedigreed bird dog when we owe so much money. I can't say it was all right for you to plan for us to move in with your mother without consulting her or me. I can't say I'm willing to move into a boarding house with old men because it's cheaper.

"I can say I love your zest for life. I love and appreciate how hard you work to make a living for us. I envy your talent with people. I love to go places with you. I marvel that you never meet a stranger. I love your having so many friends.

"I've thought about divorce. It would set you free to marry the kind of person who would suit you better. But I know you care deeply about your family. You would be embarrassed to be divorced even though you wouldn't be lonely long. The women would swarm, and you'd revel in the attention, and you'd marry quickly.

"But you love your family and your children, and most second wives don't like to give time and energy and divide money with a man's children. Her resentment would make you miserable. I've noticed most men who remarry get weaned away from their own children, even other kinfolks, because they spend more time with the second wife's relatives than their own and the second wife's children and grandchildren.

"As for myself, I see that women who divorce are no happier than I am. I was so miserable when the jeweler said my diamond had cracked. Now I know that an imperfect marriage is better than divorce. I got to the point I couldn't live with you and the other woman, but with that over, I can settle for imperfection. If you can."

Papa and the Bull

(Sanna in a conversation with Will)

"I WAS EIGHT years old and quiet, shy. I had drawn a bucket of cold well water and was standing at the shelf on the back porch, drinking from the tin dipper and watching Papa. He was working just inside the nearby pasture, hammering a loose board on the milk shed.

"Papa was small and stringy. He wasn't old, but his hair was white and silky, and so was his long beard, which he had tied in a loose knot that afternoon to keep out of his way. I adored him.

"When he looked up and saw I was home from school, he waved, and I waved the dipper, sloshing water everywhere. I decided to take Papa a drink, and poured some water into a fruit jar.

"I saw that our big Jersey bull was plodding towards him, but I wasn't alarmed. Shoot, that was just old Sultan. I laughed when the bull nudged Papa from behind. Papa turned around, smiled, and scratched Sultan between his horns, where he liked it. Then he wiped his forehead on his shirt sleeve, took off his big straw hat, and commenced fanning himself with it.

174

"Everyone agreed later, it must have been the movement of the hat that aroused the bull.

"Sultan backed off, lowered his head, and snorted. I could tell that my papa hadn't noticed. He had gone back to his work and was bent over picking up nails when Sultan hooked him in the stomach and tossed him like a sack of potatoes onto the tin roof of the milk shed. Papa rolled down like a log. He tried to grab something, but there was nothing to grab and he dropped right back onto those horns, as if they were loving arms waiting to receive him.

"I still don't know if I was crying or screaming, or what, but I saw the bull toss him up again, higher, almost over the roof peak.

"Afterwards I told Sister Maggie it was like Sultan thought he'd made up a game. Like he thought Papa was a play-pretty. When Papa hit the ground, Sultan turned away and ambled off towards his cows standing in the creek to get cool.

"I was halfway to Papa when I tripped over a root and fell, but as I was getting up I thought to run back and ring the big farm bell. We had a bell that called the field hands to dinner and called quitting time at sundown. It would never be rung at four in the evening unless for something awful. I grabbed the bell rope, jerked it hard, and with each clang screamed, 'Papa! Papa!'

"Mama came running from the side yard, carrying Tattie, who was four then, and she saw immediately what had happened. She set Tattie down among the chickens and the cats and raced

175

towards the milk shed. Violet and Daisy came out on the back porch and Zinnie ran from the privy. Scrawny, bow-legged Possum rushed out of the kitchen and down the steps. Her husband, called Christmas for being so slow, hobbled up from the back of the barn.

"Everybody's eyes were on me, ringing the bell. They didn't see Papa bleeding on the pasture grass or Mama running towards him out of the milk shed, holding a pitchfork to slay whatever had got him down.

" 'It's Papa! Sultan hurt him!' I pointed, and all eyes followed my finger. The girls ran for the shed. Old Christmas followed them, but Possum stayed with me, and we rang in everybody from the cotton fields—the colored wages hands and sharecroppers, their wives, their children, some with cotton sacks still slung over their shoulders.

"I was still ringing the bell, and crying for my papa not to die, when Violet came back from the pasture and twisted the bell rope out of my hands. 'Stop it! Stop rangin' that bell! They all comin' now, honey. Gimme the rope. Turn it loose.' She picked me up and ran towards the pasture.

"Little Tattie was left alone, bawling, wandering about the yard. Mama heard her and yelled, 'Daisy? Sanna Maria? One a-y'all go git the baby!' But not one of us went, cause Papa had started groaning. I leaned over the fence and saw that the front of his overalls was soaked with blood. There was a red spot on the white beard where it was knotted.

"He suddenly rolled onto his side, facing us, and pulled his knees up. Vi whispered to me, 'He's bent double with pain.'

"Papa was mumbling. 'Don't . . . let nobody . . . hurt . . . my bull. We . . . need him . . .' Then he went limp.

"I buried my face against Vi's stomach and screamed again. Mama glared at me. 'Shut up, young'un.'

" 'Papa's dead!' I wailed.

"Mama said, 'No, he ain't.'

"I begged her not to let him die and she said, 'He ain't a-go'n to.' Then Mama turned to the field hands. 'How come all y'all standin' there like fence posts? I got to git him in the house.'

"Mama hadn't seen old Christmas standing behind her, his hat off. 'I'm here, Miss Flo,' said Christmas. Christmas lifted Papa like he would a hurt dog. With Mama leading the way, he carried him out through the shed and past the silent watchers.

"I ran and grabbed Mama's skirt. She slapped my hand. 'Turn me loose, Sanna Maria!' she said, and rushed to pick up Tattie, who was squalling. 'Po' li'l lamb,' she crooned. 'Ain't anybody got sense enough to see to you? Here, Lily, take her. Possum? Don't just stand there wringin' your hands. Go be gittin' out some clean rags and some turp'mtime, and th'ow a clean sheet over my bed.'

"I pulled at Mama's arm and said, 'Don't let him die, hear, Mama?'

"Mama said, 'Git out of the way, girl. Yore pa ain't go'ndie.'"

"And he didn't. He lived five more years. But he was never the same after that day.

"And nothing was ever the same again for me either, Will. That was the day I realized that I was yesterday's child.

"I had got slapped. Tattie had got comforted.

"Joe Pye, sixteen, had to come home from Gordon Military School to run the farm. Papa supervised. He scheduled the plowing and plantings and kept the books. But he never again nailed a board or plowed a field. He just got weaker and weaker. No doctor guessed why. I heard him say to Mama, 'Miss Flora, we could make it if we'd had nine boys and one girl instead of nine girls and one boy.' If a man owned his land, his daughters couldn't work in the fields or go to market or do carpentry or fix fences. I helped him put on his shirt and socks and shoes, but he finally got so he couldn't walk alone.

"My mama, harder worked than ever, turned me over to my big Sister Zinnie. Zinnie did all the sewing for the family—the sheets, the dresses, Papa's shirts, everything. She was nineteen years old, beautiful, the way all my sisters were beautiful, with dark eyes and black hair, and a bright mind and agile fingers. But Sister Zinnie had no beaus and no hope. Never would have a beau out there in the country, and no way to meet anybody. Sometimes I think my mama wanted to keep her there. She had finished the seven grades of school at thirteen and had been minding children and sewing ever since. As soon as Zinnie was big enough to hold a bolt of cloth, Mama put her to making sheets, then Papa's shirts, and then dresses. I think she felt trapped by the sewing machine.

"If I ran down the hall, Zinnie might make me sit beside her at the sewing machine all day long —just for running down the hall, for heaven's sake. I started to hate her and I wouldn't mind her unless Mama was around. One day Joe Pye chanced to come in when Zinnie was going after me with the buggy whip. He grabbed the whip and raised it at Zinnie. 'You touch that baby, dammit, and I'll beat you to hell,' he shouted, and Zinnie never raised a hand to me again. From that day on, Joe Pye was my hero.

"The other one I loved was Sister Maggie. She and Brother Hen had been married for nine or ten years, with no children. So they finally adopted a premature baby boy whose mother died in childbirth. Sister Maggie had a heart big enough for all the orphans of the world."

"When I was ten an awful thing happened in the family. Violet was having a baby and wasn't married. Sister Maggie's husband came down and *made* the boy marry her. The next morning Sister Maggie found me crying in the privy and asked me if I'd like to come live with them in Mitchellville. 'The school is so much better,' she said. 'You want to be a teacher, it matters to go to a good school.'

179

"I wiped my eyes and asked, 'At the new school, will you say my name is Sanna? Not Sanna Maria?'

" 'Yes, if you want to be just Sanna.'

" 'Will you ask Mama can I go? She's got Tattie. She loves Tattie better'n me.'

" 'I already did. Come on, precious, let's go get up your things.'

" 'But I don't want to leave Papa. I help him put on his shirt and shoes and socks.'

" 'You'll come home for Christmas and summer vacation.'

" 'I hate the farm. It'd be so nice to be in town and have a bathroom and go to parties. It's awful here. One thing I know, I ain't go'n marry no farmer. I wouldn't have to mind Zinnie anymore?'

" 'Only when you're home.'

"Even now that I'm grown, I've thought bitterly and often that Mama certainly never had spoiled me. The Christmas before I left home to go live at Sister Maggie's house, Mama gave Tattie a little gold ring with a tiny diamond in it, a real 'shonuff' diamond. Her present to me was a dollar bill, not even wrapped up. She just took it out of her apron pocket and said, 'Here.'

"Mama didn't come to my graduation from Mitchellville High School. She didn't come to my college graduation, either, though I went out home and begged her to. 'Sister Maggie said tell you she'll make you a new dress to wear, Mama, and buy you a hat and shoes to go with it.'

"Mama's expression didn't change. 'Y'all don't need me,' she said, then leaned forward in her rocking chair and spat into the fireplace.

"I hated that Mama dipped snuff."

Olive Ann Burns, age two.

§

A weary young journalist at her desk
at the *Atlanta Journal Sunday Magazine.*
"I had absolutely no confidence in myself," Olive Ann said.
"It took me two or three weeks to write a simple story."

§

Olive Ann and the former first lady
Rosalynn Carter
(Conway-Atlanta Photography)

§

The author of
Cold Sassy Tree,
ready to address a crowd.
"I am a ham,"
Olive Ann admitted.

§

The wedding pictures of William Arnold Burns and
Ruby Celestia Hight, upon whom the characters
Will Tweedy and Sanna Klein are based.

§

Olive Ann Burns
A Reminiscence

OLIVE ANN BURNS lived sixty-five years and completed only one book. Since its publication in 1984, *Cold Sassy Tree* has become an American classic, selling over a million copies worldwide and still going strong. It has inspired accolades and fan letters from readers young and old, from all walks of life. Schoolchildren and cancer patients, Broadway producers and country farmers have written to say that their lives were touched, even changed, by this remarkable novel. Barbara Bush named *Cold Sassy Tree* one of her favorite books; Oprah Winfrey, Craig Claiborne, and B. F. Skinner wrote grateful letters to its author.

Now, nearly ten years after its publication, *Cold Sassy Tree* is widely regarded as one of the best-loved novels of our time. It is required reading in English classes across the country; it still appears on best-seller lists, from Washington state to the East Coast, and fan letters continue to arrive, from people who have fallen in love with fourteen-year-old Will Tweedy and the story he tells of life in a small Georgia town at the turn of the century. Over the years, there have been literally hundreds of such letters, and rare is the one that doesn't ask for a sequel to *Cold Sassy Tree*.

People who read Olive Ann's book can't help feeling they know her—that she must be just like them, except that she happened to write this wonderful novel. That is how Olive Ann herself felt. "If I can write a book," she often said, "anybody can."

I met Olive Ann Burns for the first time in Atlanta, on the day *Cold Sassy Tree* was published. But by the time we finally met in person we were already fast friends. During the preceding year we had talked on the phone every few days, and we had embarked on a correspondence that was to transcend a typical author-editor relationship, if there is such a thing. The first thing she said to me, when we were face to face at last, was, "I thought you would be plump!" "And I thought you would be old," I blurted out. Well, I wasn't plump, and Olive Ann certainly didn't seem old. In fact, she was beautiful—tall and slender, with enormous brown eyes and curly dark hair. She wore red lipstick and a silvery blue dress, long dangly earrings and a sparkly necklace—and, underneath it all, flat sensible shoes.

Surely our friendship was an unlikely one. I was a novice, a twenty-five-year-old editor from New Hampshire, making my way in New York City. She was a born storyteller from the Deep South who was about to publish her first novel at the age of sixty. I knew just a bit more than she did about how books get published, and she knew far more than I did about the things that really matter —life and death, for example. While I helped her

cut some two hundred pages out of her manuscript, she taught me lessons that have helped de-
termine the course of my life. We discussed
punctuation, publicity, and print runs, of course,
but we spent more time talking about husbands
and children, the books we loved and the ones
we didn't, the secret of a tasty casserole and the
key to happiness on this earth. At times I provided
her a link to the publishing process that she found
so fascinating and so much fun; at other times,
she offered me motherly advice, shared stories
about her nextdoor neighbors or distant ancestors, and brought me up to date on the goings-on
in her family. Always, she was an inspiration to
me in her ability to see the humor, and even the
joy, in any situation.

Olive Ann battled cancer on and off for ten years
and spent the last three years of her life confined
to bed with congestive heart failure. And yet, in
the midst of her illness, she was able to look back
on the previous year, a year during which she had
left the house exactly twice—once to vote, and
once to see the fall leaves—and say, "This has
been a happy year." She joked about someone
who had referred to her bedridden condition as
her "lifestyle," as if it were something she had cho-
sen. But she took issue with another friend, who
had tried to sympathize with her "horrendous ordeal." "I'm not trying to be brave or put a happy
face on it," she wrote, "but it has not been horrendous. Working on *Time, Dirt, and Money* gives
structure to my days, and so many friends keep

me integrated with the outside world." Knowing that she would probably spend the rest of her life in bed, hooked up to an IV tube, Olive Ann never felt sorry for herself, and her enthusiasm for writing never waned.

She worked on the novel for almost five years, years during which she also had to cope with the demands of fame, with a recurrence of cancer and debilitating rounds of chemotherapy, and finally with the death of her beloved husband, Andrew Sparks, following his own long battle with cancer. Given the obstacles she confronted, it is a wonder she was able to work at all.

As readers of *Cold Sassy Tree* may know, the irrepressible character of Will Tweedy is based on Olive Ann's father, William Arnold Burns, who was fourteen years old in 1906, when the events in the novel take place. In *Time, Dirt, and Money*, Olive Ann introduces us to Will ten years later, and to the young woman he is about to marry, Sanna Maria Klein, who is based on Olive Ann's mother. The novel was to be the story of her parents—of how they met, fell in love, and raised a family during the Depression. Above all, it was to be a portrait of their marriage, a marriage that was nearly destroyed by poverty, disillusion, and disappointment, but that survived and flourished again, years after both husband and wife had all but given up on finding happiness together.

Time, Dirt, and Money was due to be delivered to Ticknor & Fields on January 1, 1991. Olive Ann knew she wasn't going to make the deadline, but she always believed that she would finish the book. During the last years of her life, she so perfected the art of being both sick and productive that it was hard to imagine she wouldn't always be there, in her bed at 161 Bolling Road, a lacy afghan over her legs, a basket of letters to answer at her side, a Dictaphone or a pen in her hand. Andy once said that Olive Ann could be sicker than anyone else ever was, and he was right. But she had been desperately ill, and had pulled through, so many times that the news of her death, on July 4, 1990, came as a shock. She had just been talking about *Time, Dirt, and Money,* and I'm sure that her dying surprised her as much as it did everyone else—just as becoming a published author had surprised her. "I always thought selling a book was rather like dying," she once said, "something that happened to other people, but never to me."

Even now, as I read through the chapters published here, it's hard to accept that there are no more to come. Illness may have slowed Olive Ann down, but it never stopped her imagination or dulled her passion for storytelling. Months might go by, but then there would be another letter, full of funny anecdotes and wisdom. And there would be another batch of chapters to read after any long silence, miraculously produced through her painstaking process of jotting notes by hand, dictating, editing, and rewriting. (She never sent anything that was less than perfect—and she could never resist the urge to pick up her pen and start improving an impeccably typed page.)

189

Only during her final hospitalization did it occur to Olive Ann that she might not live to finish her book. Sometime after midnight, on June 22, 1990, she dictated a letter to her close friend and neighbor Norma Duncan, who had transcribed all the tapes for *Time, Dirt, and Money.* If she couldn't finish the book, she said, she hoped that the chapters she had already written would be published. Olive Ann was thinking of all those readers who wanted to know about Miss Love's baby and how Will Tweedy turned out. She had promised them a sequel, and she didn't want to let them down. This book, then, is Olive Ann's gift to her readers, and it is one way of saying good-bye, both to her and to the unforgettable characters she created.

Olive Ann started *Time, Dirt, and Money* the summer after *Cold Sassy Tree* was published. By the time she died, she had completed these chapters, had notes on several others, and had the rest of the novel in her mind. It was a story she knew well—in fact, she had already written the story of the real Will and Sanna. Long before she thought seriously of writing a novel, Olive Ann undertook to record the stories of her parents' lives as a keepsake for herself and her family. She began early in 1972, shortly after she learned that her mother was dying. That year, Olive Ann spent countless hours with her, asking her to recall her childhood and the early years of her marriage. Olive Ann took notes as her mother spoke, and the long afternoons drew them close, diverting

190

their attention from pain and illness. They also indulged Olive Ann's lifelong love of storytelling.

Ruby Celestia Hight Burns died that September, but by then Olive Ann had become engrossed in her project. "What hooked me on family history was not names and dates," she said, "it was the handed-down stories that bring the dead back to life." She interviewed aging aunts and uncles, siblings and cousins. She found and copied love letters her parents had written during World War I and grocery bills dating from the Great Depression, which had somehow survived in the family possessions. Report cards, telegrams, early photographs, letters, and anecdotes contributed by other relatives—even a floor plan of the family home—all went into the book, evoking an era that Olive Ann knew would soon be lost forever, save for these memories and mementoes.

With her mother gone, Olive Ann turned to her father, a man who "could always make a good story better in the telling." Mourning the loss of his wife and in failing health himself, Arnold Burns still found enormous pleasure in practical jokes and funny stories. "I'm sure he could have made a million dollars as a stand-up comic on television," Olive Ann said. Now, he embellished the tales she had heard all her life, some of which had assumed the proportion of myth, and he recalled events he had forgotten but that came forth with her gentle urging and well-placed questions. Arnold's voice later became Olive Ann's inspiration for Will Tweedy, and many of Will's boyhood adventures can be found, in their original versions, among Arnold Burns's most delightful recollections. He painted a vivid picture of Commerce, Georgia, at the turn of the century, a picture that later served as a model for Cold Sassy. And one of his favorite stories was about his Grandpa Power, a store owner in Commerce, who got married again three weeks after his wife died. According to Arnold, Grandpa Power said he "had loved Miss Annie, but she was as dead as she'd ever be and he had to git him another wife or hire a housekeeper, and it would just be cheaper to git married." Olive Ann recalled that, even as she heard her father tell the story, she thought it would make a fine first chapter in a novel. "But I never thought I would write it," she said.

Arnold Burns died less than a year after his wife, and finishing the family history became a way for Olive Ann to cope with the loss of her parents and to preserve their voices for her own two children. She had taken down their stories in their own words, exactly as they told them, adding her recollections and contributions from other family members as she went. The result is two typewritten volumes crammed with letters, photos, and countless other small treasures, and brought to life by a chorus of voices from the past, preserved in all their raw beauty, humor, and eccentricity. "Details matter," Olive Ann often said, and she paid attention to them. In searching for her ancestors, she wrote, "I was after the facts of their lives, of course, but also for anything anybody remembered about someone's habits, sayings, or physical appearance." She called the book *Yellow Paint on the Cows' Tails . . . and other Stories,* in reference to one of Arnold's boyhood pranks, and she dedicated it "to the memory of my parents and all those who come after them."

When she began to write *Cold Sassy Tree,* Olive Ann found the family history an invaluable source for the authentic expressions and anecdotes that give the novel its flavor. Much as she loved to write, Olive Ann's real passion was collecting such bits and pieces. Whenever she heard a phrase that captured her fancy, she jotted it down and saved it; she kept lists of colorful country names and local expressions, and slap-dash files of amusing stories, dialect, superstitions, and lore. Like a quilter with a bulging bag of scraps, she loved to find ways to work these colorful fragments into her large design. As her daughter, Becky, observed, "Mother wrote backward. She had all these little bits and pieces, and she was always trying to find places to use them."

A year after Olive Ann's death, I spent several days in Atlanta going through her papers. It was hard to know where to begin. With the boxes of fan mail stacked up in her neighbor's spare bedroom? With the piles of revised manuscript pages that represented so many years of work on *Cold Sassy Tree* and *Time, Dirt, and Money?* With all those scraps of paper and backs of envelopes on which Olive Ann had written bits of dialogue, ideas for scenes, and lists of funny names? With the files of correspondence to and from her family and friends? That first morning, I poked around just enough to become overwhelmed by the sheer amount of material and by sadness. I remembered the hours Olive Ann and I had spent one afternoon, side by side on the sofa, with the family history open in her lap. As we paged through it, she pointed to a photograph here, a letter there, and told the story behind it. Now, faced with the task of telling some of Olive Ann's story, I realized that the family history was the place to start, for it holds not only the seeds of both *Cold Sassy Tree* and *Time, Dirt, and Money,* but also an account of Olive Ann's own beginnings, on a hardscrabble farm in Banks County, Georgia.

Olive Ann Burns was born in 1924 on land originally farmed by her great-great-grandfather. According to her mother's recollections in the family history, "The pains started in the night and we called Dr. Rogers about six. He came about nine, said, 'Oh, it'll be several days before she's born.' He gave me a shot, I went back to sleep, and about two your daddy called the doctor to come back. It was forty-five minutes before he arrived, and you had been here five minutes. Your daddy pulled the film off your face and sat down to read the paper to show me he wasn't upset. I said to him, 'Honey, you're reading the paper upside down, that's how calm you are.' He later told it that the paper wasn't upside down, that I was

194

looking at an ad for the circus with a clown standing on his head. Anyway, we could hear the doctor's car across the covered bridge at the river, so daddy went to the front door to meet him and left me with the baby. Your daddy laid you on some newspapers with the cord still uncut. You were born easy, you were always easygoing and good-humored, just the way you came into the world. That was on July 17, 1924, at two-forty. I only had three hard pains.

Ruby Burns gave birth to four children in four years, creating a strain on her new marriage and on the family finances. She had never planned to have so many babies so fast. She and Arnold were married on September 8, 1918; Margaret was born one year later. Ruby confessed that she had screamed all afternoon. "It's a good thing I was out in the country," she told Olive Ann. "There was nobody to hear me." In April 1921, Emma Jean appeared, and then Billy in 1922. Olive Ann was the baby of the family. "I realized there were ways to keep from having babies," Ruby said, "but we didn't know anything but old wives' tales, like keeping a pan of water under the bed, which I knew couldn't help. Anything that's a mystery always has untruths told about it, so I didn't pay any attention to all the things people told me about that. But I read everything I could find, about not having babies and about having them and what to do with them."

Ruby said she never could have survived those early years without Arnold's help. When it was time to bathe the children, they set up an assembly line, with Arnold washing and Ruby drying and dressing. Olive Ann recalled that her father cooked breakfast every day, was around for any emergency, and had a wonderful way with children. "He was always an imaginative and flamboyant father," she wrote. "Even after the Depression hit, he didn't act poor. He bought a pony named Beauty and brought her out to the farm in the back of the car, with the seat out."

But money was a constant problem, and the farm on which Arnold—like Will Tweedy—had pinned all his dreams was a losing proposition. Recalling her earliest childhood, Olive Ann wrote, "In my mind I still see what meant country then —red dirt roads, dilapidated unpainted houses and barns, porch flowers growing in old coffee cans, mules in the pastures, shy, scrawny children with white rags tied around impetigo sores playing in swept dirt yards, and on hot Sunday afternoons, tenant families sitting on the porch watching cars go by and yearning for the fast lane."

In 1931, the family could no longer afford to stay on the farm and were forced to rent it out while they moved in with Arnold's mother in Commerce, where Olive Ann attended school through fourth grade. Two years later, Arnold took a job in Dawson, and Ruby and the children moved into a tiny rented apartment in the home of some Commerce neighbors. The year of separation took a harsh toll on her parents, and Olive Ann intended to draw on her own memories of that time to show the initial strains between Will and Sanna. "They were both so lonesome," Olive Ann wrote in the family history, "and so worried about money—they owed everybody in Commerce—and for Mother it was hard, having all the responsibility of the children." When Arnold did make it home, he was often impatient and distracted, with little tolerance for his boisterous children. Once he stung Ruby by telling her that she was raising the worst children he had ever seen. But he loved her as much as ever, and pined for her when he was away. In one letter, written after a brief stop at home and preserved in the family history, he said, "You don't know how much I did enjoy being with you last night and how I hated to leave this morning . . . I just miss you so I can't hardly stand it."

Olive Ann missed the farm—the cows, the sheep, the woods, the sound of the river. One Christmas, the renters gave the family a surprise: they were going away for two weeks and would let the Burnses move back in for the holidays. "It felt strange, seeing somebody else's furniture where ours had been," Olive Ann wrote later. "Maybe that was part of the magic, but part of it was being seven and full of Christmas hope."

When she was nine years old, Olive Ann began to keep a diary. But all it amounted to, she said, was, "Got up, ate breakfast, went to school, came home, studied, ate supper, read my book, went to bed, and prayed for everything." It wasn't until she got to high school that she began to take writing seriously. The family was reunited in Macon, Georgia, where Arnold was working for a cotton cooperative, and it was here, Olive Ann wrote, "that we all grew up." For her, that meant thinking about a career as a writer. Her first encouragement came from her ninth-grade teacher, who was teaching the class to write similes.

"*Violin* was one of the words she put on the board, and the one I picked out," Olive Ann recalled. "I wrote, 'A violin sounds like a refined sawmill.' The teacher thought that was wonderful and made me feel I was a poet or something. She told the woman who ran the high school newspaper to put me to work. So, really, those seven words changed my life." The award-winning school newspaper was a good training ground. From the beginning, a by-line meant something to Olive Ann—no sloppy work. For a while, she also dreamed of being a doctor, but said, "I knew I wasn't efficient enough to be a mother and a wife and a doctor, and I wasn't willing to study that hard. . . . Besides, I was more interested in catching a husband."

By 1942, neighbors were calling the Burns house "little USO." There was a brother in the Army and three pretty sisters at home, so it was not surprising that a steady stream of soldiers and air cadets came to call from nearby Camp Wheeler and Cochran Field. Olive Ann recorded her memories of that time in the family history: "Some weeks we went to as many as five dances a week, in the summer especially. To the three of us, names like Art, Jim, Clay, Jacobson, and Ralph have special meaning. At dances, all the dark-complexioned men lined up to dance with Margaret. [She was the sister on whose looks Olive Ann modeled Sanna Klein's.] Whatever they were —Jewish, Italian, French, Spanish, etc.— they were sure that's what she was. There weren't many dark people in the South then, except Negroes, of course. We were all in and out of love many times," she wrote, "and it was a time when you grew up fast. We had been so insulated in the South. . . . When all these Yankees came to town it was a tremendous integration of former enemies. . . . Oh, the hours we argued the Civil War with those boys, and the hours we argued Protestant versus Catholic with those of the Roman faith."

That fall, Olive Ann entered Mercer University, a small Baptist school in Macon, where she edited the campus literary magazine. After her sophomore year she transferred to the University of North Carolina, at Chapel Hill, to major in journalism. Having read that it was not enough to get training for just one job, and having watched her father struggle to stay in work during the Depression, Olive Ann got a teacher's certificate in addition to her journalism degree. "I was so practical," she said, "just awfully practical. My family had a long background in teaching—my mother taught, and my sister—and I had loved teachers all the way through school." As a result of her practicality—which required that she split her course work between education and journalism —Olive Ann never took a literature course in college, something she always regretted.

By the time she graduated, in 1946, her parents were living in Atlanta, and Olive Ann joined them there, In their modest brick house at 161 Bolling Road. In addition to her degree, she brought home from college some newly formed opinions about politics and about racial matters in particular. "Racial slurs and anti-Semitic remarks made me livid," she recalled years later. A Methodist, she had fallen in love with a Jewish boy at Chapel Hill, but had ended the romance when she realized that she lacked the nerve to tell her parents about it. "I was very much in love," she said, "but I wasn't strong enough to face the difficulties with his family or with mine." Instead, she proudly proclaimed herself a liberal and was adamant about her opinions, which she aired at every opportunity. Her father told her she was going down a one-way street and had lost sight of the fact that some people have to go the other way. The criticism hit home. "He wasn't a philosophical man, but he made me realize I was prejudiced against people who were prejudiced, and that my prejudice was as bad as theirs. And this freed me to live among all kinds of people and accept them as they are."

Within a year, Olive Ann had landed a job as a staff writer at the *Atlanta Journal Sunday Magazine,* under its founding editor, Angus Perkerson. A remarkable editor with a sure instinct for what people would read, Perkerson was already legendary, known for his magnificent tantrums and respected as a great teacher. Although dour and shy by nature, he was fully capable of letting rip a stream of profanity that would leave even seasoned newspapermen trembling. Olive Ann always remembered him with great affection, but she also admitted, "Mr. Perk fired me three times in the first six months and scared me to death for five years." Angus Perkerson had given a young Margaret Mitchell her first job, in 1922, and he remained in charge of the magazine for most of Olive Ann's ten years there. She gave him full credit for turning her into a writer.

"Everything I know about writing began with Mr. Perkerson," she said. "He never rewrote a writer. You had to do it yourself. You learned not to be sensitive about the *x*'s he put in the margins. He'd go through the copy with you like this: 'Don't you think a *the* would be better than an *a* here?' 'Dammit, that whole page is boring.' 'This word is too long. We ain't putting out the magazine for Ph.D.s.' 'You used the same word five times in two sentences.' (Once when I said I repeated a word on purpose, for emphasis, he said, 'Hell, it's bad enough to be careless without being stupid.') If he said, 'That's funny,' he meant suggestive; being young and unworldly, I was often 'funny.' He never gave praise. You knew he liked your story if he put it up front in the magazine. He was obsessive about two things: being interesting and being accurate. Once he asked me when George Washington's birthday was. I said, 'February twenty-second.' 'Well, call the reference department and make sure.' "

Much as she loved her job, Olive Ann had no confidence in herself; it often took her two or three weeks to write a story—a pace that wouldn't cut the mustard at a weekly magazine. Whenever Angus Perkerson couldn't stand her pained efforts any longer, he'd come over to her desk and yell, "Hell, Olive, if you don't finish that story by three o'clock, I'm goin' throw it in the trash can." In 1952, she accompanied her family on a trip to Europe, despite Perkerson's opposition. This time she was sure he meant it when he told her she was through. But when she returned two and a half months later, she found that he had kept up her payments to Social Security and that the job was still hers. Once she realized that Perkerson had confidence in her, Olive Ann was able to laugh when he scolded, "Olive, you gnaw on a story like an old dog gnawing on a bone," or "You rewrite so much, your copy looks as if you wrote it by hand and corrected it on the typewriter." She came to love him very much. She also credited her newspaper work with giving her the tools she needed to write a novel. "I was used to listening to what people said and how they said it, quoting dialogue exactly the way it was said and paraphrasing only when a speech was boring or too long. Also, newspaper work made me think and look for what was interesting. If it's not interesting, readers put that newspaper down! And they may plod on through a book for three pages if it starts out boring, but then they put it back on the shelf."

The memory of Margaret Mitchell still cast a spell over Atlanta in the 1950s. Although it was nearly twenty years since *Gone With the Wind* had been published, readers had continued to hope right up until her death in 1949 that Peggy Mitchell might write a sequel, and her many friends continued to talk about her as if she had been with them just yesterday. Certainly, for any young writer in Atlanta in those days, Mitchell's legendary success was vivid. She had come out of obscurity with a novel that had taken the entire country, if not the world, by storm, and that had gone on to sell more copies than any piece of fiction before or since. Little wonder, then, that Atlanta was a fine town in which to be an aspiring novelist, or that a group of young hopefuls banded together to read and criticize one another's work.

The Plot Club convened on the shady front porch of the home of Wylly Folk St. John, who later became a successful children's book author, as well as one of Olive Ann's most treasured friends and supporters. Other members were Margaret Long, Celestine Sibley, Robert Burch, Genevieve Holden Pou, and Mary Cobb Bugg— published writers all. Olive Ann was pleased to be included—indeed, she was a member of the group for thirty-five years. But she never thought she would write a novel, and, according to one veteran of the club, neither did anyone else. She had never read Faulkner or Hemingway or any "important" writer; she was too restrained, too innocent, "the wide-eyed one." Olive Ann herself claimed that she never took her writing seriously. "I was too busy dating to write more than two or three pages for those evenings, and I never finished anything I started," she said. "I figured I'd never get married if I spent every night at the typewriter."

Getting married was very much on Olive Ann's mind, for she was over thirty, and, although she had plenty of dates, there was no serious beau in sight. She had, however, become friends with Andy Sparks, a fellow staff writer at the magazine, who was the first person she met when she came to the *Atlanta Journal and Constitution* to apply for a job. Angus Perkerson was out, so she handed her portfolio of college stories to the handsome young man behind the desk. They worked side by side for the next nine years, and Andy thought she was so funny that he sometimes took notes on things she said at the office. He planned to use them, he teased, for the role of the ingenue in a play he was writing that would be called *Peachtree Island.* One line he thought worth saving was Olive Ann's confession that "at cocktail parties, I never know whether to order ginger ale, so people will think I'm drinking, or milk, so they'll know I'm not." On another occasion, she told her colleagues that she had been kissing a man she wasn't in love with. "I just wanted to teach him how," she said. "I think it's a pity, a thirty-year-old man, so uneducated. I'm just doing it for the sake of the girl he'll really fall for someday." (After Andy's death, Olive Ann found his transcription of this line among his things. On the scrap of paper he had saved, she wrote, "How silly can a young girl be?")

Olive Ann was always willing to provide a full account of her previous night's date, good or bad. One day Andy remarked, "If you and I ever fall in love, I don't want you to tell ANYBODY at the office what I said last night and what you said." "All right," she promised, taken aback.

On New Year's Day 1956, Olive Ann was interviewed on a local radio show, "a young-girl-reporter sort of thing," she recalled. Andy was listening as the host asked his guest what she wanted most in the year to come. "Well," Olive Ann replied, "I just want to get married." As soon as the show was off the air, Andy was on the phone. "Why didn't you ever tell me that's what you wanted?" he asked. He picked her up at the station, and at midnight they kissed for the first time. And then, said Olive Ann, "the magic started." She kept her word, and "didn't tell anybody anything." Their colleagues at the office didn't even know they were dating, much less in love, and when they went together to tell the Perkersons they were getting married, Medora Perkerson was shocked—she thought that Olive Ann was in love with someone else. Arnold Burns was glad to hear that his youngest daughter was finally leaving the nest. "Good," he said when she told him the news. "That will be someplace else to go."

The wedding took place on August 11, 1956; Olive Ann was thirty-two and Andy thirty-seven. She continued to write for the magazine, using her maiden name because, as she explained it, "two hot names like Burns and Sparks would look silly together in a by-line." Several weeks after the wedding, Andy developed mononucleosis and was told to stay away from his new bride lest he infect her. Olive Ann was convinced that he had gotten the "kissing disease" by kissing every girl who had offered her cheek at the wedding, and she found their enforced separation hard to take. Finally, in desperation, she held a piece of plastic wrap over her mouth and said, "Kiss me, Andy. I can't stand it anymore." "It wasn't very effective," she said later, "but it made us laugh." For them, being in love meant always being able to laugh, no matter what, and one of the things they most appreciated in each other was a sense of humor. As one close friend observed, "They might come close to having words, but they could never do it—they would always end up giggling instead. They just adored each other."

On December 6, 1957, Olive Ann gave birth to a daughter. She had Becky under hypnosis. At a time when women were routinely drugged for labor and delivery, Olive Ann knew that she wanted to experience fully the birth of her baby. "Not even an aspirin," she wrote. Afterwards, she was alone for a few minutes in the delivery room, "after the OB, nurses, assistants, and gallery of OB observers (who didn't believe it would work) had all left. The big lights were off, and an old Negro man came in to mop the floor. I was crying with joy. I told him everything was fine, I was just happy. He said in the sweetest voice, 'You jes' go on and cry, ma'am. Yes, hep yo'sef.'"

On February 1, 1960, Olive Ann gave birth to a son, John. During those years, she didn't write much at all. "Although I'm not a great house-keeper (I use a dust cloth when I can see the dust without my glasses)," she admitted, "I care about the house being a home. I don't resent the fact that cooking, cleaning, and washing clothes has to be part of homemaking, but I do wish I were more effective at it."

When Medora Perkerson died, Olive Ann was offered her job as the newspaper's advice colum-nist, "Amy Larkin." She snapped up the chance to work at home, and for the next seven years, she said, she "lived like a queen. I had a full-time maid and cook. I took care of the children and wrote the column, even when I was sick. It's easier to write than vacuum when you're sick, and I was always getting sick with sinus or chest infections." At times she was too ill to care for the children, and John and Becky would go off to stay with their grandparents on Bolling Road, or at Olive Ann's sister Jean's. Even then, she realized that there was one great advantage to illness—it created space and time for writing. The mail to Amy Larkin made Olive Ann shock-proof and taught her much about human nature. But she knew that as long as she was answering letters, nothing more substantial would come from her typewriter. So she gave up the column and resumed writing three or four stories a year for the magazine.

In the fall of 1971, Olive Ann's mother underwent surgery for stomach cancer. On the morning of the operation, Olive Ann prayed all the way to the hospital, "Dear God, please don't let it be inoperable." But the cancer had already spread. Afterward Olive Ann reflected that, of course, her mother's cancer was inoperable regardless of her prayer; it was simply too late for God to change it. These thoughts marked a turning point for her, for it occurred to her that she had always prayed wrong, that almost everybody did. It was a mistake to ask God for material things, "like Cadillacs, and a pay raise, and for the body to get well." Still, it would be several more years before she carried this idea any further, or before she moved beyond what she called "appreciation prayers"—"Thank you, God, for this; thank you, God, for that."

Because Ruby Burns was susceptible to bouts of depression and anxiety, the doctor suggested that she not be told the outcome of the operation, and Arnold agreed. Olive Ann thought that the challenge of keeping the truth from his wife was part of what sustained her father over the following months. "Deception for a cause never bothered him at all," she said. The doctor predicted that Ruby would have one or two good months following the surgery, after which it would all be downhill. At the most, he thought, she had about six months to live. For Olive Ann, the hardest part was lying to her mother. "I seldom had in my life," she explained. She also felt Ruby was fully capable of handling the truth. "She had always been the kind to go to pieces over a Disposall not working or a water heater exploding," Olive Ann wrote, "but the big things she could stand. I knew she could stand anything if Daddy was holding her hand and loving her out loud. But I couldn't tell her if Daddy didn't want to, and what if he did know best?"

After Ruby's surgery, the family history became a family project and, as Olive Ann wrote later, "we had a wonderful winter and spring." A relative had already worked on early genealogies, which Olive Ann's sister Margaret began collating and typing.

When Ruby Burns died in September 1972, Olive Ann wrote, "I have to mention Mother's beauty—physical beauty. As she lost weight in the last weeks I thought I had never seen anybody so beautiful. Her bone structure, her face, was an artist's perfection. It was the beauty of youth; I could now imagine how absolutely perfect her beauty must have been when she and Daddy married. She was five foot three and only weighed 112 when she married, but in maturity she had always been overweight, and though glowing and lovely, her face was just not revealed. I shall never forget her on her birthday—so physically beautiful, her dark eyes alive and sparkling with hope and love."

By the time Olive Ann's father died, the next July, the family history was nearly complete. Olive Ann ended it with a eulogy for both of her parents, now "side by side in the twin beds of death." Her mother's death was the first she had ever experienced in her immediate family. "After all that's happened," she wrote to friends of her parents, "it almost seems now that Daddy died within weeks instead of ten months later, and that grief for one was all wrapped up with grief for the other, as if it were all one package."

Olive Ann and Andy bought Arnold and Ruby's house on Bolling Road and moved in the next spring. There, Olive Ann typed the final pages of the family history. "It's fall now," she wrote, "and we Sparkses have lived in Daddy's house for six months. Outside we've got turnip greens planted—he was always generous with turnip greens, which he planted in his flower beds. And there are two blossoms on his roses. Every morning he would pick a bouquet for Mother and hand them to her and kiss her. He could write about love, but he couldn't talk about it much, and she always felt the roses were a special thing between them. When the season was ending he might have only one or two for her, and he'd always say, 'These are the last ones, I guess,' but then he'd find another the next day. I think maybe what is out there now may be the last ones; I wish I knew how to keep them thriving and prolific, as he did."

By 1974, Olive Ann Burns had lost her mother and watched as her sister grew desperately ill from chemotherapy treatments. Now, cancer was about to strike even closer. At a routine physical that October, her doctor detected a blood abnormality that led him to predict that, within the next two months to two years, Olive Ann would develop either leukemia or lymphoma. Olive Ann listened carefully to his explanation, wondering just how she could sit at home *waiting* to get cancer. Clearly, she would need something to keep her mind off her white blood cells and her own mortality. And then it came to her—she would write a novel. The idea, she said afterward, surprised her even more than the diagnosis. Before she left the building, she found a phone and called Andy at his office. "I may get cancer," she told him, "but I am definitely going to write a novel." Back home, she spotted her neighbor in the backyard. She told Norma Duncan the same thing, adding, "And I don't want you to feel sorry for me." Norma could tell that Olive Ann was serious. "From that day on," she said, "we would talk about the book, but she never gave me the chance to pity her."

From her father, Olive Ann had gained a lively sense of what it was like to grow up in a small town in Georgia at the turn of the century. And she already had an idea for a first chapter—the story of Grandpa Power. She would call him Enoch Rucker Blakeslee and give him one arm, a physical detail inspired by Andy's mother's recollection of a one-armed relative who had tickled her with his stump when she was a little girl.

Olive Ann figured she should start the book the way she had learned to start a magazine article: by grabbing the reader in the first paragraph. If any passage seemed slow or boring, she rewrote it. But, she confessed to her fellow Plot Club member Wylly Folk St. John, "I don't know anything about plot." "Well," her friend advised, "don't worry about plot. You just get your characters into trouble, and then you get them out." So Olive Ann got Miss Love and Grandpa in trouble right in the first chapter and forged ahead, aware that she really didn't know the first thing about writing a novel. "I never knew that the bookstores had shelf after shelf of books about how to write novels," she later admitted. "I could have saved myself a lot of time."

She finished the first chapter while visiting her sister Margaret in Pennsylvania, and sent it home to Andy, who was by then the editor of the *Sunday Magazine*. He returned it with a note: "I think you had better try again." Back in Atlanta, she reworked the beginning, added more chapters, and showed them to Norma, whose judgment she also trusted. "You're just trying to tell all those funny stories your daddy told you," Norma observed. "You've got thirty-five pages of Will Tweedy and the boys putting rats out at the school play while I'm wondering what's happened to Grandpa and Miss Love." Norma had more useful criticism: "Every time you introduce a character," she said, "you write an article, instead of feeding the information into the action."

Another friend, who taught writing, read the early chapters and observed that there were flashbacks within flashbacks within flashbacks. Olive Ann knew she was floundering. She began to watch a soap opera and followed it for a year, learning how to weave plots and subplots together, and to keep the action moving. "And where at first I made all the characters into people I could like and respect," Olive Ann recalled, "I noticed that the soaps always had a main character that viewers can hate. Hating is still a problem for me. I made Aunt Loma an unsympathetic character and I hated how she was, but I kept trying to help the reader understand her."

When she was ready for more feedback, she read a few portions of the manuscript to the Plot Club. "I was surprised," one member admitted. "I had no idea she could write something . . . so *good.*" Then, in December 1976, her monthly blood test brought the dreaded news. She had lymphoma, and she would need to undergo chemotherapy.

By this time, Olive Ann was having a fine time in Cold Sassy, Georgia, but the prospect of chemotherapy and its possible side effects terrified her. She was already running a high fever, and she knew there was no turning back. The worst thing that could happen was not that she would die; she had already accepted that. The worst thing would be to go on living with terrible fear

—to be afraid any time she wasn't busy; to wake up in the middle of the night, "cold and shivering in the pit of my soul." On the gray January day before she was to begin treatment, Olive Ann knelt down alone in her living room and began to pray as she had never prayed before. She knew now that she could not ask God to make her well. Instead, she prayed with all her heart for courage. "Lord God," she said over and over, "please help me not to be afraid." A half hour went by, and Olive Ann rose from her knees with the realization that her prayer had been answered. The fear was gone. It was a moment she would remember with awe and gratitude; in the years that followed, she said, she never had to repeat that prayer.

As it turned out, this first round of chemotherapy consisted of a monthly dose of twelve tiny pills —not much to fear after all. The treatment didn't make her sick, but it did cause her white blood cell count to drop, making her particularly vulnerable to infection. As a result, she was forced to stay at home and to stay rested—which meant that she could spend a good deal of her time working on the novel. Years before, a doctor treating her for arthritis had advised her not to vacuum anymore. Olive Ann was always grateful to him, for he had, in effect, granted her permission to spend less time on housework. Now, she tried to see her confinement in a positive light. "I realized that if I was going to be sick a long time, it would be hard on my family, so I'd better try to be as cheerful as possible," she wrote.

Soon after the day she had prayed to be released from her fear, Olive Ann had a sudden insight into how to cope with her loss of health. On a sheet of yellow lined paper, which I found in her files, she told herself that instead of thinking of her cancer as a *burden*, which seemed intolerable, she would think of it as a *challenge*. "Each time of life has its peculiar problems," she wrote. "A young girl doesn't think of finding the right husband as a burden—she sees it as a challenge." Rather than resent her cancer, she would figure out a way to get through it with grace. "A challenge is something to be faced and met. A burden is just heavy, and unbearable if it goes on too long. When seen as the biggest challenge I had ever faced, not only the illness itself, but my attitude about it—I felt that my spiritual resources were marshaled, not beaten down."

Olive Ann had to summon those resources again and again in the months and years to come. As the chemotherapy progressed, she lost all of her hair and was plagued by a constant fever. The fever she dealt with as best she could, refusing to let it keep her down. "I got great pride in keeping the clothes washed and the supper cooked," she said. "I would lie in bed and string beans, and when the fever went down I'd go fix a salad or put on a chicken, then go back to bed to write or read, then get up and empty the dishwasher." Going bald presented its own challenge. She dealt with it by maintaining her sense of humor. In an article for the *Sunday Magazine* called "Co-Ed in

215

the Bald Club," Olive Ann wrote, "I hated being bald. I saw myself as a sideshow, right up there with the tattooed lady and the two-headed calf. I'd like to say that I bore the affliction with grace. I certainly never felt that hair was more important than life." Exactly two weeks after her first chemo treatment, Olive Ann noticed that her brush was thick with hair and, she said, she literally went weak in the knees. That night, she wrote, she told fifteen-year-old John that she was molting.

"Aw, MOM!" John groaned, then with a sick look on his face said, "Well, please don't talk about it."

"Don't you care?"

"Yes. But I know you. You won't just lose your hair, you'll tell everybody—even show them."

"Tell, yes. Show, never." There was an awkward moment as he stood miserably munching his Pop-Tart, avoiding the sight of my thinning hair. "Think of it as a new style," I said brightly.

"Don't make jokes, Mom. It's not funny."

"Had you rather I cry? I could cry for hours any minute." I don't know why I expected my son to like the prospect of having a bald-headed mama when I hated the prospect of being one.

Olive Ann's vanity never got in the way of a good story, and she wasn't shy about telling this one. "There are said to be 100,000 follicles on the average human head," she wrote. "Imagine the nuisance when they all start migrating from your scalp to your mouth or down your back, sticking like Velcro to clothing, upholstery, blankets, sheets, and pillowcases." When she was completely bald, Olive Ann realized that covering her pate was a matter of necessity as well as esthetics —it was winter, and it was cold. She first tried a lace-trimmed white Colonial cap she'd bought in Williamsburg—"fetching," she wrote, "but not as warm as the stretchy blue cut-off pajama leg I pulled out of the dustrag bag. This knit tube didn't shift around, gave me a madonna look, as in Bible pictures, and prevented sinus headaches in cold weather if I slept with it pulled down over my eyes to the end of my nose." Andy called it the Hooded Falcon Look.

Finally, she got herself a wig, although she never got over feeling "fakey" in it, as if she were pretending she wasn't bald. Because she couldn't go out to a store to try wigs on, friends and neighbors threw her a wig shower, hauling out their old bouffant hairpieces from the 1960s—over a dozen in all, from blazing orange to jet black to prim and proper iron gray. Olive Ann arranged them all in the bedroom until Andy complained that it looked like a headhunter's trophy room. Six months after she had molted, Olive Ann began to sprout baby-fine black hair that gradually covered her head. In another three months, she wrote, "I had go-anywhere hair." But there was nowhere to go. The doctor still wouldn't let her out of the house.

Throughout that winter, Olive Ann's goal had been to accept her illness, come what may. She took comfort in reminding herself that "any person in Atlanta, including me, could be dead on the highway next week." But as the weather warmed and green shoots began to push through the earth in Andy's garden, it occurred to her that perhaps she had been too accepting. "At first I was happily fatalistic," she wrote. "I was so sure that whatever happened was all right that I forgot we're here on earth to *live*. I accepted so totally, and was indeed content with my lot, that I forgot for a while how much life matters. Then all of a sudden, when spring came I was *consumed* with the joy of living. I accepted the illness, but I wanted to live, and every new day seemed like a treasure or like a passion that couldn't be satiated."

A few weeks before Christmas in 1977, Olive Ann's doctor told her that the chemotherapy appeared to be working. After more than ten months of fever, her temperature was back to normal, and, although her white blood cell count was still low, she felt well. In a letter to the Sunday school class that she and Andy attended throughout their marriage, she wrote, "You must be mighty tired of hearing how I am. It's been hard for me to keep a sustained interest in it. So I will report, once and for all, that as far as day-to-day living goes, I am now a well person. I can wash windows, cook casseroles, and run the dishwasher and typewriter with the best of you."

She said she loved to hear about art exhibits or shops that were so unsuccessful that nobody went—because then she could go. But the year at home had been a happy one, she said. "I'm convinced true fulfillment is living in God's world one day at a time, savoring it, leaving today's disappointments behind and borrowing no troubles from tomorrow. It's done not only by accepting life, fever, and things that go bump in the night, but also by cultivating love and new and old friendships, and especially by finding a new work or project that makes it exciting just to get up in the morning."

Working on the novel made it exciting for Olive Ann to get up in the morning. Day after day she sat at her kitchen table, surrounded by notes she had made on scraps of paper. She wrote on the old Royal typewriter on which she had composed her magazine features and her advice column. She edited and rewrote as painstakingly as ever, covering every typed page with dense scribbles in ink, always "cutting out the dull stuff." She had taken her early readers' advice to heart and by the middle of 1978 had several hundred typed pages that she felt good about. When Andy read them, he said, "Stop writing articles and finish the book." It was all the encouragement she needed. She sent the chapters to an editor in New York, who turned them down, gently. Olive Ann took the rejection in stride. "I have to hope that in its finished form the book will seem salable to some other editor," she responded. "Meanwhile I take encouragement from your appraisal that it is 'splendidly written,' for when I started I had no idea how to structure a novel. Even if it doesn't sell, I will have learned alot, and I've never had more fun."

Olive Ann was hooked on her story and determined to go on with it, but she was also realistic about her prospects as a first-time novelist. Rather than set her sights on publication, she thought of the novel as "just a hobby." "Who would want to publish a novel by someone who doesn't know how to write one?" she asked herself. "I thought if I finished it, I would just make some Xerox copies and give them to my family for Christmas presents. I really wasn't sure I'd ever finish it, though. If I lived to be ninety, I might not finish it at the rate I was going."

Oddly, it was a clean bill of health that slowed her down. After three years of on-and-off chemotherapy, a blood test showed that Olive Ann's lymphoma had gone into remission. It was time for her to turn her attention away from Cold Sassy and back to the world—and to all the things she had missed during her confinement. Now she had choices to make. "I wrote when I wasn't busy doing something else," she said. "If I wanted to go camping with the family for three weeks, I didn't say, 'Oh no, I have to stay with my novel.' I might go for weeks without writing; I might write every day for a while. Real writers tend to get up at four or five in the morning and write until they have to go to work, or they start at eight and that is their work, and they write steadily until about two or three o'clock."

When Olive Ann was well enough to fulfill her

responsibilities as a wife, mother, and home-maker, there was often little time or energy left for writing. It was being well that now presented the challenge. "My surprise, after conquering cancer, is to find that renewed health is something to cope with," she wrote to the Sunday school class. "I've got postpartum blues! All the time I was sick I was happier than ever in my life. I *accepted.* I had everything to gain by fully and joyfully living one day at a time and worrying about nothing, not even the cancer. Viewed in the light of cancer, other problems never seemed worth a worry. Now that it has remissed, I'm realizing that I've gradually withdrawn from that sense of spiritual well-being. In other words, I've become a chronic worrier again, always impatient for progress. Cancer teaches that life is too short to be lived like that; you take your knocks when they come, not in advance.

"So my current project is to deprogram myself as a worrier. I find I can *notice* when I'm depressed or anxious and switch on another attitude —the way a man on an expense account can freely choose shrimp scampi over hamburger. Andy, who has always taken life in full stride, isn't much help in the project. After I put a card on the bathroom mirror that said WHY WORRY? in big letters, he wrote under it WHY NOT?"

Friends who watched Olive Ann cope with cancer and the side effects of chemotherapy would not have characterized her as a worrier. She could always see the positive side of her illness, even saying, "It's almost worth being sick awhile to come to such glorious joy and realization of how great it is to live." She could transform any problem into an anecdote; she found the humor in every situation. But the stories themselves were often a means of prevailing over her worries. She believed that she had inherited her tendency toward anxiety from her mother. "I worried about my children's problems," she admitted. "I had no patience to just let their lives evolve; I wanted to make things happen. And I worried about not getting the house dusted and things like that." Getting back to work on the novel provided a necessary distraction.

And so, instead of worrying about things she couldn't change, she stewed over tricky scenes and bits of dialogue, turning them over in her mind until she had them right, jotting them down, and then fiddling some more. She struggled to make the dialect authentic, convinced that if you get a person's words right, you don't have to go on and on describing his or her personality. She loved to find ways to use the pieces of real life that seemed stranger and more wonderful than fiction could ever be. Granny Blakeslee's hallucinations on her death bed, for example, were inspired by visions Andy's mother had seen shortly before her death in 1978. After visiting with her in the hospital one day, Andy came home and told Olive Ann that his mother had grabbed him and tried to pull him right down onto the bed. The room was full of angels, she told him. Couldn't he see them? Olive Ann comforted her husband. She also got him to elaborate on what had taken place, and later sat down and told the story of Granny Blakeslee's death through Will Tweedy's eyes.

At the end of the novel, when Grandpa is critically injured during a hold-up at the store, he is as feisty as Olive Ann's own father had been after a bad fall. Nearly eighty and unwell, Arnold had stumbled on the front walk on the way to the car. He called Olive Ann and told her that he had broken his nose, cut his forehead, and was bleeding like a hog, but was going fishing anyway. When his daughter suggested that he stay home and rest, Arnold replied, "Haven't you ever noticed? Folks die in bed." Olive Ann jotted that down—and she remembered it when Grandpa broke his nose and ribs, banged his head, and twisted his knee.

All her life, Olive Ann had written down bits of conversation that interested and amused her. One country aunt, a particularly colorful speaker, once got so put out with her niece that she warned, "If you don't stop takin' down notes, I'm goin' stop talkin'." Olive Ann later said, "Well, I didn't stop taking notes, and my aunt couldn't stop talking." Now, all those years of listening and paying attention to detail were bearing fruit. She had a feeling that the novel was finally coming together, and the reactions of others confirmed it.

In 1980 she spent time at a writers' colony on Ossabaw Island. One evening she read some chapters aloud. Her fellow writers, she said, "were mostly Yankees who couldn't understand my Southern accent. When I asked if they thought the dialect was overdone, a man said, 'We can't tell how much is the way you pronounce things and how much is the way it's written, but it sounds great.' " One member of the group was Menahkem Perry, a publisher and professor of literary criticism at the University of Tel Aviv. "He insisted on reading the whole manuscript," Olive Ann said, "and shocked me by comparing it with Mark Twain's work. He said it was not a regional novel, but a universal love story. He said a lot else —enough to make me believe that I had somehow stumbled into learning how to structure a novel. After that, I took the writing seriously."

She bought herself a computer and set it up down in the basement, in the pine-paneled room her father had built. With the help of her son, she learned how to use the word processor, and realized that now she could rewrite and edit to her heart's content. What's more, she could steal away to this little room at all hours of the day, put on some classical music in the background, and lose herself in writing, without the sight of dishes piled in the sink or unmade beds to make her feel guilty.

Having made up her mind to finish the book, Olive Ann arranged to spend a month at the Hambidge Center, an artists' retreat in the north Georgia mountains. Away from the familiar routines of home and family, however, she found it difficult to work. Later, she wrote an article about her experience there: "Whenever I hit a snag in the writing, the need for human companionship became overwhelming, but nobody lived within hollering distance of the Hopper House. I found myself neglecting the novel to write extravagantly long letters. I talked out loud to myself, and whenever I wasn't working, I turned on the radio. Hungry for other voices, hungry for news, I listened eagerly to country music, school doings, even funeral news on 'The Obituary Column of the Air.' Only late at night was there good reception out of Atlanta or Chicago or New York—usually hard rock music that set me dancing like a teenager. Dancing gave me something to do and somebody to watch: surrounded by night, the kitchen windows became black mirrors in which my gyrating image was indistinct. Not quite me, a woman with grown children, but instead a lithe and lovely girl who, if I do say so myself, seemed rather winsome." Olive Ann admitted that there were times during that month that she almost gave up and went home, but she stuck it out. In the end, the affection she felt for her characters was more powerful than her loneliness and isolation.

During those years of writing, Olive Ann had never made publication her goal. All she really wanted, she insisted, was to perfect the dialect, to tell a good story, and to have fun doing it. "I wasn't trying to preach or write a sociological study," she said. "I wanted it to be funny. I'm tired of a world so dead serious, in which silliness passes for humor. I wanted to present fictional characters who are human but fundamentally decent. I wanted Grandpa to be true to himself and care about work and goodness, yet be free of the burden of perfectionism. I wanted him to live with courage and gusto, and know how to look death in the eye."

There is so much passion, so much life and humor, and so much wisdom in *Cold Sassy Tree* that it is hard to imagine that Olive Ann might have finished her novel only to circulate it among her family and friends. As it happened, a publisher was practically delivered to her doorstep.

In 1982, Anne Edwards was in Atlanta doing research for her biography of Margaret Mitchell. One day, Andy gave her a tour of the *Sunday Magazine* office and helped her locate copies of the feature stories that Peggy Mitchell had written under Angus Perkerson. Grateful for his help, Anne and her husband invited Andy and Olive Ann out for dinner. The two couples hit it off, and before they parted, Olive Ann suggested that Anne be their guest the next time she came to Atlanta. As Olive Ann admitted later, she didn't realize it might be an imposition to ask an author to read a manuscript in progress. When Anne returned and stayed with the Sparkses, Olive Ann said to her, "If you'd like to read a chapter or two of my novel, you'll know me better." Anne was complimentary, but, Olive Ann said, "I didn't dream she'd ever remember it."

Anne did remember, though. A year later, in

May 1983, Ticknor & Fields launched Anne Edwards's *Road to Tara* with a publication party at the Atlanta Historical Society. Although it was her night to celebrate, Anne also wanted to do some matchmaking between Olive Ann and the president of Ticknor & Fields, Chester Kerr.

Chester Kerr had become the president of Ticknor & Fields after a distinguished career as the director of the Yale University Press. On his retirement from Yale, he had been invited by Houghton Mifflin Company of Boston to preside over a new trade book subsidiary that would resurrect a famous nineteenth-century firm that Henry Houghton had acquired in 1880. In its heyday, Ticknor & Fields had published such American writers as Emerson, Thoreau, Holmes, Longfellow, Whittier, and Harriet Beecher Stowe, and had imported from England the works of Tennyson and Dickens. Under Chester Kerr's leadership, the revived imprint published its first titles in the spring of 1980, out of a modest office in New Haven, Connecticut. (Three years later, the offices were moved to New York.) In January 1981, I came to work at Ticknor & Fields as an editorial assistant.

Anne Edwards's biography was an important addition to our 1983 list, and Chester and his small staff were determined to do everything right. Anne was pleased by Chester's attention to detail, and she suspected that Ticknor & Fields might be just the right place for Olive Ann's novel. On the plane trip to Atlanta she told Chester and his wife, Joan, about Olive Ann and her manu-script; she was eager for the Kerrs to meet her.

Olive Ann loved to recall her first impression of the man who was to become her publisher: "He was a tall, big man, with a shock of white hair and a shock of white mustache, and very dignified. . . . I thought he was the kind of person you should call 'Your Eminence' when you speak to him."

While Chester was busy making introductions for Anne Edwards, Anne's husband introduced Olive Ann to Joan Kerr, who put the aspiring au-thor immediately at ease. "Oh, tell me about your book," Joan prompted. "Can you describe the characters and what it's about?"

"I did," Olive Ann wrote afterwards, "and she said, 'Will you send it to us?' "

When Olive Ann asked if she should finish it first, Joan told her not to bother. "Send it tomor-row," she said.

Olive Ann knew she couldn't send it tomorrow —"it was the biggest mess"—but she now had a great incentive to get the manuscript in shape. "I had already spent eight years on the novel, and it was really time to wind it up," she said. A month after their meeting, she wrote to Joan Kerr, "I plan to send my manuscript as soon as possible. In the rhythm of the South (actually my rhythm), that is not as fast as it sounds."

But by the middle of August, she was almost done. She typed a title page for the novel, then entitled *Call Me Love,* packed up the manuscript (minus the ending, which she had yet to write), and sent it to Joan Kerr in New Haven. "The book will be about 825 pages, finished," Olive Ann predicted, "but I am quite willing to cut it. I am also willing to tone down the colloquialisms and the Southern accents if they seem overdone. . . . I think (fear) that submitting a manuscript is a lot like entering a Reader's Digest Sweepstakes!" She enclosed a check to cover the cost of shipping the manuscript back to Atlanta.

Joan Kerr was not on her husband's staff, but she *had* encouraged this charming Southern woman to submit her unfinished novel and she was eager to see if her hunch was right. It didn't take eight hundred pages for Joan to know she had had the right instinct in urging Olive Ann Burns to send her book. The novel was too long, it sagged a bit in the middle—but there was certainly something special here and Joan felt certain that we should publish it. She asked me whether I would take the manuscript home over Labor Day weekend and read it.

I will always remember meeting Will Tweedy on that early fall weekend. Thanks to him, I had to abandon my holiday plans—yet any regret I may have felt melted away as I fell under the spell of this extraordinary novel. I remember feeling privileged to be among its first readers, privileged even to hold those pages in my hands. I had left the office on Friday afternoon with a pile of unexpected work, and I returned on Tuesday morning carrying one of the best books I had ever read.

Olive Ann told us that when she received Joan

Kerr's letter the following week, she was so happy, she cried. "Boy howdy," it began, "that is a fine book you have sent us. Katrina Kenison, our editor, and I can hardly wait for the concluding chapters!" Olive Ann had never let herself set her sights on getting published; now she had a publisher eagerly awaiting the rest of her manuscript. "Hurry up with the conclusion," Joan wrote, "so Katrina and I can take the ms. to Chester for preparation of an offer. And congratulations on a superb job."

Olive Ann treasured this letter for the rest of her life. "Reading your warm, encouraging letter," she wrote to Joan, "is the most exciting thing that has happened to me since Andy and I got married and had babies." She estimated that it would take her till mid-November to finish the book, depending on how much rewriting she decided to do. "I have never seen a first-draft sentence that couldn't be improved," she wrote. "As you can imagine, your letter has put wings on my imagination." But while Chester and Joan waited in New Haven, Olive Ann found herself waylaid in Atlanta.

As would be the case all too often in the years ahead, her inspiration and good intentions were thwarted by illness. After a week of high fever, she ended up in the hospital with an infection. Then, just as she felt up to working again, an inner ear problem brought on a few days of dizziness. "That too is passing," Olive Ann wrote to Chester, "but so is time. If I were not a wife, mother, and housekeeper, and if I did less rewriting, I could go like a nine-day wonder and still finish before Thanksgiving. As it is, a more realistic deadline is mid-December."

It was worth the wait. "If you think it is unsatisfactory in anyway," Olive Ann wrote, "I will try again." In fact, there was remarkably little to be done. All those years of polishing had paid off. Olive Ann may have created Grandpa "free of the burden of perfectionism," but she allowed herself no such freedom. She had been as meticulous with the details as Angus Perkerson himself might have been, carefully checking all the historical facts, confirming the authenticity of the dialect, and scouring the manuscript for typographical errors. She had also taken Anne Edwards's advice and engaged an agent in New York. Five days before Christmas 1983, Chester called her to say he was ready to make an offer.

That day, in a gesture so characteristic of her, Olive Ann took the time to share her good news with her old Plot Club friend, Wylly Folk St. John, now widowed and in a nursing home. "Today has been a red-telephone day," she wrote. "The first thing I could think of after calling Andy was to write you and thank you for saying all those years, 'If I could do it, you can too.' I never believed that made it so, because you knew instinctively what I had to write for eight years to learn—how to put together a novel. But your encouragement —back when writing a novel was not even a gleam in my eye—has meant everything to my keeping

231

on trying. One thing I have to accept is that I can't tell Mother and Daddy or Ma Sparks or Tom [Wylly's husband] about it. But accept we must in the death part of life."

The encouragement of others meant a great deal to Olive Ann. Now that Chester had actually offered to buy her novel, Olive Ann wrote to Joan, "I think anybody who suffers from low self-esteem should get letters from you, Joan. I feel quite confident as an article writer but one reason I had to work on this book for eight and a half years is that I was, and felt like, a total amateur at fiction. So to have you tell me enthusiastically and warmly that things I tried have mostly worked is very gratifying."

Eight years after she had begun to write, with the threat of cancer hanging over her, Olive Ann Burns found herself in remission from lymphoma, a finished novel to her credit, and an enthusiastic offer from the very first publisher to have read it. *Cold Sassy Tree,* as we now agreed to call it, would be published in the fall of 1984.

After so many years of working alone, Olive Ann loved the collaboration of the editing process, which we began the day after New Year's, 1984. I knew from our first telephone conversation that this would be more than a business relationship. That day, I took a deep breath and picked up the phone to tell our new author that, much as I loved her book, I thought it could be made even better if we cut it by about a fourth; there were too many incidents that did nothing to advance the plot.

"I'm game if you are," she said, adding, "I look at it as a challenge to cut and at the same time make the book better."

It was clear that all of this was simply great fun for her. Business would be done, of course, but above all, we would have a good time. For Olive Ann, that meant getting to know each other. I wanted to hear all about her and how her book had come to be—but Olive Ann said, in her gently insistent and irresistible Southern accent, "Tell me about *you*." Years later, as I sorted through her papers after her death, I found notes she had made during that very first phone call—about our publication plans for her book, yes, but also about where I was born, where I went to college, and how many people were in my family. Even then, in that first rush of excitement at becoming a published author, Olive Ann was as interested in the people she would be working with as she was in what would happen to her book. She was tremendously happy that *Cold Sassy Tree* was going to be published at last, but she was not at all impressed—and she knew there was a difference.

The next day, Olive Ann sat down and wrote a letter answering all my questions—and some I never would have presumed to ask. She described her childhood in Banks County and in Commerce. She wrote, "1906 is a whole generation before my time, of course, but it is interesting that even in 1934 they still could produce a few tottery old Confederate veterans in uniform to sit on the stage for our Southern Memorial Day exercises at school, and there was always a Confederate flag —though by 1934 they had a U.S. flag, too. The war was still bitterly discussed on front porches, and I never met a Yankee till I was in high school in Macon, Georgia. When I told my mother's mother I was in love with a Yankee (she was five years old when Sherman's soldiers ransacked her home), she said there must be a few good ones." I think this was her way of letting me know that, despite my own Yankee heritage, she would be willing to give me the benefit of the doubt, and would consider me a "good one" until she was proven wrong.

We had decided that I would suggest cuts and editorial changes on one copy of the manuscript while she made her own on another, and then we would put both versions together and decide what should go and what should stay. Despite her fear that the dialect might be overdone, I felt she had written it to perfection—that it was, in fact, one of the novel's greatest achievements. We worked to hone the story line while preserving as many as possible of what Olive Ann called "the non-essential stories and dialogue that make the characters alive and what they do believable, and that also help to color the time and place."

She was particularly fond of her "dying stories." Andy described *Cold Sassy Tree* as "a funny book about death"—a theme that had never occurred to Olive Ann. As she said, "There's just no way to avoid the fact of life called death in a book set in the year 1906. Folks died a lot back then." But it wasn't quite that simple. Like many Southerners, Olive Ann had a well-developed appreciation for good dying stories. "If Southerners get going on dying and funeral stories," she said once, "a party can last till 3:00 A.M." After Granny Blakeslee dies, at the beginning of the novel, Will Tweedy spends a morning alone in her house, missing her. He says, "One thing I got on to that morning, with the house full of Granny and empty of her at the same time, was the notion that she'd have hated dying so plain. Like doctors and undertakers, she really told good dying stories. There wasn't a grown person in Cold Sassy who couldn't pass away the time after Sunday dinner by recollecting who'd died of what when, but Granny was the only one I ever heard be interesting about it." Needless to say, Olive Ann could be pretty interesting on the subject herself. In the end, we arrived at a compromise—her favorite dying stories would remain intact, and the ones she could bear to sacrifice would go, in the interests of space and pacing. Typically, Olive Ann turned our deliberations into a good story; she loved to tell how her Yankee editor had never heard anyone tell dying stories and couldn't understand why there were so many of them in the book. That would always set people shaking their heads, asking "You mean, you had stories that she made you take out of the book? Well, what were they?" One way or another, Olive Ann got to tell her dying stories; after the book came out, she even wrote a *Sunday Magazine* article on the subject.

During the spring of 1984, we sent revisions back and forth and talked on the phone almost daily. Olive Ann loved every minute of it, but her happiness was tempered by the discovery that Andy now had lymphoma himself. She had suffered from side effects during chemotherapy, but she had never been terribly sick. Andy endured the treatments with his usual good grace and humor, but, in addition to losing every hair on his body, he was violently ill almost continuously for two or three days after every treatment. In February, he was hospitalized, and Olive Ann sat at his bedside, editing the manuscript. She sent the first batch back to me right on schedule. "I look back in amazement to all I've done besides be a compassionate wife in the five weeks since Andy went to the hospital," she wrote. "Sitting with him at the hospital, I went through the first 600 pages, coordinating your copy and mine. Counting the above, I have read through and revised it five times since the original I sent you, including the revisions I made as I ran it through the computer again twice. Much has been smoothed out that way, including the cut parts, and I had a grand time doing it, despite fatigue."

Before, Olive Ann had written for her own pleasure; now she had a book contract and deadlines to meet. The sense of urgency was new to her, and she rose to the challenge. Olive Ann met every deadline and she went through the entire manuscript yet again to respond to the copy editor's queries and suggestions. She also managed to take care of Andy, attend an aunt's funeral, and help her son pack his belongings for a move to Colorado. ("He left home this morning and I haven't even had time to cry yet," she wrote in one letter.) Little wonder that, nearly nine years after beginning to write, she took pride in the fact her job was done; *Cold Sassy Tree* was finally ready to go to the printer. "You have to understand that I am not a workhorse type," she wrote to me. "Besides writing and cooking and housework, I take naps and camping trips and go swimming and read. All such has taken a backseat lately to what in this household is called 'Mother's Book.' I have really enjoyed the push, though I still find it hard to believe I could do so much."

Olive Ann added a P.S. to this letter: "I am about to get so I don't shout when I talk to you all in New York. I could say I talk loud so you can hear me way up there. The truth is, I think, that I'm feeling more at home with you all and am getting over the shock and surprise of being publishable as a fiction writer." For her, one of the best things about having her book published was that it led to friendships with people she never would have known otherwise. She was delighted to find herself suddenly in the company of all these "Yankees," and she loved to hear the details of the Kerrs' lives in New Haven and mine in New York City—a name she always said with some awe, as if it were as far away and as foreign as the moon.

With the editing done and the manuscript out

of her hands, Olive Ann had only to sit back and wait for the second installment of her advance. "I look forward to getting the second check," she wrote to her agent in New York. "I'm going to have the sofa recovered and buy an electric skillet with mine. What are you going to do with yours?"

Now that her novel was about to be published, well-meaning friends warned her not to have high expectations. "Most first novels sell only about five thousand copies," several Atlanta authors told her, and she had no reason to expect that hers would be different. In a letter to Chester she wrote, "I find myself hoping that the book is a success for all of you even more than for myself. Fame and fortune have come to few writers that I know, so I have no illusions or delusions or frivolous expectations. Having had a marvelous time writing it, and never having thought it would get finished, much less published, I can't lose. But I want it to make enough money to justify the time and enthusiasm you all are bringing to the project."

Years ago, she and Andy had decided they would live off his salary, and that any money she made from writing would be for nice "extras." Now, she assured us that "making gobs of money or becoming famous myself isn't even in my day-dreams. This sounds naïve or insincere, since obviously if T&F makes a lot of money, I will make some too. The point I'm trying to make is that, having no craving for fame and fortune, I expect whatever I do in the way of promotion will just be fun, not a time of anxiety or overblown expectations."

Just because Olive Ann didn't have any illusions about publicity didn't mean that we weren't thinking about it. We had already decided to pique interest in *Cold Sassy Tree* by producing a thousand bound samples of the first sixteen chapters. In an accompanying letter, Chester Kerr wrote, "When a cheese seller has faith in his cheese, chances are he'll offer you a taste before you buy. We have faith in *Cold Sassy Tree*—in fact we're ebullient about it—and that's why we want to give you a taste of it now. We're sure these pages will whet your appetite for more." He was right. As soon as these "teasers" were distributed at the American Booksellers convention that May, word began to travel among booksellers that Olive Ann Burns was a first novelist to watch. Early readers of the manuscript were responding with glowing letters and phone calls. Olive Ann claimed that she wasn't "looking any farther ahead than the next project, which will be the galley proofs and getting the house cleaned up," but it was becoming clear that we would be able to drum up attention for our first-time novelist. Olive Ann was more than willing to help, but she was also wondering what to expect. In a letter to the Ticknor & Fields publicist, Gwen Reiss, she wrote, "Since I'm such a neophyte in this business and have no idea what to expect next fall, could you tell me when the publicity will start? . . . I assume there will be a lot of autographings in and around Atlanta, and around Georgia, but do you think I'll have to go farther than that? And does that usually slack off, say, in a month, or had I better get my Christmas presents bought before then?"

"Incidentally," she added, "I will be sixty in July, and if there's any reason to use that fact, I certainly don't mind. I'd rather be sixty than dead, and also I realize I couldn't have written *Cold Sassy Tree* when I was thirty. I didn't know enough about life. Anyhow, I've only just begun to realize I'm middle-aged . . . I don't really think I'm old enough for my age to help promote the book. If I were a hundred, that would be something you could make hay out of."

As far as we knew then, even if *Cold Sassy Tree* did enjoy modest success, Olive Ann wouldn't have to worry about finding time to do her Christmas shopping. Despite a generous handful of pre-publication comments, we figured that *Cold Sassy Tree,* like any first novel, would need every push we could give it. But with publication still several months away, there was not much more to be done, so at the end of June, Olive Ann and Andy set off for two weeks in England, for a reunion of Andy's World War II military unit—a luxury paid for by her advance.

Andy had grown accustomed to his chemotherapy treatments, eventually scheduling them for late on Thursday afternoons so that he could be sick Friday and all weekend, and still be able to go to work on Monday morning. But the drugs had taken a toll. Andy Sparks was the embodiment of an old-time gentleman journalist, with his lively blue eyes beneath scraggly, bushy eyebrows. He wore snappy ties, hats that would have looked silly on anyone else, and a mustache that only emphasized the width of his smile. He had boundless energy and enthusiasm, and was one of those rare men who can work all their lives in one job and yet never assume the demeanor—the tired posture, the tension, the lines of worry or resignation—of a working man. He loved his life and he loved his work, and he radiated happiness. Whether he was on his way to the office downtown or to his beloved garden in the backyard, he walked with a bounce in his step and a look of anticipation on his face, like a kid stepping into Saturday morning.

Now, for the first time, he looked his age. And without those eyebrows or the mustache, not to mention the hair on his head, he didn't look like Andy. In a letter to John just before they left for England, Olive Ann wrote, "A strange thing has happened about Dad. About me, really. Until recently I have felt I had a new husband from the skin out—he looked so different. I'd find myself just sitting staring at him, trying to get used to it. Because he has gained weight, the lines in his face have filled out and he really does look good, but he doesn't look like Andy. Now I guess I've become used to the difference, because I'm really enjoying the new him all of a sudden. I can't remember how he looked before!"

Olive Ann had nursed Andy through the worst

of it, telling him that she wished they could just trade places; she had learned to be such a good cancer patient, she felt, that it would be easier on her than it was for him. "No," he told her, "you had your turn; now it's mine." Olive Ann found that it was harder for her to deal with Andy's illness than her own. "I could face the possibility of dying myself," she said, "but I didn't want to live without him." Throughout the spring, Andy kept assuring her that the book was more important than his throwing up; that's what they would focus on. "It's something to remember," Olive Ann wrote to John. "If you ever have a prolonged problem, do something that gives you something else to think about—like have your wife publish a book, or the two of you go off to England for a second honeymoon."

By the time they returned, the prepublication excitement had prompted Chester to move the publication date up from November to October. Gwen Reiss was busy scheduling autographings and interviews, and the Book-of-the-Month Club had named *Cold Sassy Tree* a featured alternate for October. Gwen wrote to Olive Ann and asked how she felt about public speaking, for it was becoming apparent that *Cold Sassy Tree* was generating more attention than a typical first novel. "I found out long ago that talking to a thousand or two hundred or ten is all the same," Olive Ann replied. "I mean it doesn't scare me, and if it's a small group I enjoy the ones who are there instead of lamenting that it isn't a crowd."

She did want us to know, however, that she was not a "fancy speaker." "I don't declaim," she wrote, explaining that her talks were "really kind of like *Cold Sassy Tree*—funny, with stories and throwaway comments, but carrying significant and, I hope, inspiring messages. I don't mean I try to be inspiring, but when I say things that are heartfelt, things that other people are surely dealing with, too, they seem to respond. Also, I don't try to act brilliant or as if I take myself to be the world's greatest gift to audiences. If I did, I'd feel like a fool and fall on my face. As it is, they take me for one of them and it seems to be effective."

Characteristically, she wanted to make sure that Ticknor & Fields didn't incur any extra expense on her account. Olive Ann prided herself on never spending a penny she didn't have, and she certainly didn't expect her publisher to spend any more than necessary on accommodations. "My ego needs are small," she assured us. "Being Andy's wife and a fulfilled person are enough, and all this is just icing on the cake. I can be just as happy about talking to the little literary club in Cornelia, Georgia, as to more important groups. And I don't need any VIP treatment. Do whatever you need to for T&F's image, but limos and ultra hotels are unimportant to me. I'm game for anything that will make the promotion budget stretch. To me, ordinary taxis will be a luxury because driving tires me if I've never been there before and have to feel my way, and any place to sleep will be fine if it's not on a busy highway beside an uphill curve where trucks scream into lower gear all night long."

The only thing she insisted on was some time to lie down in the middle of a busy day, and a taxi instead of the services of "a little old-lady driver who drives scatterbrain or tailgates and with whom I must carry on a conversation. I like such conversation," she said, "but I would arrive out of breath at my destination."

She meant what she said: Olive Ann loved to talk and she could somehow ask questions and tell a funny story at the same time. She once told me that her talking had caused one of the few arguments she and Andy had, when, early in their marriage, he suggested on the way to a party that she try to keep her mouth shut that night. If she could do it, he told her, she might hear something interesting. Much as Olive Ann talked, I never once heard her say anything that wasn't worth listening to. It was impossible for her to be boring. And her letters were almost as wonderful as Olive Ann in person—long and leisurely, funny and intimate, and thoroughly entertaining. When she returned her author questionnaire with a ten-page single-spaced essay about her intentions while writing Cold Sassy Tree, everyone in the office gathered round to read it. "I think what I've written is more than you want to know about anybody," she apologized, "and certainly more than you need to know for publicity purposes. But I decided to send it on as is. At least you'll have some idea of what you're dealing with."

244

Her essay became a publishing story in itself. "I don't know if it will help sales to say *Cold Sassy Tree* isn't a dirty book," Olive Ann wrote, "but I don't think I'm the only person who is tired of sordid stories about unsavory people. I'm tired of books and movies full of paper-doll characters you don't care about, who have no self-respect and no respect for anybody or any institution. I hope this book is compelling and realistically sensual; I have great respect for human sexuality. But I'm tired of authors so lacking in sensitivity that they wallow in vulgarity and prostitute sex —making exhibitionists out of the characters and peeping Toms out of the readers. And I don't want to sound preachy or Victorian, but I'm tired of amorality in fiction and real life. Immorality is a fascinating human dilemma that creates suspense for the readers and tension for the characters, but where is the tension in an amoral situation? When people have no personal code, nothing is threatening and nothing is meaningful."

Olive Ann's words were far more captivating than any sales line we might produce. Here, Chester realized, was the perfect way to introduce Olive Ann Burns to everyone else in the company; to let them know, as she put it, "what they were dealing with." He sent copies of this letter to all of the Houghton Mifflin sales reps, and they, in turn, started showing it to booksellers they knew. Everyone was charmed and intrigued. B. Dalton Company, a large bookselling chain, reprinted six pages of the questionnaire in their merchandising newsletter. By early September, the *New York Times* and the *Washington Post* had both caught wind of the story and responded with features about Olive Ann and *Cold Sassy Tree*—several weeks before books were in the stores. "It remains to be seen whether the book has any merits," Jonathan Yardley wrote in the *Post*, "but there can be no doubt that its author does."

On September 27, the first copies of *Cold Sassy Tree* came off the press. Already there had been a cover story in the *Sunday Magazine* (now renamed the *Atlanta Weekly*) and a special boxed review in *Publishers Weekly*, proclaiming Will Tweedy "one of the most entertaining narrators since Huck Finn." The advance reviewers were unanimous in their praise, and early readers of *Cold Sassy Tree* concurred. Ferrol Sams, author of Run with the Horseman, said simply, "Olive Ann Burns has laid claim to all the literary territory between Tobacco Road and *Gone With the Wind.*" The Georgia governor, Joe Frank Harris, announced that October 18, publication date, would be Cold Sassy Tree Day in Georgia. When Olive Ann received the first copies of her book, she set them all up on top of the hunt board and the mantelpiece in her living room so that Andy would see them as soon as he walked through the front door. She was delighted that the colors on the book jacket perfectly matched the autumn hues of her upholstery. "Sometimes I feel like Cinderella," Olive Ann wrote to a friend, "scared I'll forget to leave the ball before my coach turns back into a pumpkin. But I'm about to believe I will at least get to the ball."

The ball was a party at the Atlanta Historical Society, attended by over 550 people, including about twenty-five of Olive Ann and Andy's relatives; the former first lady Rosalynn Carter and the governor's wife, Elizabeth Harris; Joan and Chester Kerr and four of us staff members from Ticknor & Fields; and an assortment of local writers, booksellers, and friends. *Cold Sassy Tree* was already a hit—the first printing of twenty-two thousand copies was nearly gone and we had gone back to press for twenty thousand more the day before—and the party was really a celebration of Olive Ann and her success.

When Chester Kerr stood to introduce his "star" author, she admitted that she had been more than a little intimidated by him when they first met, at Anne Edwards's party. Chester took the ribbing in stride, delighted that in a year's time Olive Ann had gone from thinking of him as "Your Eminence" to being able to joke with him in front of a crowd.

Although he had retired from Ticknor & Fields five months earlier, Chester was clearly the host of Olive Ann's publication party in Atlanta—in the very room in which they had first been introduced. The Kerrs and Olive Ann remained good friends and correspondents, and Olive Ann never forgot that it was they who had given her the confidence she needed to finish her manuscript. "If the Kerrs hadn't encouraged me," she told one interviewer, "I might have gone on like Miss Santmyer did with . . . *And Ladies of the Club.*" Olive Ann always recalled the day that she opened that very first enthusiastic letter from Joan Kerr as one of the high points of her life. "My joy at receiving that letter would rate at least twelve on a scale of one to ten," she said.

Just the year before, Olive Ann Burns had stood in this room trying to describe her sprawling, unfinished manuscript to a stranger; now she was the guest of honor at Atlanta's literary event of the season. She had a wonderful time. For a few hours Olive Ann seemed to forget that writing a 600-page novel had actually been hard work; she was having so much fun entertaining her friends and family. "I think everyone should write a book," she said happily.

Later that evening, all of us from Ticknor & Fields sat around Olive Ann and Andy's living room, getting acquainted in person at last. Norma and Charlie Duncan came over from next door, and we had another party, reliving the first one. I don't remember all that we talked about, but I do remember that Olive Ann and Andy and Norma began to tell dying stories, just so we Yankees could see that Southerners really do entertain one another with accounts of dramatic deaths and good funerals. Later Olive Ann told me that she and Andy had lain awake most of the night. She was almost as happy and excited as she had been on her wedding night, she said, knowing that she was surrounded by people who loved her as she embarked on a new life, not as a bride this time, but as a published author.

She was about to discover just what that meant. The next morning, the first autographing party for *Cold Sassy Tree* was held at one of Rich's department stores. Olive Ann had asked Norma to come, because she had been warned that sometimes no one shows up at book signings. When Olive Ann and I arrived a half hour early, people were already lined up, holding their books. Most of them had two copies, and one woman had a Rich's shopping bag full of books: she was going to give *Cold Sassy Tree* to everyone on her Christmas list. Olive Ann talked and signed, signed and talked, until we were out of books and time. It was only the beginning. Rich's had arranged for the first autographings to be held at their stores, and they had placed an initial order for twenty-five hundred books. According to the former bookstore manager, Faith Brunson, "It should have been five thousand."

Faith Brunson had been with Rich's, Atlanta's largest department store, since 1945 and had a reputation as one of the shrewdest buyers in the industry. As soon as she read a bound galley of *Cold Sassy Tree,* she knew we would have a best seller on our hands. She requested galleys for every bookstore clerk and made the book required reading. "After that," she recalled, "it was a snap." Over the years, Faith had built a formidable book department on her ability to get people excited, and she went all out talking up *Cold Sassy Tree* to her employees and customers. In the first few days after publication, Olive Ann autographed books at each Rich's store, and there was a crowd every time. People came because they knew Olive Ann—from church, from her days at the magazine, even from grade school or high school or college. They came because they loved the book and wanted to meet the woman who had written it, or because they had heard about *Cold Sassy Tree* and wanted to find out what all the fuss was about. All over Atlanta, bookstores sold out their initial orders, and many people showed up at autographings with books that they had stayed up all night reading. Most came with their own stories to tell—about growing up in small towns and how things really hadn't changed, or about parents or grandparents who were just like the folk in Cold Sassy, Georgia.

The stories Olive Ann enjoyed most were the ones about relatives who, like Grandpa Blakeslee, had married scandalously soon after a spouse's death. She wrote to us about meeting a young woman who said, "My parents were Grandpa and Miss Love. I'm the product of the union. They married six weeks after his first wife died." Another woman said that her father was a fifty-five-year-old bachelor when he married her twenty-four-year-old mother. Her family protested that she would spend her life taking care of a sick old man. "The mother died at forty-eight," Olive Ann reported. "He was healthy and died two years later at eighty-one." Olive Ann had something to say to everyone; she asked questions and cracked jokes and made sure that the people who had come out to meet her were all having as good a time as she was.

Within a week of publication, Olive Ann had talked herself hoarse. Exhausted and unaccustomed to such a relentless schedule, she landed in bed with a racking cough. But, true to form, she took a week off, marshaled her resources, and declared at the end of October, "I'm coming back to life."

In the months that followed, she attended parties and autographings almost every day. Norma remembers how wonderful it was to look out the window and see her neighbor all dressed up and heading off to another event in her honor, after so many years of sickness and confinement. Several weeks after publication, Olive Ann wrote, "I think I'm going to like being an author. I'm now looking at my schedule as a job instead of as an interruption of writing or as an intrusion on this do-my-own-thing life I've had." For her, the best part was not the pile of glowing reviews, which continued to grow, or her sudden fame and popularity; it was meeting new people every day. The most interesting ones found their way into her letters—more stories and characters for her collection. "Saturday in Fayetteville," she wrote, "I met a ninety-one-year-old lady who grew up in Commerce and worked for my great-grandfather when the store was Power and Williford. She was a milliner! Trained by Miss Love herself—by a milliner who came to the store from a hat company in Baltimore." She was excited about attending a homecoming reception in Commerce, which was suddenly famous itself as the model for Cold Sassy. "I am to give a talk, eat homemade cookies, and sign books—all from 7 to 9 P.M.," she wrote, "and everybody plans to come."

Cold Sassy Tree was a phenomenon in the South. The reviewer for the *Atlanta Journal and Constitution* admitted, "About a quarter of the way through Olive Ann Burns's *Cold Sassy Tree*, I stopped taking notes. But I continued reading, and now, several hours after finishing the book, I am still searching—sweating, if not blood, at least the last good drops of several pots of black coffee—for the words to do it justice. This is the best I can do: *Cold Sassy Tree* is simply great. And Atlanta's Olive Ann Burns, who suddenly has bloomed into a novelist at age sixty, is as good a writer about the South as you're going to read for a long, long time."

Still, Olive Ann and Andy were amazed to see the book in the number one spot on the Atlanta Journal's best-seller list week after week. By Christmas, it was popping up on best-seller lists across the country. "Not since Flannery O'Connor has the state of Georgia produced a storyteller to compare with Olive Ann Burns," wrote one reviewer. "Not since Eudora Welty and Alice Walker has the whole country spawned an author with so flawless an ear." The *Boston Globe* called *Cold Sassy Tree* "no less than brilliant," and the *Wash-*

ington Post described Will Tweedy as a "rare literary character who is so perfect that his existence can be credited only to magic." Readers agreed. At the end of the year Ticknor & Fields had fifty thousand copies of *Cold Sassy Tree* in print, and we were waiting for the fourth printing to arrive. Paperback rights were about to be auctioned off, and inquiries were coming in from foreign publishers and the film industry. Olive Ann had appearances booked throughout the spring and into the summer, and the mailman was delivering her fan mail in bags.

In January, in a letter to Chester and Joan, she wrote, "Somebody quoted Will Campbell, the folk hero of the civil rights movement, as saying you don't need to worry about success. 'Fame don't mean much,' he said, 'and it don't last long.' I'm so naïve about books that I don't even know what success really means. Five thousand books would have been success to me. Fifty thousand is hard to believe." She still expected that the dust would settle before long, and that she would be able to resume some semblance of normal life. "I began the winter in bookstores," she said, "and I hope to end it working on the next book."

The next month, Andy retired from the editorship of the *Atlanta Weekly*, after thirty-nine years, and celebrated his final chemotherapy treatment. "Around here," Olive Ann wrote, "that is even bigger news than paperback rights." There was still evidence of lymphoma in his bone marrow, however. "We feel disappointed that he isn't well," she wrote, "but we're delighted that he'll have a chance to recuperate from the treatment a while before diving back in." Andy embarked on retirement with as much zest as he had brought to his work on the magazine. In his first three weeks at home, he wrote three articles and conducted an interview in South Carolina, and Olive Ann joked that she was beginning to think he wouldn't get the kitchen painted after all. Andy always claimed he was thankful that he didn't want to write a book —he knew better than anyone how hard Olive Ann had worked on hers. But he was a first-rate writer himself and, in addition to the articles he continued to do for the magazine, he composed long, delightful letters to friends scattered all over the country. He carried on a passionate gardening correspondence with the writer Mary Hood, and he stayed in touch with members of his Eighth Air Force unit from World War II. He was enormously proud of Olive Ann and didn't mind it a bit when people referred to him as "the husband of Olive Ann Burns," or even as "Mr. Burns." In February he wrote to a friend, "Olive Ann told her publisher that she was going to start her second book in January and so far she hasn't written a word. She is running here and there to autographings and speechmakings, and generally having fun."

"Running" was just the word for it, too. Between the middle of March and the first of June, Olive Ann attended three library receptions in her honor, over half a dozen autographings, and one concert. She addressed four writers' clubs, students at five schools, and the Sunday school class of over a hundred members at her church. She preached one Methodist sermon, in Thomasville, Georgia, and she did a TV interview in Macon. She was the featured speaker at one luncheon and two dinners, did two days of publicity in Tallahassee, Florida, taught a three-day course in novel writing at the Hambidge Center, signed books and performed at a three-day literary symposium at the University of Georgia in Athens, and spent a week teaching writing on St. Simon Island. She and Andy also found time to fly to Colorado to spend a week visiting John. In April she flew to Virginia to give a dinner speech for a library fund raiser. "Imagine anyone that far away thinking I can draw a crowd," she marveled. "But they say the book has caused a stir there. Isn't that something?" There was one day on which she gave both breakfast and dinner speeches, at two different locations. "Some of those weeks are really overloaded," she conceded, "but I think I will enjoy them." Still, she was beginning to realize that she could easily spend the rest of her life on the road promoting *Cold Sassy Tree*. "Anybody else who calls," she said, "I'm saying call me back next year, or in two or three years. At my age it is important to get on with the next book if I intend to write it."

One of Olive Ann's favorite opening lines in her talks was "I now know the difference between a writer and an author. Writers write, and authors speak." She told everyone that she didn't intend to be an author much longer. But even with her good intentions, it was hard to say no and return to the lonely life of a novelist. Writing *Cold Sassy Tree* had been tremendously fulfilling; it had given her a new identity. "Writing the book was like getting born again as ME instead of remaining forever a wife and mother," she wrote. "I like wifery and motherhood, but it's like being young again to create something of one's own—young again, only better." She was having a grand time taking advantage of this second youth. In the course of autographing books all over the state of Georgia, she claimed, she had seen every boyfriend she'd ever had—"all those that hadn't died." Some of them came accompanied by wives, who didn't believe that their husbands had actually dated the author of *Cold Sassy Tree*. She even signed a book for a man who told her, "Well, I'm glad you didn't marry me. My last name is Olive." Olive Ann laughed and said she was too old for him anyway.

If Olive Ann had had to say what pleased her most about the success of *Cold Sassy Tree,* the fact that her book was read by schoolchildren would surely have been at the top of her list. Her favorite audiences were "the eager ones among high school and college students," because she could encourage them to pursue their own writing. She was living proof that anyone with the determination to stick with it could write a novel. Now that she had published a book herself, she was delighted to share what she had learned, lessons gleaned not from any writing workshops, but learned during forty years of journalism and nearly a decade at her own desk, as she figured out for herself how to write a novel.

"Use words that make pictures," she would tell every group of schoolchildren. "If you say the word *animal,* you can't see it. You don't know what it looks like. If you say *horse,* you can see it very well. If you say somebody is riding the horse, you don't know who. If you say the word *boy,* it makes a picture."

Even before *Cold Sassy Tree* was published, Andy's sister Jane, a high school English teacher in College Park, Georgia, had invited Olive Ann to visit her classroom. Not only did Olive Ann encourage Jane's students to write; she urged them to seek out stories from their families just as she had done in her family history. "Stories bring the dead back to life," she told them. "With only a name and dates, all you can see is a tombstone. Yet if all you find out is that Uncle Quillian was short and his wife tall, you can see them."

Inspired by Olive Ann's visits to their classroom, the students embarked on an oral history project, honoring their black heritage by interviewing relatives and members of their community, who described a vanishing way of life. The annual magazine that grew out of these efforts was a source of great pride to Olive Ann—she knew that, in a small way, she had made a difference in these students' lives. *Cold Sassy Tree* provided her with countless such opportunities to reach out to children, and she seized them all. She was just as happy talking with a group of sixth-graders as she was giving a dinner speech or being interviewed. She cherished the letters she received from schoolchildren and made a point of answering each one personally. When the American Library Association and the New York Public Library put *Cold Sassy Tree* on its list of books recommended for teenagers, Olive Ann was unabashedly thrilled. "The New York list had my name right there between Emily Brontë and Willa Cather," she exclaimed. "Think of that!"

Reading through the letters Olive Ann wrote during 1985, I'm struck by how happy she was. In the midst of all the publicity she once said, "It's as if everybody I know is dancing with me." She meant it when she said that fame was never important to her, and never once did she write to inquire about sales figures or advertising plans. Instead, she wrote to tell us about her adventures with *Cold Sassy Tree*. She was the first to admit that she loved being in front of an audience, and she found herself in steady demand. "I said no to invitations three times today," she announced in one letter, "but last week I said yes to PREACH at a morning service in a Methodist church. I've always wanted to write a book entitled *Flattery Will Get You Somewhere*. It got me to say yes to this." The same day, her aunt called to say that a professional speaker had come to her church to review the book. "Maybe I can cut out all my going and just let other people talk about it," she joked. But in the next sentence she said, "I never knew there were so many literary clubs. It's ego-stroking to attend one—all those excited women coming in with my book under an arm."

When a woman hurried up to her at a writer's conference and exclaimed, "You've changed my life!" Olive Ann admitted, "Oh, I felt so important. I thought one of Grandpa's sermons in the book did it." But no, that wasn't it. The woman continued, "I read that interview with you in the paper where you said you wear all your underwear inside out. I tried it, and sure enough, it is more comfortable to have the inside outside 'cause it's smoother." "That's what I said," Olive Ann conceded. "I didn't think about anybody remembering that, but she did."

Someone told Olive Ann that "the real pros" accept only one speaking engagement a month after their book promotion tours are over. "Unfortunately," she admitted, "I keep accepting invitations because they are so attractive—like going to Mercer for two days, and to the University of Georgia where I can see, hear, and touch Mr. Erskine Caldwell, not to mention James Dickey. . . . And I do indeed love to talk to the eager ones among high school and college students, and to old folks, as at Cornelia, Georgia, last week— lots of them were cousins I'd never met. I got a teacher's certificate in college as well as the degree in journalism, and this has been my first chance to indulge. Also, it is exhilarating to get out of my basement hole and back in the world again.

I was such a hermit for so long that at first I felt resentful of the calendar ordering me to be here today and there tomorrow instead of at home doing whatever I pleased. But I do look forward now to almost every place I speak. I am a ham."

The book continued to sell steadily, and the invitations showed no sign of abating, but we all agreed that the best thing Olive Ann could do for her fans now was begin on novel number two. She decided that June would be her cut-off point for "speaking wholesale," as she called it. "It has been and still is a very happy experience," Olive Ann wrote to a friend, "and I have had a grand time speaking. (I really always wanted to be a stand-up comedienne or an actress, and I really can make an audience laugh. They connect with me. What fun!) But I've stopped it all for the time being, and I am emotionally and physically ready just to be me, housewife and writer. I have no itch for any more attention. I am satiated with it. I know that I'll be a one-shot writer if I don't say no to most invitations next year, and I'm already finding it hard; libraries and schools are gearing up for fall and winter and the invitations keep coming, and saying no to them is a little like a girl having to stop kissing a boy she's crazy about. Maybe my pleasure in talking (I don't really give speeches) is a little like Marjorie Kinnan Rawlings' and Betty Smith's thirst for drink, but I don't think for the same reasons. Also I know that I really enjoy writing more, so once I get the book going I'll be more tempted to be right here in front of a computer instead of in front of an audience."

Certainly Olive Ann hoped that would be true. "I plan to start the new novel the last week of June," she wrote to me, "when all my commitments will be done with. I have now run the gamut of life as a new author—everything except starting to write again." She got home from a week of teaching on June 22, and on June 23 she sat down in her basement room and began to write. The next morning, however, she couldn't go on. Instead, she sent me a letter. "I've learned that when I feel blocked," she said, "it's always because what I've done is not going to work, and my subconscious knows it." She spent a week rereading her family history, thinking, and planning; she read *Cold Sassy Tree* cover to cover (and admitted that she was surprised by how good it was); she turned over ideas for the first chapter, but she couldn't seem to go back to it. She had begun to write *Cold Sassy Tree* out of desperation, knowing that she was facing, as she put it, "nausea, pain, and death —the great uncertainty." But in the summer of 1985, she had no such crisis to back her against the wall. Indeed, life was offering all sorts of new pleasures and adventures. In addition to the invitations to speak and travel, she and Andy were embarking on a project together. They had decided to build a small vacation cabin in the mountains about two hours north of Atlanta.

"Mostly," Olive Ann wrote to a friend, "it will be a writing place. I'm not so famous that I need an unlisted number or that anybody bothers me here at home (fan mail is no bother!), but the house and all I need to do here besides write are always pulling me this way and that." The cabin would be a quiet retreat for work. Meanwhile, planning and building and furnishing it together would be more fun than sitting alone in the basement, facing a computer screen. For the first time in her life, Olive Ann felt that she could relax about money—which is not to say that sixty years of thriftiness could be abandoned overnight. She often said that, for her, being rich meant being able to throw away a soup that didn't work; usually, if a pot of soup didn't turn out well, she kept adding things, trying to make it better. John would always complain, "Mom, you're not making it better; you're just making it BIGGER." Being rich, she went on, "is buying fish and fruit without feeling guilty, buying books and nice gifts for friends without worrying about the cost, buying maid help." After *Cold Sassy Tree* was published, Olive Ann and Andy began to allow themselves all these things, but they still seemed like indulgences.

Once, writing had been Olive Ann's indulgence; now the success of *Cold Sassy Tree* had brought her unexpected fame and, at the same time, the pressure to produce another novel. She was no longer a cancer patient with a hobby; she was a best-selling author with an audience. In some ways, the latter role was more of a challenge.

Olive Ann knew the story she wanted to tell in *Time, Dirt, and Money,* but she kept changing her mind about how best to tell it. She had felt confident writing *Cold Sassy Tree* from Will's point of view as a fourteen-year-old; she had her father's stories, told in his own words, to inspire her. This time, though, she wanted to write in a different voice—that of Sanna Klein, Will's wife. "I have already figured out everything that will happen to each character in the new book," she assured me, "and I KNOW the characters—not only those left over from *Cold Sassy Tree,* like Miss Love and Will and his family, but also the new ones."

She hoped that a month at the Hambidge Center, free of all other temptations, would enable her to get "a big glump of writing done." In fact, the weeks she spent there were difficult ones, as she grappled not only with the first chapter of her novel, but with a return to the discipline and isolation of writing. She was surprised by her own lack of confidence. "I had a good writing day today," she reported to Andy and Becky two days after arriving. "Redid the first chapter and I now believe I can still write (more than yesterday). I remember now that I do my best writing off the top of my head and *then* developing it further later." But before she sent the letter, she added a P.S.: "It was a faulty remembrance. I tried it today and got bored to death." She tried writing in Sanna's voice, and stopped after five pages. She turned on the radio and danced to rock music; she ate meals with friends, attended a bluegrass concert, and wrote more letters home. After two weeks, she went home herself, sick with a fever and feeling that she had made little real progress. She now had four different first chapters and didn't like any of them.

Though she was not feeling well, Olive Ann made a trip to New York on September 9, 1985, to speak at the annual dinner of the Bookbinders Guild. She had accepted this invitation because it meant that she and Andy could have a holiday in the city, and they had been looking forward to it for months, planning trips to museums, meetings with Olive Ann's agent and her paperback publisher, and visits with old friends. When Gwen Reiss and I arrived at their hotel to take them out to dinner on the first night, Olive Ann was running a temperature and hadn't been able to eat for several days. Nevertheless, she was determined to enjoy herself—and she did. I think she was as surprised as the rest of us when she handily put away two good-sized lamb chops at the Yale Club that night, and her speech the next evening was a smashing success. She stood before a crowd of well-fed businessmen, most of whom had never read her book, and won their hearts. "The Yankees laughed as hard as they do in the South," she wrote afterward. But she spent most of the rest of her time in New York in bed. Back home, she signed books and gave speeches. But every day that she spent before an audience was a day that she was not working on her novel. At the end of September she returned to the Hambidge Center, hoping that this time inspiration would strike.

All of the other residents had left by the time

she arrived, and the retreat was about to close for the winter. This time Olive Ann really was alone; she cooked her own meals in her tiny cabin. "It is a beautiful time here," she wrote, "fall nip in the air, leaves beginning to turn." She suspected that she had had so much trouble those first two weeks because she was sick and getting sicker without being aware of it. Now she felt strong, but still not sure of her direction. "I could really get all my correspondence done now," she wrote to a friend. "It is so easy and gratifying, and starting the book is so hard." Three days later, she wrote to me, "I seriously sat myself down the first day back here and asked myself, 'Do you really want to write a novel? You've done that.' I asked myself if it wouldn't be fun just to take a year off from have-to's and just cook good food and go to Italy with Andy and read lots of books, and get my kicks with a speech here and there."

She was still pondering that question when a letter arrived from Mary Hood, the Georgia writer who had become a friend. Mary knew that Olive Ann was still rewriting Chapter 5, and she enclosed a copy of an essay by Robert Pope entitled "Beginnings," about authors' efforts to write first lines. "Beginnings may be entrances to a time and place, a culture and a faith, a moment, an eternity," Pope wrote. "The struggle to find first words creates great anticipation, if not great anxiety, in the writer searching for the voice in which to speak, for each writer hopes to reach that voice inside himself which is immortal." It was the right thing at the right time. "How can I ever thank you?" Olive Ann wrote back. "I was actually about to give up and come home. I haven't liked anything I've tried. It wasn't alive. And of all the things you might have copied from writing philosophers, you chose the one that made me see what was wrong . . . I realized suddenly that I was using the wrong voice to tell the story."

Sanna Klein may be the main character, Olive Ann realized, but that didn't necessarily mean that Sanna should narrate the story. "Sanna is modeled after my mother," she wrote in her letter to Mary, "who was beautiful, and good, shy, often depressed, always trying so hard, always doing *the right thing,* a brilliant woman, under-used intellectually, a chronic worrier; I loved her very much and thought of her as my best friend—we had many interests in common, I valued her thinking, she was intellectually stimulating. But from the time I was a teenager it exhausted me to be with her, listening to her and trying to pull her up from depression, anxiety, endless rumination about all her problems from childhood to now. Because I was her therapist, her telling me so many details of her life [gave] me a sense, and understanding, of what she was like and why. She was an amazing person, and her family was unbelievable, and I couldn't have made up such a person without knowing her. Sanna will be different in ways, but I think I was afraid of dragging the reader down as I was often drug down."

Reading Pope's essay had forced Olive Ann to

confront the fact that she simply didn't want to assume her mother's voice, as she had her father's. "To write as Sanna would be to BE her for two or three years," she wrote, "and felt exhausted by the prospect. And I realized I wanted to keep on writing as Will Tweedy. My father had so little understanding of my mother, and she knew him inside out, but he had a zest for life and challenges and change that made him very appealing. Without Grandpa Blakeslee to grab the book and run away with it, Will and Sanna will have a chance to have their own troubles and triumphs—and there is no doubt that the way Sanna is is a challenge to him."

For the first time, Olive Ann knew in her heart not only that she wanted to write another book, but that she could do it in her own way and feel good about it. Having decided that she would be Will Tweedy again after all, she sat down at her typewriter and "wrote some first words, and words following words—so free and spontaneous and alive that I felt resurrected." At last she was having fun again. "I had almost forgotten that writing can feel wonderful," she wrote to Mary. "I don't think I'll worry any more about whether it gets published than I did about *Cold Sassy*. I've always been a perfectionist about writing—wanting to make it my best and all that—but I haven't really been ambitious. Ambition can be a spur, but if it uses up energy it can be a cruel taskmaster." It wasn't ambition that Olive Ann discovered at Hambidge; it was a renewed confidence. Even though she didn't come home with a tall stack of manuscript pages, she had done something just as important: she had decided that she would write another book because she *wanted* to, not because the world expected it of her.

It would be a mistake to assume that *Time, Dirt, and Money* would have been strictly a biographical novel, for while her parents' marriage was certainly to be at its heart, from the very beginning Olive Ann was taking liberties with their story in the name of fiction. Real life was her jumping-off point, it was even the basis for her plot, but it would not have been the whole story. She had learned how to weave fact and fiction together while writing *Cold Sassy Tree*. Although she began that book thinking Will would be her father, she quickly discovered that he needed a life of his own. "After three pages," she said, "I realized I couldn't keep trying to recreate my father because then I couldn't let Will become himself—a person, not a reminiscence." In the same way, Sanna Klein is both Olive Ann's mother and her own creation, and she is all the more compelling for that.

Olive Ann said that her parents' marriage was a great love story. She thought of *Time, Dirt, and Money* as a love story, too. The title came from a psychiatrist friend, who had once told her that the three things worriers worry about most are time, dirt, and money. "What about sex?" Olive Ann asked. No, her friend assured her, sex wasn't in the top three. The phrase captured Olive Ann's imagination, and she knew that she could create a character whose worries would threaten to deprive her of any real happiness. Will and Sanna would meet, be attracted to each other, and marry. But they would not be *in* love. True love would come to them years later, once they had learned to accept each other just as they were, for better or worse, and for all time. When we leave Will and Sanna at the end of Chapter 55 their life together is just beginning. However, the family history does shed some light on the challenges they were to face, and it provides a glimpse of their final reconciliation. It is also a fascinating document in its own right; it reveals how Olive Ann drew on real life to write her fiction. Here, for example, are Ruby Burns's memories of meeting her future husband, from which Olive Ann created Chapter 1 of *Time, Dirt, and Money:*

I met Arnold at a watermelon cutting in the park. The school board gave the party for the teachers, and a lot of young men came because there were a lot of new teachers. Arnold was working in Athens and brought several friends with him from the college. There were quite a lot of attractive young men there that day. I was impressed with Arnold Burns, but not overly. I didn't think he was exactly handsome, he was so skinny. He just weighed 135. But I knew I liked him. The next Sunday he asked me for a date and I had a date with him every Sunday from then till summer, when he went to the

Army. He had a motorcycle when I first met him, but he always used his father's car for dates and I never remember having a date with him by myself. He always filled up the car. He wasn't too good at talking in those days—I mean saying sweet things or handing out a line. Arnold was good at DOING. I mean he showed me how he felt, by wanting to be with me.

That's Will Tweedy, all right, but only Olive Ann could bring him to life. Her notes for the novel make it clear that Ruby Burns's struggles were to provide some of the book's major themes—namely, Sanna's lifelong search for a sense of belonging, and her need for constant reassurance that she came first in her husband's heart.

Ruby Burns told Olive Ann that she didn't let Arnold kiss her until the day she told him she would marry him. "She always said she thought part of what kept Arnold after her was being hard to get," Olive Ann wrote in the family history. "He was so popular and attractive that girls had always fallen for him and he wasn't used to anybody as feisty and independent as she was."

If Ruby was feisty and independent, it was because she had been forced to be. Her life had been shaped by her father's early death and by her mother's rejection of her. "Ruby's father got sick when she was eight," Olive Ann wrote, "and after that nothing was ever right again . . . From then on she always expected the worst to happen, not the best." Sanna's childhood was based on Ruby's as Olive Ann had recorded it. "When Ruby was ten," she wrote in the family history, "Sister Ollie and Brother Ed invited her to stay with them in Greensboro so she could go to a better school. This made a good education possible for her, yet it was the beginning of an isolation complex from which she still suffered as an adult. To belong somewhere became an obsession. Her education cost her a mother, for she never again felt that Mama was interested even."

Olive Ann had grown up hearing about the unloved little girl who was given just a dollar for Christmas while her six-year-old sister received a diamond ring; whose mother hadn't attended her high school graduation or her wedding. "I went to see my mother when school was out," Ruby told Olive Ann, "and showed her my engagement ring and she didn't say anything. She just looked at it. Arnold and I were married on the eighth of September at Sister Ollie's house. Mama didn't come to the wedding." Olive Ann found it hard to believe that any mother could reject a daughter like this. Such experiences went a long way toward explaining Ruby's bouts of moodiness and anxiety, and the sometimes unreasonable demands she made on those around her. In creating Sanna, Olive Ann tried to see the world as her mother had seen it. Soon after she returned from the Hambidge Center, she sent me a photograph of her mother, taken when she was a dark-haired young beauty with large, sad eyes. "This is Sanna," Olive Ann wrote.

Olive Ann describes Sanna as "a perfectionist and a worrier." She is obsessed with the idea of finding happiness, and for her, as Olive Ann wrote in her notes for the novel, "happiness means being first with somebody, having her own home, being loved by a perfect man and perfect, loving children." Much of the dramatic tension was to come from the difference between Will and Sanna, each wanting such different things from their marriage. Rejected by her mother, Sanna spends the rest of her life seeking love and acceptance. "The theme of Sanna is disillusionment," Olive Ann wrote. "Her life is the pursuit of happiness and perfection, but she finds happiness and perfection impossible to obtain—her idea of happiness is constant joy, no changes."

By contrast, "Will's idea of life is to be challenged. [He] loves trying anything new, loves change—is impatient with Sanna—living is a matter of making things work if you can. . . . In fact, the harder things are, the more he is excited and challenged."

Ten days before their wedding, Arnold Burns sent Ruby Celestia Hight a diamond engagement ring. Olive Ann wrote in the family history, "All her life she treasured the fact that it was a perfect stone. Then perhaps five years before she died the jeweler who cleaned it said it had a crack—he said a diamond can survive all manner of licks and then get hit just the right way, maybe on a sink, and crack like that. It was a great blow to Ruby, who treasured perfection. But to me—I wear it now

—it is a symbol that a marriage that was a victim of the Depression, and the fact that these two, so in love in the beginning and so in love in the end, with so many troubles in between and personalities so opposite—it's a symbol that an imperfect marriage can still survive and be good, and much good can come out of it. And if any grandchildren or great-grandchildren reading this has a cracked marriage and is thinking of divorce, remember Ruby and Arnold and try harder before you give up."

The Depression nearly crushed the fragile bond between Arnold and Ruby; he had to struggle just to keep food on the table, and Ruby yearned for romance and affection. Her dreams of perfect married life were replaced by a reality that included four rambunctious children, piles of unpaid bills, cramped rented rooms, and a husband who was away from home five nights a week. Olive Ann remembered those years all too well; she had sympathized with both her parents. Her notes for the novel show that Will, like her father, was stretched too thin, trying to help his parents, to earn a living, and to be a good husband and father. But Sanna wants all of him. Olive Ann intended to show "Sanna caught in another situation where she feels second, except with the children. She centers her life in them. So does Will, so this is their togetherness. Their separateness comes from his being pulled between his family and Sanna, and from conflicts over money."

At one point, trying to explain her unhappiness,

Sanna was to say to Miss Love, "I read some psychology books in college. Everything that's supposed to warp a child happened to me." Miss Love, who had been raped as an adolescent, replies, "Everything that could warp a child happened to me, too. But understanding that doesn't help. It's interesting but it doesn't help. I figure that what you do with your life now is all that counts. I try not to look back."

This is Will's philosophy, too. Much as he loves Sanna, he can't understand her constant brooding, and he cannot bear the feeling that no matter what he does, he can never meet her expectations. Olive Ann knew how hard her own father had tried to make her mother happy, and she saw the disappointment on both sides. In the family history, she transcribed a 1943 letter that Arnold had written to Ruby from a hotel in Alabama, where he was working for a cotton cooperative. "Dearest Ruby," it began, "so tomorrow's your birthday and the night when you took me for better or worst 25 years ago. Well, I guess it's been worse for you, but if I had it all to go thru again my pick of all the women would be the same. You have been a wonderful mother and a very patient woman to put up with me. You could probably have done much better, as your life with me has been one continued hardship. About the only good thing I can think of, is you have never actually gone hungry, even tho for six months your only meat was rabbit. I am enclosing a little plain ring. [Olive Ann added: "Her original wedding band wore so thin it broke. For years she had only had the engagement ring and looked divorced."] It's not what I wanted for you," Arnold apologized; "it should be filled with diamonds and made of the finest platinum, but with so much to buy and the war on I'll have to put off just what I wanted to get you until later. You have four diamonds around you and after seeing other people's children I am satisfied they are the finest in the world. You deserve all the credit. I'll be thinking of you tomorrow and Wednesday, and of the vow I took 25 years ago, 'Until death do us part,' and I'll make the same vow again."

Ruby and Arnold did indeed stay together until death intervened, but they were sorely tested. Olive Ann had figured out how she would test Will and Sanna, too, from the influenza epidemic of 1918 to the grinding poverty of the Depression. She also knew that she would take Will and Sanna to the brink of divorce.

In her notes for the novel, Olive Ann refers to two women who were to enter Will's life at a time when his foundering marriage had made him particularly vulnerable. One of them is his college love, Trulu Philpot, who is living nearby, unhappily married, with no money. Although Will assures Sanna that their affair means nothing, that it was only bad judgment on his part, Sanna is devastated. "Sanna finds out," Olive Ann writes in her notes, "breaks it up, decides divorce is better than living like that." In time, though, Sanna informs Will that if he gives his word that the affair is over, she will stay with him, having concluded that she will probably be "happier in an imperfect marriage than most divorcees are."

Ruby Burns had come to the same conclusion. In the family history, Olive Ann recalls an extraordinary afternoon she spent with her mother shortly before her death. One of Ruby's grandchildren was there, with a young friend, and everyone was sitting around the dining room table. Ruby said that she wished young people wouldn't give up so easily. "There was a time when your granddaddy and I just couldn't get along," she admitted. "It was as much my fault as his, and it started with the Depression. Before that, nobody could have been happier than we were. Plenty of things happened that I resented, and I'm sure he didn't like everything I did, but we were so in love it didn't affect our relationship. But then we lost everything we had and his father went bankrupt—you see, in his family there had always been money, and the family pride was based on what they had as well as their prominence in the life of the town. . . . To lose everything humiliated Arnold. We owed everybody in Commerce when we left. MONEY became the cross of our lives. When he was upset over bills he fussed at me and I fussed back, until finally I lost my spirit."

Ruby believed that Arnold would be better off with a different kind of person. "I told him that we had to either change or separate," she said, "and that's when he made his decision. He didn't become an angel overnight and he's still not an easy person to live with, and I'm certainly not easy for him to live with. We are just as different as we ever were. I'm such an awful perfectionist, and he really doesn't care whether a job is perfect or not, just so it's done. He still is totally concentrated on whatever he's busy at, whether it's a drive to sell more debentures at the office or getting ready for a fishing trip, so that I still don't get the attention I need to really feel secure. But when I have needed him most, since I've been sick, it is me he has been concentrated on."

Olive Ann was moved by her mother's reflections, and she never forgot that afternoon; it prompted her to look at her parents' marriage in a new light, and to feel that the pain they had endured had not been for nothing. Not only had they survived it, but, toward the end of their lives, they rediscovered the best in each other and fell in love all over again.

According to Olive Ann, Ruby finished telling her story "with the most beautiful glow on her face." At last, she felt the love and security she had been seeking all her life. "So I've gone from thinking I couldn't possibly keep living with him to knowing, now, that he is the one thing I don't want to live without—can't live without. He is my whole reason for living. He always has been, of course. I've never stopped being in love with him. When he would be sweet and affectionate to me the whole world seemed mine. When he ignored me or was irritable I was shattered. That's why it mattered so much. I couldn't ignore him. So don't give up too quickly when you marry and things aren't right. I wish long ago I could have accepted your granddaddy as he is, not as I wanted him to be. I might have made him happier too. I was not the person he needed, I know that, but I thank God we have lived long enough to love each other again."

Arnold felt the same way. He had never stopped loving Ruby, and when he finally realized that she felt her life had become intolerable, he did everything in his power to win her back. He tried to find ways to show her, every day, that he was thinking of her, that her happiness was the most important thing in the world to him. When he was sixty-two, he wrote her, "I am looking forward now, not to 63 or 64 but to 65. Then I'll quit this job and fish and piddle and sit and watch you. You are just as sweet, pretty, and lovable as you were in 1918 . . . I don't know of one thing I would want changed in my life and the only thing in yours I would change would be from a pessimist sometimes to an optimist. Just think, if it's raining today, the sun will be shining tomorrow, and just remember that I'll be loving you every day until that day when there's no tomorrow for either of us."

Olive Ann adored her father and shared with him a sense of humor and a love of storytelling that led her to write the novel that changed her life. And she knew that there was nothing she couldn't share with her mother. With her talent for listening and for drawing people out, Olive

Ann felt she had come to know and understand both of her parents even better than they knew each other. Their marriage shaped her, and in the end, it astonished her. Watching her father, sick himself, care for her mother during the last year of her life, Olive Ann felt a new respect for both of them, and for the amazing power of love. "And all the time there was Daddy," Olive Ann wrote. "Always there at the hospital, bringing her cantaloupe, which she could eat, and wine, and making jokes that made her laugh. There were times, of course, in their life together when he had failed her, as she had him, but no woman ever felt more loved and secure and supported than she did when it mattered most. She said one day, 'I couldn't have stood it if it hadn't been for all of you. I've felt as if the arms of God and everybody I love have been around me, holding me, and your daddy most of all.' "

This was the story Olive Ann wanted to tell in *Time, Dirt, and Money,* and she worked hard on it because she was determined to do it justice. "I want to write this book because it can say something," she wrote from the Hambidge Center. "I don't need any more fame or fortune than I have and have never craved it. But when I thought about NOT writing this book, I knew it would haunt me. I think I've been writing it all my life —Sanna and Will, I mean. I think it can say something to all these people who have problems or are mismatched and just give up and get divorces."

Back in Atlanta in October, Olive Ann was still saying no to speaking invitations at least once a day; now, though, it was easier, because she was genuinely eager to keep writing. But she also wanted to make time to enjoy life, the great gift that had been handed back to her. She would work steadily, she decided, but not let herself feel guilty about taking time off for naps, for friends and family, or for the occasional *Cold Sassy Tree* appearance. Bookstores were already gearing up for Christmas. Olive Ann agreed to do a round of holiday autographings and publicity, and *Cold Sassy Tree* jumped right back onto the Atlanta best-seller list. This time, most of the people who appeared at her signing parties were already loyal fans, out buying more copies of their favorite book. Olive Ann wrote about meeting a mother and her fifteen-year-old son, who were buying two books as gifts. "We already own six," the mother explained. "We lend them out."

Over a year after publication, *Cold Sassy Tree* had taken on a life of its own. It seemed that publicity, or even appearances by Olive Ann herself, had little to do with it. The word simply traveled. Nearly everyone who read *Cold Sassy Tree* passed it on to someone else; teachers used it in their classrooms; ministers preached it from the pulpit. After selling the hardcover for a year, Faith Brunson reported that *Cold Sassy Tree* had sold more copies at Rich's than any other fiction except *Gone With the Wind,* which had a forty-five-year head start. The actress Faye Dunaway bought the movie rights to the novel, in January 1986, and announced her plans to play Miss Love in a film version. After the *Atlanta Journal* quoted Olive Ann's agent as saying that the deal had been in the six figures, the author reported that everyone in Atlanta now thought she was rich. She also began getting telephone calls from stage mothers wanting her to arrange auditions for their children.

Any notion Olive Ann may have had in the fall about sticking to a regular writing schedule became moot that winter, when she found herself seduced by a whole new batch of invitations. "Yesterday I got a call to teach at a writers' conference for a week on a horse farm in Kentucky, which I turned down," she wrote to me in February, "and then an invitation to go to New York for lunch, which I accepted." She couldn't imagine why the Georgia Department of Industry and Trade was willing to send a bunch of Southern writers all the way to Manhattan for lunch at the Russian Tea Room, but she couldn't pass up the opportunity. "I don't personally see how we are famous enough outside of Georgia to interest a bunch of Yankees, even if they're hungry," she said, "unless they're just mad to hear Southern accents." The tourism board would put them up for two days. Olive Ann conceded, "Now conscientious fiction writers would let it go at that and come on home and get to work. Being me, and like my father, I can't imagine not extending the trip, hoping that this time I will be in action instead of in bed. . . . After being a hermit so many years, what with doctor's orders not to go anywhere and then really trying to finish the book, it's as if I'm starved to go places."

That year, there were lots of places to go. She and Andy contemplated another trip to Europe, and they made plans to attend the American Booksellers Association convention in New Orleans in May. The paperback edition of *Cold Sassy Tree* was due out that summer, and the publisher, Dell, was launching it at the ABA with a special luncheon for booksellers. Olive Ann hadn't been to New Orleans since 1952, on a trip with her parents; this time, Andy would be her escort and she would be a guest of honor. "I'm sure you understand why, for me, going is more delightful with him than without him," she wrote. "I am not a helpless female who can't carry my own bag or weight, but with him even a simple trip is sprinkled with starlight."

Happy as she was visiting all of us in New York and being wined and dined by booksellers and publishers in New Orleans, these two trips were also sobering for Olive Ann; they made her realize that she didn't have the strength to do everything she wanted. She already had had to cancel a couple of appearances and talks that spring because of the mumps, of all things. ("But just on one side," as Andy kept reminding her.) Mysterious fevers continued to come and go. And five days of bookstores, Broadway shows, galleries, and socializing in New York landed her in bed on the last day.

"I am finally facing the fact that I need an afternoon nap just as much in New York or New Orleans as at home," she wrote me when she got back to Atlanta. "New York made me sick." After a week of bed rest she felt better, but knew that a trip to Europe was out of the question. That summer, Cold Sassy Tree was once again climbing the best-seller lists—now as a paperback—and Olive Ann Burns was as much in demand as ever. A fifth-grade student wrote her a fan letter, after reading the book for school, and begged for a reply: "Please answer this letter. If you do, I'll get extra credit, and I need all the help I can get." ("I answered the letter," Olive Ann reported.) On Sunset Boulevard in Los Angeles, a huge *Cold Sassy Tree* billboard advised California drivers to "leave the fast lane for a country road." Olive Ann was pleased that *Cold Sassy Tree* was suddenly being read by thousands more people, and she would have loved to be out and about, meeting some of her new fans, but in December she confessed that she didn't feel well enough to write or do publicity. It was one of the few times I ever heard her sound discouraged about her health.

Ever since she was first diagnosed with cancer Olive Ann had thought about one day writing a book called *How to Be Sick,* for people with terminal or chronic illness. Now she joked that she had been unwillingly gathering material for *How to Be Sick* all fall. "But," she said, "it isn't meant to be for people with intestinal bugs, mumps, vertigo, bronchitis (my latest ailment), or too much New York or New Orleans." Reading her letters, one might be tempted to accuse Olive Ann of being a hypochondriac; there was always something wrong. In the fall of 1986, she had run a fever every day for a month. Standing up made her dizzy, and two days of watching work progress on the mountain house had landed her in bed with bronchitis. She didn't complain; instead, she wrote about how much fun it had been to sit outside in a director's chair and watch as the backhoes and front-end loaders felled trees and dug trenches for the drain field and septic tank. Norma said that no matter how bad she felt, Olive Ann could find something to enjoy in every day, and that was certainly true.

The day after she wrote to me that she had not been feeling well enough to work, I received another letter, titled "Chapter II—Dec. 7, 1986." It read, in part: "Now as for the sequel, I think circumstances are giving me a chance to make my fiction-writing career repeat itself. Five weeks ago I had a bone marrow biopsy that showed some evidence of lymphoma (the first time in eight years!), but it didn't seem worth mentioning since it might be months or years before chemo. But I've been running fever with the bronchitis that should have been long over. Trying to be sure of the situation, the doctor ordered a CAT scan that revealed a mass (probably of tumor-laden lymph

284

nodes) at the back of the abdomen." She was scheduled for a biopsy and surgery the week before Christmas, after which she was to undergo more chemotherapy and radiation. The day she got the news, Olive Ann said, she had been so busy cheering up relatives that the fact that her cancer had recurred didn't even sink in. But later she realized that she was scared. "I admitted this to Andy," she wrote, "and I haven't felt scared since we talked about it. Hooray for an in-house therapist—one who can hold me." But, in parentheses, she added, "He said he was a little scared, too."

As one of their friends has observed, Olive Ann and Andy weren't cheerful just by nature; they were cheerful by policy. Certainly Olive Ann summoned all her resources in an effort to view this new development in a positive light. "I'm really not much dismayed or upset right now," she wrote, perhaps trying to convince herself, too. "I've had lots of practice living one day at a time and accepting the unacceptable. This is one more adventure in living—another challenge—and what a difference to know for sure that I can deal with it. It has *not* been easy to deal with feeling bad most of the time."

As usual, Olive Ann knew that what she needed from her friends was not sympathy but encouragement. And after all those years of living next door to Olive Ann, Norma Duncan knew that the best thing she could do for her now was urge her to get back to work on her book. After making Olive Ann promise not to die, Norma said to her,

"Well, maybe we'll get another *Cold Sassy Tree* out of this." Olive Ann had already had the same thought. "That is exactly my intention," she wrote to me. "A few letters to do now, and Christmas presents to wrap and mail, and then I expect to get to work in earnest—before that biopsy next week. I really haven't felt like getting at anything lately, but I had *better.* " Ferrol Sams liked to tease Olive Ann by saying, "Some writers need to get drunk in order to work. Olive Ann Burns needs to get cancer." She thought this was a wonderful joke; I suspect she also believed that there was a grain of truth in it.

Unfortunately, cancer was not much of a help this time around. Olive Ann was out of the hospital for Christmas but was back within days. "I felt what dying must feel like," she wrote. As it turned out, she was severely anemic and dehydrated. But worst of all, her abdomen had swollen up so much after the surgery that, as she joked in one letter, "it looked as if the surgeon did a caesarean and put the baby back in." She was in the hospital for almost two months, sicker than ever before, and it was then, I think, that I realized that she was not indomitable after all. Always before she had done such a good job of coping with illness that I had come to see it as just another part of her life, something she accepted with good humor, but not something to worry about. Even now, she was referring to the hospital as her "health spa," so extended was her stay turning out to be.

She didn't come home until March. "I had chemo on Tuesday," she wrote, "a bigger dose than before, but as Andy pointed out, only the cat threw up that night." She believed that she could beat lymphoma again as she had beat it before, so she set about choosing appliances, carpets, and cabinets for the mountain cabin. They were calling it the Write House in honor of all the writing that she and Andy intended to do there. Reading through Olive Ann's letters from the spring of 1987 is in itself a lesson in living in the moment, for they are an odd juxtaposition of alarming health bulletins and lovely plans for the future. At the end of March, Andy had an enlarged lymph gland removed from his neck; it proved to be malignant. Now he and Olive Ann were both receiving chemotherapy, alternating treatments so that one of them would be well enough to cook and keep house while the other was sick from chemo.

Olive Ann described one night when Andy began throwing up and didn't stop until four-thirty the next afternoon, at which point the Prednisone he was taking kicked in and produced such a high that he couldn't sit down. "He tackled every project in the house and garden, both here and at the mountain house, and without sleep," Olive Ann wrote. "By the time he finished the pills on Sunday he was getting a little tired but had had a good time. At one point I was afraid we'd give out of work to do and I'd have to hire him out." Olive Ann herself was in and out of the hospital for blood transfusions and was confined to the house after each round of chemo until her white blood cell count rose to an acceptable level. Hearing all of this, I began to fear that if I didn't make a trip to Atlanta soon, I might not get another chance to see either Olive Ann or Andy. Even though her letters were upbeat—she wrote about meeting a fan who had bought forty hardcover copies of *Cold Sassy Tree,* about Dell's seventh printing of the paperback, about her cozy writing loft in the Write House—I also sensed a precariousness, as if either one of them might be snatched away at any moment.

So my fiancé and I planned a visit for May, timing it so that we would arrive just before one of Olive Ann's chemotherapy treatments. "Just before treatment time," she advised us, "the white count is always 5000 or 6000, and I can do wild things in public." She didn't do anything wild, but she and Andy did take us to the Write House for lunch. What I remember most about that trip to Skylake was how much life and laughter and vitality could emanate from someone who appeared so frail. Olive Ann covered her bald head with a colorful turban rather than a wig, but she wore it with style, complemented by long, swingy earrings. Her eyes were enormous in her thin face, magnified even more by her large glasses. She didn't look healthy, but she certainly looked happy, so it was easy to forget how sick she was. We had a wonderful time. She joked and told stories and asked questions all the way to the mountains, and then she and Andy proudly showed us around their little house—including their bright red bathroom. There was no furniture yet, and the electricity hadn't been hooked up, and just as we arrived the day darkened and it began to rain. We set up a makeshift table on the screened porch, covered it with an old cotton tablecloth, and sat down to a meal of fried chicken, Vidalia onions, and iced tea that Olive Ann had brought from home. The spring rain fell all around us, thunder rumbled in the distance, and we all agreed that it was a beautiful afternoon. Olive Ann and Andy knew how to make a rainy-day picnic into a festive occasion, just as they knew how to turn cancer into an adventure in living. I remember that meal, and that day, with great pleasure and with more than a little awe. We had come to Atlanta with the notion of perhaps saying farewell to two sick friends; instead, they orchestrated a party in our honor and thoroughly enjoyed themselves in the process.

That summer Olive Ann did feel well enough to get back to work on the book. What's more, after nearly a year of poor health and little or no progress on the novel, she was excited again. Just after our visit, she wrote, "Sunday morning I woke up at 3 o'clock and just suddenly I, who could once honestly say I didn't understand what a theme meant, suddenly saw where I wanted to go with this book. I had everything before—setting, characters, incidents, scenes, conflicts—but I hadn't decided what I wanted the book to say, so I just saw endless writing days ahead. Now it's as clear as looking out a newly washed window."

A month later, Olive Ann and Andy's dream of a writing retreat finally came true. She got her computer set up at the Write House, and they spent a peaceful week there, returning to Atlanta for chemotherapy treatments and then heading right back to the mountains. "I wish you were here with us now," she wrote, "the house fully furnished and the tree frogs outside an antiphone chorus so loud we have to raise our voices to be heard clearly. . . . I got interrupted on the writing last week by a high fever (an infection) . . . but I'm still excited about what I've written and am writing, and I feel really good." She and Andy were planning to come to Maine that September for my wedding, and they were confident that they could not only make the trip, but do some sightseeing and visiting as well. Olive Ann's doctor had told her that the lymphoma appeared to be in remission again; she would need only one more chemotherapy treatment, three weeks before the wedding. "That should leave me in good shape," she wrote. "Andy will have three more after the wedding, but the doctor will let him put one off for a week, for the occasion." She added, "I expect my eyebrows to be in for the wedding. I have missed them."

Olive Ann *had* beaten lymphoma, but a couple of days after she wrote this letter, it became clear that something else was terribly wrong. She was too weak to do anything but sit at the computer for a couple of hours, and when she went in for her weekly blood study, the doctor warned that her white blood cell count was low again. The next day she was weaker still and was having trouble getting her breath. The diagnosis was congestive heart failure. In a letter to a friend, Andy wrote, "I am not sure when she will be home, but soon I hope. It is awfully quiet around here at 4:30 A.M. which is about as late as the Prednisone will let me sleep, even with a sleeping pill." To me he wrote, "September 12 on Bailey Island has been a dream for us just as it has for you and Steve. We even got a New England guidebook from the library and dug out our old camping road atlas. But we've had an unexpected change of plans."

According to Olive Ann's doctor, Andy wrote, the only cure for a weakened heart was rest. That meant no walking, no sitting, not even talking. Olive Ann always got a laugh in speeches when she told about the arthritis doctor who had advised her never to vacuum again. "Now," she would say, "if I could only get one to say I shouldn't cook . . ." She remembered that joke now, hearing her doctor's orders for complete bed rest. "Be careful what you wish for," she said to Andy. Still, she hoped that the bed-rest sentence would result in progress on the book, and she inscribed a copy of *Cold Sassy Tree* "to the doctor who says I can do nothing but write." At the end of Andy's letter to me, she added her own handwritten note: "I have to not think about all we will be missing in Maine . . . I learned long

291

ago to accept what has to be and not waste energy on what cannot be changed. There are good things to everything. Since I've been in the hospital I figured out how to put Loma on page one, and I'm giving her a pet monkey and snake, the better to make her even more inconsiderate, and suddenly the whole book has a life and focus and excitement I didn't feel when Will and Sanna were carrying it by themselves."

From the first time I saw Olive Ann and Andy together, they had been an inspiration to me. Here were two people who had been married for over thirty years and who still got starry-eyed looking at each other. They were each other's best audience, equally matched in their storytelling abilities and in their appreciation of a good joke. Even when Olive Ann was telling a story Andy had heard a hundred times before, he would listen with full, adoring attention, stopping whatever he was doing to gaze at his wife as she spoke. Sometimes Olive Ann would turn to him, and say, "Andy, tell the one about . . ." just because she wanted to hear his voice. The pleasure they took in each other's company was unmistakable and absolute, and I often told them that I aspired to a marriage like theirs. Having discovered true love at the office herself, Olive Ann presided over my romance and my engagement to a Houghton Mifflin colleague in fine Amy Larkin style, sharing our happiness and dispensing romantic advice at the same time. She and Andy had looked forward to being at our wedding just as much as we had looked forward to having them there. Now, trying to put the best face on her having to spend September 12 in the hospital instead of on an island in Maine, Olive Ann suggested that we freeze some fish chowder for her and Andy. "If you were our daughter we wouldn't love you more or be any happier for you and Steve," she wrote. She hoped that she would be going home the day after she and Andy sent this letter. Instead, she took a sudden turn for the worse, and two days before the wedding she slipped into a coma. Just as I was packing my wedding gown into the car to head for Maine, Andy called to say that Olive Ann's doctor didn't expect her to live through the night. His voice breaking, he told me that he and Olive Ann would be there in spirit when we said our vows.

The next day, we heard nothing from Atlanta. And so, first thing on the morning of our wedding, I called the hospital, not knowing whether Olive Ann was alive or dead. Andy answered the phone in her room, and his voice held the answer. She had opened her eyes that morning and asked if she could have her hair washed. Hours later, as sun broke through the clouds on Bailey Island, the first glass of champagne was raised to Olive Ann Burns.

Olive Ann remained in the hospital until just before Thanksgiving, and there were many more days when the doctor summoned the family to her bedside, as her blood pressure dipped dangerously low. When she finally did come home, she was so weak that she could barely talk. She couldn't leave the hospital bed that they set up for her downstairs, and she couldn't have company. As Norma said, "For someone as gregarious as Olive Ann, that was hard." Of course, "company" didn't include Norma, who was almost part of the household, always there to do a load of laundry, drop off a casserole, or share in the daily reading of the fan mail and get-well cards. Olive Ann often said that God must have put Norma Duncan in the house next to hers, so grateful was she for Norma's presence in their lives. But Norma herself takes no such mystical view. "I was just their neighbor," she says simply.

Surely, if there was ever a time when Olive Ann needed Norma's love and encouragement, it was that fall, when even holding a pen was too much effort for her, and when day after day went by with no improvement. Though he was just finishing his own chemotherapy and not feeling well, Andy was determined to take care of Olive Ann himself, and he did. Olive Ann knew how hard it was for him. And feeling that she was a burden on Andy was more difficult for her to handle than being sick. Later, she recalled that shortly before she went to the hospital, Andy had said, "If I had to prepare three meals a day, I'd eat out." "Now," Olive Ann quipped, "he cooks three meals a day."

Olive Ann was never one to waste much time or energy worrying about her health, but that fall she did worry about money, and with good reason. Her hospital and medical bills had been astronomical, and she had run through her insurance. From now on, she and Andy would have to pay all her expenses themselves, a frightening prospect. Royalty checks came twice a year and were earmarked for medical bills, but it still wasn't enough. Even the day-to-day cost of home care was staggering, because Olive Ann couldn't leave her bed, and the doctors made house calls. She required a hospital bed, a wheelchair, and a variety of expensive medications; the daily cost of the oxygen alone was nearly a hundred dollars.

Olive Ann and Norma and Andy often talked about *Time, Dirt, and Money,* and about how she would get back to it when she was feeling better, but, recalls Norma, "it seemed to be taking an awfully long time." Late that fall, Norma went over to check on Olive Ann one afternoon and found her reading a pamphlet on congestive heart failure. "I guess I had just had enough," Norma says. "I asked her if she would be willing to try dictating the sequel, because I thought that would be a lot more fun than reading about heart failure."

At first, Olive Ann didn't think she could do it; she was accustomed to typing, to having the words come through her fingers, not out of her mouth. Norma suggested that Olive Ann just pretend she was talking to her; then Norma would transcribe the tape and give the typed page to Olive Ann to revise by hand. They arranged to try a dictating machine for a month, and, Norma says, "We started off, not with the novel, but by answering fan mail."

"I wish now that I had kept one of those early tapes," she says. "Olive Ann's voice was so weak and the sound of the oxygen so grim that I would have to type a little bit and then cry a little bit. But as she got stronger and started having fun with what she called 'the dictator,' I could type and laugh, not only at what she was writing in letters, but at the asides she would make to me, sometimes complete with punctuation."

When she began to dictate in January, Olive Ann had five months worth of fan letters to answer, not to mention correspondence to resume with countless friends and relatives. She composed what Andy called "a generic letter" to her "Dear Loved Ones," explaining that, although she was once again in remission from cancer, she was also bedridden, and the end of that was not in sight. "I did have a period of despair about it," she admitted, "but I've accepted future limitations and am aware of an inner joy and peace that a low-salt diet and backaches can't alter."

That done, she tackled the fan mail, finally agreeing to write an all-purpose letter to her readers, too. Even so, she couldn't resist adding personal notes when Norma brought the letters back for her to sign. "Andy and I would tease her that we wouldn't give her the mail until she had dictated a chapter of the book," Norma recalls, "but that fan mail was as important to her as writing, and she answered every letter."

At the end of January, Olive Ann reported, "If I can dictate the book as easily as I can dictate letters, this is going to be no problem at all. Norma knows how much I rewrite and says that won't bother her a bit. I can just talk it out any way I want to and she will doublespace it and I can correct and rewrite and she will do it again . . . What a great, great blessing! It has already changed my life. All of a sudden I have something to do instead of lie here with my mind turned on to most anything or nothing, whiling away four hours a day on 'All Things Considered.' "

It may sound dramatic to suggest that *Time, Dirt, and Money* saved Olive Ann's life, but it certainly gave her the escape she needed, for the only way she could get away from her bed, her financial worries, and her physical discomfort was on the wings of her own imagination. Her hair was just beginning to grow back, but, by her own admission, she looked like "a ridiculous refugee, with rib cage and arms being just skin and bones, and this huge stomach." She had been unable to eat normally for months, but her weight had gone up as high as 151 pounds—all from fluid retained in her abdomen. The pressure was so great that it was all she could do to sit up for a half hour before backache forced her to lie down again. With the dictating machine as a means of communication, Olive Ann began to feel a certain pride in her ability not only to cope, but to enjoy life in spite of all the obstacles. She found a great sense of accomplishment in answering a hundred fan letters that month, and she was deeply moved by a book about a blind leader of the French Resistance movement in Paris, who had overcome his handicap with joy—even when he was imprisoned in a concentration camp. "The impact it had on me was partly because I realize that—wherever it came from—I have this kind of joy, too," she wrote to me. "My back can hurt, but I am still undismayed. A lot of it comes from acceptance, but I know that's not all of it, and I hadn't realized this before. The longest I can be depressed is about two hours and that's not often. I was depressed for about a month when I got home from the hospital with this problem—the congestive heart failure—because I realized I might never get to write the book and because I might be more or less bedridden for the rest of my life. At some point I did accept this and was back to my usual self." She promised that she would have some chapters ready for me to read "any minute now."

Working on the book turned out to be much harder than doing letters, but Norma was patient, transcribing every page twice, once as a rough draft, and then again after Olive Ann had edited it by hand and read it back into the machine. "For the first time I believe it will work!" Olive Ann wrote happily.

It did work, but in fits and starts. Just when she would get on a roll with the writing, the pain in her back and shoulder would flare up, and, as Olive Ann said, she would feel "waylaid as a person and as a writer." Her back hurt if she got up, and her shoulder hurt in bed, and a few days of this, combined with lack of sleep, would result in another setback. Progress—on the book and on getting well—was slow indeed. "I still look as if I'm carrying surrogate twin grandchildren," she said in one letter.

As spring rolled around, Andy began to make day trips to the Write House, and Olive Ann realized that any hope she might have of accompanying him would lead only to disappointment. Instead, she took pleasure in the way the world seemed to come to her. Craig Claiborne wrote her a fan letter, and they became pen pals, a new friendship that she enjoyed immensely. Faye Dunaway called to introduce herself and to say that she would love to come to Atlanta and talk with Olive Ann about turning her novel into a film. Meanwhile, *Cold Sassy Tree* was banned in a high school in Florida, which only resulted in more publicity as parents and teachers came forth to defend its virtues. (Much to Olive Ann's amusement, the principal of the school appeared on television to explain why the book was banned. "With hands shaking, she said, 'It's just an awful book. Full of rape, incest, and SOUTHERN DIALECT!' ") One day Oprah Winfrey announced on her show that she was reading a great novel called *Cold Sassy Tree;* that night Olive Ann heard from every friend in Atlanta who had seen the program. "But I decided I had really arrived," she wrote in a letter to Chester and Joan Kerr, "when I heard that last summer a high school girl went into a bookstore and asked for the Cliff Notes on *Cold Sassy*, which was required summer reading in her school."

Being bedridden may have been the greatest challenge Olive Ann had faced so far, but every day brought its own reminder that she continued to touch people's lives. What's more, after three years in which she had made almost no real progress on her novel, she was now in a situation where the only thing she *could* do was write. She had a good laugh when a friend called to say she had heard that Olive Ann's publisher had sent a secretary down to Atlanta for her to dictate the sequel to. "Thanks but no thanks!" she wrote. "Norma suits me just fine, and I think she'd shoot anyone who tried to take her job. The ms. is now 40 pages." Norma never complained when Olive Ann scribbled all over her perfectly typed pages. More important, she knew just when to urge her to keep writing and when to insist that she rest. "I know if it weren't for Norma I would still be wishing I could write but not doing it," Olive Ann admitted in one letter. "Maybe planning scenes, but not writing them."

Olive Ann's goal that spring and summer was to perfect a hundred pages to send to Ticknor & Fields. As long as she had a telephone and a commode by the bed, she could be alone for a few hours, and she looked forward to that time for dictating and rewriting. When Olive Ann had two finished chapters, she gave the first to Andy one night to print out on her computer. "In the morning," she wrote me, "he waked me like Prince Charming with a kiss and the words 'I read the first chapter and I think it's delightful. I knew you could do it.' Isn't that a nice way to wake up?" In August, John came home for a visit from Colorado and read several versions of the first chapter. Olive Ann was still in a quandary over how the book should begin, but it helped her to have a fresh pair of eyes on the manuscript. She reread one of her old beginnings, written in the third person, and felt that it worked. "I can't wait to get this all together and see what you think," she wrote. "I'm more excited about TDM now than ever before. Not from anything John said but from my own confidence. At last."

On October 5, Olive Ann sent me 113 pages of *Time, Dirt, and Money* for my birthday. It was the best present an editor could have received. Olive Ann felt that she, too, had been given a great gift—the courage and the inspiration to keep writing. Finally, she had something to show for all those nights of lying awake, planning scenes in her mind; for all those hours spent dictating; for all those first chapters. "As I've told you before," she wrote, "anybody who ever worked for Angus Perkerson can't get hurt feelings from criticism, so you don't need to try to veil your words in kindness." A stack of manuscript pages wasn't the only thing Olive Ann had to celebrate. She felt stronger, and she was finally able to get up and walk from one room to another. "The fluid retention in my stomach has been reduced to about the size of a large baking hen," she reported. Olive Ann's doctor was impressed by her progress; he told her he had never been able to get a patient to stay in bed this long. As Olive Ann wryly observed, "It was no temptation to be up. Between the backache and the fact that I had a definite forward list when I walked, it was easy to stay in bed."

After a whole year of that, though, it felt wonderful not to have to be waited on for every little thing. "Now, other than the fact that Jack (the cat) and I have fleas—we've got a flea collar for him and we may well get one for me—everything here is going well," she wrote. When Steve and I went to visit that fall, Norma cooked the meal for our reunion dinner, but Olive Ann and Andy were definitely the hosts. They opened a bottle of homemade scuppernong wine in honor of the occasion, set out the fine china and lit candles in the dining room, and talked of the past year as if it had been one of the happiest of their lives. After dinner, Andy read a funny scene from T. R. Pearson's novel *A Short History of a Small Place*. He was a marvelous reader, with a rich, expressive voice, and he knew just how to play up the humor, but he couldn't keep a straight face himself. Once he started to laugh, he couldn't stop. The more he read, the harder he laughed, and that laughter was so infectious that all of us ended up gasping for breath, urging him on. Sitting around the table that night, it was hard even to imagine what Olive Ann and Andy had just been through; not a mention was made of pain or hardship.

In a November letter to her *Cold Sassy Tree* fans, Olive Ann said, "I'm up more now. I've been out once to ride, I've had on lipstick seven times and a dress five times, I've put on a chicken to roast, last night I fried some fish, and the doctors think the heart muscle is getting well, not just better. (They say the only way to be sure is with an autopsy, but I say never mind being so sure!)" The same day, however, she wrote to me that about ten pounds of the abdominal fluid had reinstated themselves. After just a month of the very mildest activity, she was being sent back to bed. It didn't seem to faze her. This time, she knew she could handle it and, besides, she had work to do. Ticknor & Fields had made an offer for the novel based on the first hundred pages of manuscript, and Olive Ann now had a contract in hand and a deadline toward which to work. "Just knowing about it has liberated me," she wrote. "Suddenly I don't want to read the newspaper in the morning before I even think about writing. The first two chapters are already improved, and I'm now on chapter five."

Although she had tried out several different narrative voices, the chapters Olive Ann had sent in October were written in the third person. Will's voice was nowhere to be heard. When I told Olive Ann that I missed Will, she admitted she missed him, too. It was hard to suggest that she start all over again, knowing how much effort and sheer force of will it had cost her to produce these chapters, but I also knew that she wanted a truthful reaction and that she could handle the criticism. She did handle it, magnificently. In fact, she hardly needed to hear it, for her instincts were telling her the same thing I was. Andy, who had watched the painstaking writing process day by day, was moved and deeply impressed by Olive Ann's willingness to go back to square one. In a letter to friends he wrote, "Olive Ann sent 113 pages to her editor, who said she liked it, but would she mind starting over. . . . So Olive Ann started over, writing as Will as an older young man, and says the book is much more fun. She said she had written herself into a corner, having to explain everything from the girl's point of view, when Will can just dive in. She now has 8-pages that she is happy with, although she keeps rewriting. Norma and I say, 'Get on with Chapter 7.' "

That winter of 1988-1989, the continuing success of *Cold Sassy Tree* and Olive Ann's "fat contract" for *Time, Dirt, and Money* seemed to be the only bright spots. Shortly after our October visit, Andy began to feel pain in his lower back. Late in December tests revealed that his lymphoma had come back yet a third time, now in the form of a large tumor pressing against his lower vertebrae. In February he underwent four weeks of radiation, to be followed by nine months of chemotherapy. "We are now a two-wheelchair family," Olive Ann wrote.

She wanted to care for Andy as he had taken care of her over the past two years, but with both of them in wheelchairs, the day-to-day tasks that they had just managed before were now impossible. Friends and relatives all pitched in to help, and members of Olive Ann and Andy's Sunday school class took up the cause. This group of nearly a hundred friends organized themselves, drew up a schedule, and saw to it that hot food arrived at Olive Ann and Andy's doorstep several times a week. When they were too ill for company, the cook would drop off his or her wares and slip out quietly; when Olive Ann and Andy were up to it, they would visit and catch up on news of the outside world. "All those Sunday school class people who bought books by the dozen at Rich's are bringing soup and casseroles," Olive Ann wrote. "I am still amazed by what *Cold Sassy* has done and now I'm even more amazed by the kindness of people and by how many friends in various places we have who care and help. And Norma is our mainstay. She is typing this, of course, and I'm not saying it just so she'll hear it and clean out the dishwasher real quick."

On days that she felt well, Olive Ann undertook some of the cooking and housework herself, but she wasn't able to combine being up and about with any writing. Every exertion tired her, and besides, as she said, "how could I retire into Cold Sassy when Andy was hurting?" That spring, she sent out a letter to "special friends," bringing them up to date on her health and Andy's and on other events at 161 Bolling Road. "The doctors say my heart is working fine," she wrote, "and I've lost all of the abdominal fluid. I don't look like Tweedledum or a California raisin anymore." She hoped that her return to a normal shape meant that she would begin to feel stronger; nevertheless, she had grown almost accustomed to a universe that extended no farther than her living room. "In October Andy took me to see the fall leaves," she wrote, "and I sat outside on the front lawn three times, but otherwise I haven't been out of the house since November of 1987, when I got home from the hospital. But I don't feel lonely or cut off from the outside world, partly because of *Cold Sassy Tree* and the mail it brings, and partly because so many people come here. Somebody said yesterday, 'You and Andy have such a wonderful attitude!' We have a whole houseful of attitude, and most of the time it sustains."

Even with Andy sicker than he had ever been, Olive Ann could look around her and feel grateful. In a letter that March, she wrote about signing a contract for a Hebrew translation of *Cold Sassy Tree*, about the paperback edition coming out in Great Britain, about the Turner Network Television company's plans to start filming for the movie that spring, and about her son John's engagement to be married. The wedding was to be in the fall, in Olive Ann and Andy's backyard, so that they could both attend. Meanwhile, Olive Ann's sister Margaret had come from Pennsylvania and was "keeping the house going, making oatmeal cookies, whole wheat rolls, and anything else she can think of to fatten us up." That meant Olive Ann could conserve her energy and get back

306

to her writing; she hoped to send a hundred revised pages to me within a week. "The suspense of waiting for so long for Andy's treatment, and the difficulty of accepting seeing him feel bad, is not conducive to writing," she admitted. "On the other hand, it's the other world I can go to without leaving the house. He and Norma keep me at it."

By the time Margaret returned north to her family, after three months in Atlanta, Olive Ann and Andy were able to manage on their own. For the first time in nearly two years, Olive Ann felt well enough to sleep at night in her own bed with Andy. They used her hospital bed and a twin bed in the guest room for resting during the day. "We may be the only couple in Atlanta who has his bed, my bed, and our bed," Olive Ann joked, adding, "It's wonderful to be together again." Once a week, Olive Ann's sister Jean and her husband came by to help around the house, buy groceries, and run other errands. With the help of Meals on Wheels, they could feel somewhat independent, knowing that a hot meal would be delivered once a day. Olive Ann loved that she could be on the phone with Craig Claiborne one minute, hearing about his most recent culinary explorations in China, and then tuck into her own plate of plain fare from Bradshaw's Feedmill the next. "If we had our choice we wouldn't eat at the Feedmill five days a week," she conceded, "but it's good average cooking."

Andy never did feel well that spring, but he was able to go out back and lose himself in his garden, just as Olive Ann could turn on her dictating machine and escape to Cold Sassy. John's October wedding gave Andy a goal, and he was determined that by fall the backyard would be more beautiful than ever before. His chemotherapy wasn't making him nauseated, as it had in the past, but he was terribly frail and often in pain. One day he came in from the garden, complaining of being weak. "I don't know what's wrong with me," he said. Olive Ann replied, "Well, I do. You've got lymphoma, you're taking chemotherapy, you're very anemic, and you've been hauling concrete blocks in the garden." Andy hadn't lost his sense of humor. "Oh, good," he said, "I thought it might be old age."

In May Olive Ann sent me the new version of the opening chapters, now written from Will's point of view. She had never once questioned the wisdom of starting over, and now, six months later, she felt good about what she had done and was eager to keep going. "Of course I look forward to hearing what you think," she wrote. "Please remember you don't have to tiptoe around my feelings. If this beginning is too slow or you want something more exotic to start with, I can put Will and Sanna at the Army camp where everybody's dying of the 1918 influenza epidemic—really strong stuff. I'd just as soon have that in the next hundred pages, but I can't be sure this (what I've done) grabs the reader the way I want it to. I like it, but is that enough? Please tell me if there's any section that seems slow. I'm not going to work on this (chapters 1–5) for a while. Norma and Andy both say I've got to get on with chapters six, seven, eight, nine, ten, eleven, twelve. Andy said one way to get ahead was to let Will pretend he lost one chapter and just skip from chapter five to chapter seven. But I've already done chapter six, so I'll save that idea for a real emergency."

It was a good thing that Olive Ann finished five chapters and got them sent off that May, for just a week later shooting began for the TV movie version of *Cold Sassy Tree,* and every day brought new visitors and distractions. The movie company set up camp in Concord, Georgia, a little town about seventy miles from Atlanta that Olive Ann said hadn't changed since the Civil War. Olive Ann and Andy had been invited to be on site for the filming, but they had to decline. As it happened, though, a close friend was hired to be the dialect coach, and he kept them supplied with regular briefings from the front lines.

"I wish you could see the beehive of activity in Concord," Charles Hadley wrote. "The production office, set up in a lovely old home, is awash in traffic of stars, crew, secretaries, producers, make-up artists, wardrobe people, etc. Out front a sign says 'Welcome to Cold Sassy Tree, population 586.' " For Olive Ann and Andy, Charles Hadley's "secret communications" were almost as good as being there in person, for he took time from his own busy schedule to describe the scene and all the goings on. "Strickland's old country store now reads 'Blakeslee,' " he wrote, "and tons of dirt have covered the paved street in front of it. Set designers have transformed the interior into something marvelously 1906! All is about ready for the turkey trot come Wednesday. Costumes from London are being fitted, hairdos and beards are appearing. Poor Lightfoot has undergone a chopping that left her near tears. Both she and Will T. begin the shoot with the cemetery kissing scene on Tuesday and are scared to death. They should be—I'm having trouble getting the Yankee out of their speech and there has been so little time to work. Effie Belle, Alice Ann, Mrs. Predmore, and Mr. Means, however, are a hoot! It is all ultra-exciting to see this huge operation in full swing. You would burst with pride if you could see how beloved and famous you are. Can there be a soul left who doesn't know your name? I do get so much mileage out of telling that I know you in person!"

Cast and crew members alike took advantage of breaks in the filming to come to Atlanta to meet Olive Ann. She welcomed them all, signed their well-thumbed copies of Cold Sassy Tree, and listened to their accounts of life on the set. When she first read the movie script, Olive Ann had been surprised and disappointed that all vestiges of Southern dialect had been removed. Even the rhythm of Southern speech—which she had worked so hard to capture precisely—had been lost. Olive Ann was sure *Cold Sassy Tree* was such a success in part because she had put every line to the supreme test by having Andy read the manuscript aloud. Whenever she was fussing over a tricky bit of dialect, she would listen carefully as Andy read, making changes as he went so that every sentence *sounded* right. Now the film producers seemed ready to disregard her efforts. "The script was written as if everybody in Cold Sassy was educated and had at least an A.B.," she said when she saw it. Grandpa Tweedy's "Good goshamighty, she's dead as she'll ever be, ain't she?" had become "Good gosh almighty. She is as dead as she is ever going to be." Not only was the poetry gone, but so was the authenticity. "Southerners are just too lazy to say that many extra words," Olive Ann pointed out. She quickly realized that she would be wise to take Chester Kerr's advice concerning the film—namely, Be happy that a movie was made at all, and don't waste a moment's time or energy fretting over the final product. That done, Olive Ann was able to enjoy both the film itself and the people who worked on it. For a brief time, she even became something of a Hollywood celebrity, a role which amused her thoroughly.

Certainly having actors and actresses in for tea was a good way to divert one's attention from red and white blood cell counts or the rough spots in Chapter 7, and it was good for the ego, too. Olive Ann was delighted when two visiting actresses greeted her with "You couldn't have been born in 1924; you don't have a wrinkle!" One afternoon Faye Dunaway herself came to call—an event staged mainly for the benefit of some national reporters and photographers. The story of the movie star making friends with the author of *Cold Sassy Tree* did result in some fine publicity, but Andy's version of that memorable day was by far the most entertaining. Later Olive Ann even sent a copy of Andy's account to Faye.

The photographer had come a few days in advance to scout the location and plan his shots; Faye was expected on Sunday at five. "By Sunday afternoon," Andy wrote, "we had white magnolias at one end of our antique white sofa and white hydrangeas at the other; tables were waxed and excess books and magazines banished out of sight. Things did look good, if I say so myself. Until the photographers came back. I told them they could move anything. They had enough equipment to cover half of the dining room floor. They moved furniture to install strobe lights on top of the cornices over the windows and the tall clock on the mantel. They strung extension cords from the garage to the back of the garden to have some blue hydrangeas in the background for a possible cover picture outdoors.

"Then they shot Olive Ann in bed, with her tiny dictating equipment and the red telephone and pages of manuscript. They shot her in the living room, with those bookshelves in the distance, and in the dining room with a photograph of her real great-grandfather hanging on the wall beside the grandfather clock.

"Then we started waiting for Faye."

The writer from *Southpoint* magazine, which had orchestrated this momentous meeting, confided that Miss Dunaway's requirements included a hired limousine, a suite at the Ritz-Carlton for the night, and $800 worth of make-up. Once Faye arrived, the writer explained, her German make-up artist would require two hours to get the star ready to be photographed. Olive Ann joked that she had done her own make-up and that it had taken ten minutes. At quarter of seven, a long black Cadillac pulled into the driveway at 161 Bolling Road. As Andy told it, "Doug [the writer] went out to tell Faye the arrangements—I was to open the front door, introduce her to Olive Ann, and get out of the way. The black driver got out first. Then out stepped a man who must have seemed to Doug like the enemy climbing out of the Trojan horse; he was a writer from *TV Guide* who had had two hours to interview Faye in the limousine at Doug's expense. Then Faye got out, wearing a white T-shirt, rumpled gray slacks, and a wind-blown (air-conditioner blown?) blond wig. Doug must have thought, where did my $800 go?"

Faye said she would have to go inside and change her clothes before the meeting, so Olive Ann and Andy hid in the kitchen while Faye and her assistant disappeared into the back bedroom, carrying a boxful of clothes and a large make-up case. "When Faye reappeared," Andy wrote, "she wore neat gray slacks, a tailored plaid jacket, and Miss Love's blond wig, made of real human hair by the German artist and beautiful. With those

313

cheekbones, Faye could look beautiful in any-thing, and now she really did."

The writer guided Faye back out the front door, Olive Ann and Andy emerged from the kitchen, Faye dashed back in and threw her arms around Olive Ann as the photographer flashed away. According to Andy, Olive Ann and Faye chatted for the next hour or so like old friends while the reporters took notes and the pho-tographers took pictures. A young TNT vice president arrived dressed in a tuxedo, with a glamorous blond woman on his arm; Olive Ann's sister and brother-in-law set out a gallon of iced tea and sliced some cake; the writer from *TV Guide* slipped away; and, in the last light of day, everyone descended to the backyard, where they swatted at mosquitoes while the photographer tried to get a shot worthy of a magazine cover. Faye began to scratch, but Olive Ann and Andy weren't bothered a bit. "Fortunately those biting insects hate people who are taking chemother-apy," Andy wrote.

By the time the filming was over and the Hol-lywood folk had packed up and gone home, Olive Ann and Andy were ready to settle back into what he called their "un-star-studded normalcy." Still, that summer of 1989 was a happy one, and all of Olive Ann's letters brimmed with movie news and wedding plans. "We really did enjoy all the visits," Olive Ann wrote, "and that afternoon with Faye was like a three-ring circus." She mentioned Andy's anemia and his difficulties with chemotherapy, of course, but there was no way for distant friends to know just how weak he had become. His own letters, as the account of Faye Dunaway's visit attests, were full of vitality and humor. As one close friend of Andy's later wrote, "No one ever knew when he was in pain, because that's the way he wanted it." "If you smile," Andy always said, "no one will know." He did admit to Celestine Sibley, a long-time friend and fellow newspaper writer, that he was "too weak to dig holes in the backyard, as I would like to, and almost too weak to walk up our not-too-steep driveway from the backyard."

Those who knew Olive Ann and Andy had come to think of her as the invalid and of Andy as the ever-present, good-natured caretaker. That summer, almost imperceptibly, the tables turned. In July, Olive Ann's doctor gave her permission to spend a quiet weekend at their mountain house. The house had been finished and uninhabited for two years, ever since Olive Ann had left there and ended up in the hospital, in August of 1987. Now, a weekend at Skylake seemed cause for celebration—they were in their beloved retreat at last, and even though she was still in bed much of the time, Olive Ann could begin to imagine a more normal future. "It is not the Write House yet," Andy wrote, "but it will be!" They had furnished it with old pieces from 161 Bolling Road and, as Andy observed, "they look good with the natural white-pine walls, especially painted things like an old red-and-black chest from New England, a little blue blanket chest we use as a coffee table, and a black chair from Madison that Olive Ann sat in to write much of the book." Andy had always planned to collect wildflowers and native shrubs from their property at Skylake and bring them back to Atlanta, to grow in what he called his "final wheelchair garden." But, he joked, this was before he knew they'd *have* wheelchairs. Now, he wasn't strong enough to dig holes and transplant shrubs, but he did walk all over the lot, examining every tree and flower, and thinking about the gardening he would do once his chemotherapy was over.

Back in Atlanta, he read one gardening book after another, pored over seed catalogues, and made occasional visits to the nursery. We sent him gardening books from Houghton Mifflin, and he sent back enthusiastic reviews, happily correcting mistakes that had eluded our proofreaders. Olive Ann was working, too. In one letter Andy reported, "Yesterday O.A. had a fine time in bed going through her boxes of 'goodies,' words, ideas, anecdotes, and letters from the real Will Tweedy to Ruby Hight to see what she can use in upcoming chapters. This is one way she kept rewriting the first book, making it better. Believe me, she hasn't left those first 113 pages alone, Katrina, so it's a good thing you didn't do extensive editing. But she loves the process."

Late in August Olive Ann and Andy considered a friend's offer to drive them to Skylake again, but this time it was Olive Ann who looked at Andy and questioned whether he should make the trip. "I don't think Andy's up to it," she confided. "He really has gotten very weak, and the low white blood count from chemotherapy has kept him from going places and doing things where there are people who might have a germ or virus to give away." In the end, they did decide to make an overnight visit to the Write House. It was to be their last together.

About a week before Andy's final chemotherapy treatment, Steve and I spent an evening with Olive Ann and Andy and Becky. We arrived with a huge lasagna dinner, heated it up in batches in the microwave, and served it on their good china. Olive Ann looked almost like her old self, all dressed up and delighted to be presiding over a party in her own dining room. Andy conceded that the summer had been hard—but all that was behind him now, he assured us; the chemotherapy had worked its exacting magic once again, and now he expected to see some of his hair and some of his strength return. After dinner, Norma and Charlie appeared for dessert, and we all sat in the living room, telling stories and getting caught up on *Cold Sassy Tree* news. Olive Ann read a fan letter from B. F. Skinner, and admitted that it had pleased her as much as the one from a farm woman in Virginia, who had written to say that she'd named her prize hen Olive Ann. The mood was wonderfully festive. I was nearly seven months pregnant, so there were baby stories to tell, and Olive Ann and Andy were both in high spirits, looking forward to John's October wedding and to the Atlanta premiere of *Cold Sassy Tree,* which would occur the same weekend. The wedding guests would be served Brunswick stew and barbecue on Friday night on Norma's deck, and then attend the movie premiere the following day, where they would see Faye Dunaway herself arrive in a horse-drawn carriage. "It's Ted Turner's party, naturally," Olive Ann said, "but it's heaven-sent for entertaining wedding guests!" She and Andy planned to skip that celebration so that they could really enjoy the wedding.

At one point in the evening, as Olive Ann was telling a funny anecdote she planned to use in *Time, Dirt, and Money,* I happened to look across the room at Andy. He was seated on the edge of his chair, leaning forward, his hands clasped between his knees, listening with full attention to Olive Ann's every word. On his face there was a smile of pure delight. It was impossible to look at Andy and think of him as a sick man; he was a happy man—and that's what showed. Later, Olive Ann told me that much as she had enjoyed that evening, the high point for her was just after they had closed the door behind us. Then, Andy took her in his arms and said, "Wasn't that a wonderful party!"

A week later, on September 17, 1989, Andy died. Olive Ann believed that she could accept almost anything, but she never expected that she would have to accept the death of her husband. If there was a "dying story" to tell here, it was that after all those years of nursing Olive Ann, Andy was the first to go. All summer, Olive Ann had looked forward to attending John's wedding; it was to be her first real outing in over two years, and she had every reason to believe that Andy would be at her side. Now, she was going to his memorial service instead. She managed it, and afterward she invited family and friends back to the house. That afternoon, she admitted that she hadn't slept at all the night before. Lying in bed, she realized that she had to decide whether life was worth living without Andy; it would be so easy to just give up now and follow him. By morning, she knew that wasn't the answer. One by one, she told us, "I've decided that I want to live." The way she said those words, there was no doubt in anyone's mind that she meant them. Losing Andy took an enormous toll on Olive Ann, but his death did not diminish her zest for life. There were still too many things she wanted to do.

A few days after Andy's service, Olive Ann wrote a note to a little boy down the street who had come to offer his condolences. "Dear Clark," it said, "it's not easy to say good-bye to someone you love. It helps me to know that a boy like you cares that I am sad, and I want you to know that thinking about Mr. Sparks makes me smile. He enjoyed your visits. You brought sunshine into our house. Ask your mother to make this cake for your next birthday. It is big! It is so big you could ask 799 children to the party and still have a big piece left for your mom and dad and your brother and your sister. It makes 800 pieces of cake." She enclosed a recipe that Andy had saved from the mess galley of the battleship U.S.S. *North Carolina*.

In the weeks after Andy's death, friends and relatives gathered round to make sure that Olive Ann was well taken care of. Characteristically, she thanked everyone with a letter—a letter that was also intended to let us all know that she would be all right. "Andy assumed he'd get well this time," she wrote, "just like twice before. 'If I don't, it won't be for not trying.' In the spring, he laughed and said, 'I know the chemo is working. It has taken most of my hair, my white cells, my red cells, and my energy.' But he did beat the lymphoma, as it turned out, and despite having chemotherapy that last week he looked and felt better every day. What caused heart failure and death was an overwhelming infection that started with a chill late Saturday night. He died at 8:30 the next morning.

"But we had a good year," she continued. "There's something to be said for living dangerously! We didn't waste much time worrying, we cherished the fact that we were still together, we had some really good times with friends, got to the mountain house twice, enjoyed hearing about the goings-on in our Sunday school class and with the *Cold Sassy Tree* filming, and our hearts were constantly warmed by all that was being done to help us.

"Andy's garden was never lovelier. And there was great joy in looking forward to John and

Judy's wedding. Sometime in July, on a bad day, he said, 'If I don't make it to the wedding, I want you to see that it goes on exactly as planned.' I promised, but he was obviously so much better in general that I never once thought he wouldn't make it. As planned, three weeks after he didn't make it, the wedding took place in College Park at the home of Andy's sister, Jane Willingham. The house was built by their grandfather in 1904, and their mother and father married there in 1912. It was a lovely day.

"There is now something wonderful about knowing for sure that I can cope with whatever happens. Andy taught me how. It hasn't been hard for me to accept that Andy has died, though I think I don't quite believe it. It's just that he has disappeared and I miss him. Acceptance doesn't mean I haven't cried—a lot. But I never have to remind myself that we had much to be thankful for, and I still do, most especially for our family, neighbors, friends, and doctors."

Olive Ann did go to John's wedding, but by the time it was over it was clear that the stress of the preceding month had affected her heart. Some of the fluid had returned, and her doctor ordered her back to bed. Now, in addition to having to adjust to a world without Andy, Olive Ann had to get used to someone else taking care of her. There were decisions to make, financial affairs to settle, and tasks to be done—from finding someone to make her breakfast in the morning to cleaning out Andy's closet. She hired a cook-housekeeper to come in five mornings a week, and she spent some time with her brother-in-law and an investment broker, organizing her finances and arranging for a regular monthly income from the *Cold Sassy Tree* profits. As Olive Ann wrote in a letter to John and Judy, "To have the money question sorted out for me and to have the housekeeper and cooking problems solved seems like huge progress and a lot off my mind."

One Sunday morning, two months after Andy's death, Olive Ann wrote that she had woken up at six o'clock and, for the first time, was able to think about him without crying. "It was a joy and a delight to think about him," she said. "I think one reason I've missed him so is having to try not to, in order not to cry all day. I guess I'm healing, at least emotionally."

By November she was catching up on her correspondence and getting ready to go back to work on the novel. She wrote a long letter to Faye Dunaway, complimenting her work on the movie and recalling the day they had spent together. "For myself," she wrote, "it was enough to be with you as a delightful human being, so interesting that we could both forget photographers. It really was a lovely day, which Andy enjoyed as much as I did. The whole time that you were in Concord, we were getting reports and photographs of what was going on and felt we were a part of it. It really added a great sense of fun to those last months. He has disappeared now, and I miss him, but I'll soon be back to the sequel, and writing has always been my best escape, my best therapy, and my most pleasure."

In the months that followed, Olive Ann did get back to work on her book. As always before, fiction transported her to a place where she could call all the shots. Having lost first her own health and now her husband of thirty-three years, she was glad to have at least one aspect of her life in her control. Although she was almost completely bedridden again, she spent the afternoons alone in the house, dictating and editing. "I do enjoy the afternoons by myself," Olive Ann wrote to me, "and that's usually when I get around to working on the book." Her deadline was just a year away, but, as she told us, "My first job is to stay alive, so there's no chance I'll be burning the midnight oil to make up for lost time during the last few months." Olive Ann's doctors gave her permission to sit up but said that she mustn't walk any more than was absolutely necessary. "For the most part my walks now are to the bathroom and to the front door once a day to let Jack out, Jack being the cat," she wrote.

To some, such a life might seem little more than a prison sentence, but Olive Ann didn't think of it that way. That winter, she indulged herself and wrote long, thoughtful letters, something that she truly loved to do. In answer to a letter from a young woman who had worked on the film of *Cold Sassy Tree*, Olive Ann wrote, "If balancing a career and family ever puts too much pressure on you, don't mind lightening up on the career for a few years. It's better than chronic exhaustion." My Christmas letter from Olive Ann was full of memories of the first camping trip she and Andy had made with John and Becky, and reflections on being a parent. "The wonderful thing, I think, about children is that you see the world all new through their eyes," she wrote, "whenever you try to show the world to them, whether it be a red maple leaf, a ladybug, dinosaur tracks, or the Metropolitan Museum. That's what it really is all about—that and love."

On December 18, 1989, my husband called Olive Ann from my hospital room to let her know that I had just given birth to a baby boy. Over the next few months I sent more photos than letters to Bolling Road, and Olive Ann devoted herself to her book. She was feeling well enough to write and was determined to make "real headway now." Rather than dictating the first draft, she was jotting down lines and paragraphs on scrap paper, fiddling with them till they were the way she wanted them, and then dictating them for Norma to type. "That way I have something on paper that I can see and work from," she explained, "and I think it will cut out the necessity for so much rewriting of the first draft." Arduous as the process might be, Olive Ann still refused to settle for anything that was less than perfect; she had worked out a method that enabled her to tinker more while Norma typed less. It seemed a good sign.

The eight-page, single-spaced letter Olive Ann sent me in March 1990 was, it turned out, the last. It seems a fitting farewell. As Olive Ann herself warned, "You may have to read this letter in sections between feedings. Unless my voice gives out, it will have all the things I've stored up that I've thought about and wanted to tell you since last fall." She began by reflecting on the friendship with Norma and what it had meant to her and Andy over the years. "I really love each person in my family, and we are all very close," she wrote, "but Norma being next door and being over here so much washing dishes and cooking when we needed her, and typing, and needing Andy's advice about gardening, I think she—like you and Steve—had much in common with Andy and enjoyed and really experienced him in the same way I did. It was always a merry threesome whenever she came over."

In fact, this letter is full of stories and recollections of happy times, from the days she and Andy had spent at the *Sunday Magazine* to the magical connections and friendships that had come about as a result of *Cold Sassy Tree*. Olive Ann described the afternoon she and Andy had spent with Jessica Tandy, who came to visit while she was in Atlanta filming *Driving Miss Daisy*. She gave a progress report on *Time, Dirt, and Money,* and brought me up to date on *Cold Sassy Tree* news, concluding, "*Cold Sassy Tree* does seem to have a life of its own, like a river with lots of little branches—or maybe I should say like a sassafras tree with many branches."

And, much as she missed Andy, Olive Ann also wanted me to know that she was growing accustomed to life without him. "At first I had the feeling that Andy's death was a dream and I would wake up," she said. "When I did wake up, my feeling was as if a meteorite had hit the earth in September and killed every witty, interesting, sweet, cheerful, courageous, loving, exciting, sometimes irritable, determined man of seventy who lived at 161 Bolling Road. It doesn't hit like that anymore, and I'm very grateful for the kind of marriage we had. We were married for thirty-three years but worked together every day for nine years before that." Still, she felt that her recovery was occurring in stages, and that the process was a continuing one.

"The first few weeks, every morning when I woke up I had to remind myself, with surprise and amazement and often out loud, that 'Andy is dead!' " she admitted. "Then for four months I hardly ever thought about him. I couldn't let myself. Any time I ever thought about him I cried, and even with a good heart it's exhausting to cry all day. I looked forward to the nights because I would sleep and not have to try so hard not to think."

Once all of the legal and financial affairs were tended to, Olive Ann decided it was time to go through Andy's things, something she had dreaded. "It seemed like just another painful, overwhelming widow-type task," she wrote, "until it dawned on me this was something I could do for him! He did hate to go through stuff, as is clearly evident when one opens his closet door or his drawers or his desk. I started with the desk, and it's turning out to be a happy time. The desk is like a profile of Andy and his life and his interests, with constant interesting or funny surprises."

She found Andy's uncle's gold pocket watch; a box of coal ash containing the burned remains of a diamond ring that Andy's Aunt Mamie had wrapped in a piece of paper and accidentally thrown in the fire; a box of gold inlays ("Years ago I heard inlays are worth something, so whenever I had to have one replaced I'd make the dentist give me the old one. Even Andy, who was embarrassed by such, started asking for his"); and two stamped envelopes from Andy's mother's Aunt Em, mailed during the Civil War. "This desk work has been like being with Andy again," Olive Ann wrote. "Too interesting to cry about, and full of memories of happy times, including my love letters that I didn't know he'd kept, and notes from the children when they were little. It's amazing what a difference it's made—feeling I'm doing something for Andy, almost with him. I bring batches out of the pigeonholes to my bed to go through, and I'm having a good time. But, oh, law, he's got two file cabinets full in the basement!"

Written words were never discarded in Olive Ann and Andy's household, and Olive Ann's going through Andy's desk didn't necessarily mean that she was throwing anything away; in fact, she was annotating, as I discovered a year later when I sorted through many of these same papers. To a bundle of tender and funny notes that Olive Ann had written to Andy over the years, and that he had saved, she added this explanation: "Whenever Andy was away overnight, I would tuck a card or a note into his suitcase. I never knew he kept them."

"I really am being long-winded," Olive Ann exclaimed toward the end of this extraordinary letter, so full of looking back. "Most of all I want to express my joy in everything about yours and Steve's and Henry's new life. My feeling is a little like something said by Ray Moore, a local TV newscaster whom I dated for four years—seriously but not exclusively. I never dated anybody exclusively until I told Andy I'd marry him. But the night I told Ray I was in love with Andy, he thought a minute and said, 'I envy Andy, but I'm not jealous of him.' He and Andy and I stayed good friends, and the last time he called I reminded him of what he said, thinking it was such a genius way of delineating the difference between our friendship love, which had been romantic at times, and what I then felt for Andy. He didn't remember that, or that shortly before we married, he took Andy and me out to lunch and said, 'I can't come to the wedding because the three of us will be the only people in Atlanta who will know I wasn't jilted.' The point of all this is to say I envy you all right now, but I'm not jealous. Actually I don't think I envy—I'm just happy for you. I've had my turn."

In addition to her own eight pages, Olive Ann enclosed all the letters I had written her during my pregnancy and after Henry's birth, explaining, "You may have been too busy or too tired to have kept a journal in this period. *It is hard to part with them,* they make such pictures of you and Steve and little Henry, but they could go in your baby book." And at the end she added a final note: "The doctor made a house call after I finished this—heart much better, and he said by all means accept an offer from a retired doctor-friend and his wife to take me and all food to the mountain house for a few days!"

Olive Ann made that trip, but by the time she got home she had caught a cold. Over the next weeks, she felt worse and worse, and by May she was in the hospital with bronchitis, which took a severe toll on her already weakened heart. Olive Ann believed that, with time and patience, she would rally, as she had so many times before. But in June she was in intensive care, and the doctors were considering a heart transplant. Mercifully, they concluded that she was too weak to undergo the surgery. It is impossible to know what Olive Ann thought about as she lay in her hospital bed while doctors deliberated her fate, but I don't doubt that she found some comfort in words she had written herself, for Grandpa Blakeslee to say to Will Tweedy after the boy narrowly escaped getting crushed by a train:

"Life bullies us son, but God don't. He had good reasons for fixin' it where if'n you git too sick or too hurt to live, why, you can die, same as a sick chicken. I've knowed a few really sick chickens to git well, and lots a-folks git well thet nobody ever thought to see out a-bed agin cept in a coffin. Still and all, common sense tells you this much: everwhat makes a wheel run over a track will make it run over a boy if'n he's in the way. If'n you'd a got kilt, it'd mean you jest didn't move fast enough, like a rabbit that gits caught by a hound dog . . . When it comes to prayin', we got it all over the other animals, but we ain't no different when it comes to livin' and dyin'. If'n you give God the credit when somebody don't die, you go'n blame him when they do die? Call it His will? Ever noticed we git well all the time and don't die but once't? Thet has to mean God always wants us to live if'n we can. Hit ain't never His *will for us to die*—cept in the big sense. In the sense he was smart enough not to make life eternal on this here earth, with people and bees and elephants and dogs piled up in squirmin' mounds like Loma's dang cats tryin' to keep warm in the wintertime."

In a letter she wrote just before she got sick in March, Olive Ann had said, "I guess what gracious living all comes down to is acceptance and forgiveness. Forgiveness has never been a problem for me and now acceptance isn't either." Everyone who visited Olive Ann in the hospital that June remembers that, sick as she was, she never seemed to despair. The last time that Andy's sister, Jane, saw Olive Ann, they spoke about the possibility of an afterlife. "I wish it were true," Olive Ann said. "That would be wonderful. But if it's not, that's all right too."

One day Olive Ann's brother Billy went to see her in the intensive care unit. She was having a terrible day, was very sick, breathing through an oxygen mask, and unable to talk much at all. After a short time Billy concluded that she might be better off just resting alone. But as he headed for the door, Olive Ann spoke. "Just a minute," she whispered.

"What is it?" he asked, turning back.

"I just wanted you to see me smile," she said. And she did. *That* was Olive Ann.

When Norma came to visit, on June 22, Olive Ann tried to talk with her about her hopes for *Time, Dirt, and Money* if she was unable to finish it. "There's no need to discuss that now," Norma assured her. "Of course you'll get back to work on it." But Olive Ann was not to be put off that easily. She would not give up hope, but she would be practical, too, and she knew she could rely on Norma to do whatever needed to be done. Late that night, she picked up her dictating machine and began to speak: "Norma, this is Olive Ann. Your visit and Charlie's was just like a great gift . . . I've figured out a way that if I don't get to finish the novel it might still be marketable as a small book." She expected that she would be able to revise the first six chapters, and when she got home, she said, she planned to work on a synopsis —"which won't hurt me to do—I may even write faster if I've got it, everything written down and decided." She referred Norma to several scenes that were among her notes, and said she hoped that some of these could be used and that she would have time to write an ending. That way, even if the novel itself was not finished, there would be enough to satisfy those people who were interested in what happened. "In the meantime," she concluded, "I'll just keep working on the book, and aren't you glad it's in a fairly good state of repair?" Finally, yawning, she said, "Now this is the middle of the night, Norma, Friday night, and I'm getting sleepy so I'll send this over to you . . . And so good night now."

Less than two weeks later, early on Independence Day 1990, Olive Ann Burns died. She had come home from the hospital four days before, accompanied by a portable IV tube that was to administer medicine continually for the rest of her life. She had declined the suggestion that she employ a home nurse, confident that Becky, a part-time housekeeper, and a few friends and relatives could manage the IV and oxygen. Olive Ann was delighted to be home, and she was eager to get back to work. On the morning of July 3, Billy's wife, Rosalind, had come to stay with her while the housekeeper went out to run errands. "Olive Ann was scribbling notes for her book when I arrived," Rosalind recalled. "She thought that she was missing a chapter, and I began to look around for it. We talked about the novel, and also about a book I had loaned her from my church library, called *Better Health with Fewer Pills.*" Olive Ann said she had read the book cover to cover, and she was so impressed that she'd asked a friend to buy two copies, one for Rosalind and one for herself.

In his introduction to *Better Health with Fewer Pills,* Louis Shattuck Baer quotes Socrates: "If the head and body are to be well, you must begin by curing the soul." Sick as she was, Olive Ann was inspired by the author's conviction that faith and a positive outlook are as important to health and happiness as any medicine. This was one of the best books she had ever read, Olive Ann told Rosalind, and she wanted to inscribe a copy of it for her sister-in-law. Rosalind handed her one of the new books, and Olive Ann wrote, "For Rosalind . . ." She stopped. "I feel dizzy," she said, and turned her head away, closing her eyes. Olive Ann would have thought it worth mentioning that she died with a pen in her hand, talking about a book she admired and a novel she still hoped to finish. If she could have written her own dying story, she might have done it just this way.

A week later, Olive Ann's family and Norma gathered at the family cemetery plot in Commerce, the small Georgia town that had become famous as the inspiration for Cold Sassy. The death of Olive Ann Burns was national news, and hundreds of friends and relatives from across the country had attended her memorial service in Atlanta. Now, it was time for those closest to her to say good-bye. A hole had been dug to receive the ashes of both Andy and Olive Ann, and the family stood around it, under a hot July sun. John and Becky, who had lost both of their parents in less than a year, turned away and headed for their car. A moment later, they returned with a blanket of fresh roses. The two of them had made it early that morning, knowing that nothing would have pleased Olive Ann and Andy more than this small act of life inspired by fiction. When the flowers were in place, each child took a plastic bag of their parents' ashes and slowly poured them, mixing as they went, into the ground. Then, one at a time, they tossed in the first spadefuls of earth. They looked at each other and, without a word, continued shoveling until the hole was full of red Georgia clay. When they were finished, Andy's sister, Jane, read aloud from *Cold Sassy Tree*.

Fans of *Cold Sassy Tree* mourned its author's death and asked one question: "What about the sequel?" There were newspaper reports that Olive Ann had left behind ten chapters, "all freshly typed by her secretary Norma Duncan." There were suggestions that another author be hired to complete the book. There were rumors that she had in fact written an ending, if only it could be found. Needless to say, it had never occurred to Olive Ann that anyone else might try to finish her novel; there was no ending; and there were no "freshly typed" chapters. Faced with the formidable task of collating literally hundreds of pages of manuscript in various drafts, Norma exclaimed, "Who said that? Every time I find another scrap with a sentence on it, I feel that statement is hanging over my head!"

In the end, we simply did our best to carry out Olive Ann's last wishes. Norma cleaned up and typed the chapters that Olive Ann had left for her. She transcribed all of the notes she found on the backs of envelopes and on innumerable scraps of paper tucked away in every room of the house. When it was all together, we had fifteen chapters —chapters that Olive Ann surely would have rewritten again, given the chance, but chapters that we feel are worth publishing just as they are.

Katrina Kenison
January 1992